...LING

"When it comes to writing hot, sexy heroes and strong, independent women, no one does it better than Kate Meader." —*Harlequin Junkie*

THE CHICAGO REBELS SERIES

IRRESISTIBLE YOU

"[A] heart-stealing opener to the Chicago Rebels sports contemporary series. . . . Meader's strength is creating characters who live, breathe, and jump off the page. . . . The mix of sexual tension and emotional decisions will lead Meader's series launch to many a keeper shelf."

—*Publishers Weekly* (starred review)

"A charming hero who's sexy as sin and a smart, fierce heroine who gives him a run for his money? Yes, please! I couldn't turn the pages fast enough."

—Kimberly Kincaid, *USA Today* bestselling author

"Meader's signature firefighter heat transfers flawlessly to the world of high-stakes ice hockey in her hot-as-sin Chicago Rebels series."

—Gina Maxwell, ̶ ̶ ̶ ̶ ̶ ̶ ̶ ̶ ̶ ̶ ̶ ̶lling author

"Remy and ̶ ̶ ̶ ̶ ̶ ̶ ̶ ̶ ̶ th serious sizzle!"

̶ ̶ ̶ ̶ ̶ ̶ ̶g author

"Steamy sex scenes, colorful characters, and riveting dialogue . . . a real page-turner."

—*RT Book Reviews* (Top Pick Gold)

"A smart, sexy book."

—Sarah MacLean, *The Washington Post*

"Hot, sexy, wonderful."

—Beverly Jenkins, *The Huffington Post*

FLIRTING WITH FIRE

"Sexy and sassy . . . I love this book!"

—Jude Deveraux, #1 *New York Times* bestselling author

"Sexy, witty, and hot, hot, hot. Kate Meader will make you fall in love with the hunky firefighters at Engine Co. 6."

—Sarah Castille, *New York Times* bestselling author

"Get your fire extinguisher ready—*Flirting with Fire* is HOT and satisfying!"

—Jennifer Probst, *New York Times* bestselling author

"This book is everything you want in a romance: excellent writing, strong characters, and a sizzling plot that keeps the pace up throughout the story."

—*RT Book Reviews* (Top Pick)

BOOKS BY KATE MEADER

The Chicago Rebels Series

In Skates Trouble
Irresistible You

The Hot in Chicago Series

Rekindle the Flame
Flirting with Fire
Melting Point
Playing with Fire
Sparking the Fire

So Over YOU

KATE MEADER

Pocket Books

New York   London   Toronto   Sydney   New Delhi

Pocket Books
An Imprint of Simon & Schuster, Inc.
1230 Avenue of the Americas
New York, NY 10020

This book is a work of fiction. Any references to historical events, real people, or real places are used fictitiously. Other names, characters, places, and events are products of the author's imagination, and any resemblance to actual events or places or persons, living or dead, is entirely coincidental.

First Pocket Books paperback edition January 2018

POCKET and colophon are registered trademarks of Simon & Schuster, Inc.

For information about special discounts for bulk purchases, please contact Simon & Schuster Special Sales at 1-866-506-1949 or business@simonandschuster.com.

The Simon & Schuster Speakers Bureau can bring authors to your live event. For more information or to book an event, contact the Simon & Schuster Speakers Bureau at 1-866-248-3049 or visit our website at www.simonspeakers.com.

Interior design by Alison Cnockaert

Manufactured in the United States of America

10 9 8 7 6 5 4 3 2 1

ISBN 978-1-5011-8089-7
ISBN 978-1-5011-6856-7 (ebook)

For every woman who's been left frustratingly scoreless,
may you get all the orgasms you deserve!

So Over YOU

PROLOGUE

Hockey is not for pussies. Technically, it's defined as a sport. Words like play *and* game *get thrown around liberally to shield its true nature: hockey is warfare with water breaks. In the rink, you have over two thousand pounds of brute force clashing with whittled clubs, a rubber disc that could crush a larynx, and knives attached to feet. Let's not pretend there's anything civilized going on here.*

—Clifford Chase, three-time Stanley Cup winner,
NHL Hall of Famer, and all-around asshole

Sold out. The arena was freakin' sold out.

On jellied legs, Isobel Chase skated to the face-off circle at the center of the rink in the Bayside Arena, home of the Buffalo Betties. The puck hadn't even dropped yet, but the raucous crowd of twenty thousand was already on its feet in anticipation of history about to be made.

The inaugural game of the National Women's Hockey League, playing to a sold-out stadium, and she was here! On this night of firsts, Isobel would continue her storied career. Winner of the Patty Kazmaier Award for best NCAA player, last captain standing after the Frozen Four, silver medalist for Team USA . . . She could go on, but she had a professional fucking hockey game to win.

Melissande Cordet, the famed Canadian power forward and the only woman to get called up for a game in the NHL, hovered, ready to do the ceremonial drop. They'd chitchatted before the game and posed for photos while Cordet told Isobel how far women's hockey had come. How Isobel and her fellow athletes were blazing a trail.

Come back to me with that BS, Mel, when there isn't a salary cap of $270K on each team in the women's league.

Yeah, yeah, Isobel got it. Baby steps. Until they could prove their worth with decent attendance figures, TV broadcast deals, and feminine hygiene product sponsorships, the Great Experiment would continue.

"Ready to make history?" Cordet asked in a voice liltingly inflected with her French Canadian accent.

Isobel remained still, her left hand choking her stick, her body bowed and tipped toward her opposite, Jen Grady, the captain of the Montreal Mavens. They'd roomed at Harvard together, skated to glory at the Games together, but that meant jack shit now. Tonight Isobel would be the first to touch the puck.

Drop, sweep, flick, chop—all viable strategies to win a face-off. Every day since he'd plopped her on the ice at the age of three, her father, Clifford Chase, had drilled into her the same advice. *Know your enemy. Know what they're going to do before they've even thought it.* Grady liked to go for the crisp slice, so chopping her stick would be Isobel's best move.

The old man was on his feet somewhere in the stands, though with his wealth and renown, he could have easily landed an entire box to himself. Wanting to feel the crowd, that pulsing, living thing as it rose and fell with the team's fortunes, he'd bought a Buffalo Betties cap and planted himself in the thick of it.

When women go pro, you'll be first on the line, Izzy. It's why I'm harder on you than I am on the boys. It's for your own good.

The boys, meaning the pro players on the Chicago Rebels, the NHL team her father owned and ruled with an iron fist. Substitute sons, they were sporadically successful, which only served to place more pressure on Isobel's shoulders. She inched those shoulders forward.

The puck dropped.

Grady touched it first.

The night went downhill from there.

ONE

Two years later . . .

"So this is just a flying visit, right? A couple of dances and we're out?"

Isobel's younger sister, Violet, flicked a look of disgust over her shoulder. Granted, Isobel had vowed to make more effort in the Grand Plan: get herself a real, live boyfriend versus the battery-operated one she defaulted to in times of need. But six weeks into the year and she'd gotten no further than a few awkward online chats.

What are you wearing?

A sports bra and— Hello, hello, are you still there? Oh, fuck off, dickbiscuit.

"You're never going to get laid with that attitude," Violet said as they hacked through teeming masses of nubile, tanned, scantily clad bodies that packed the floor of Ignite, Chicago's newest, hottest whatever. Most of these people looked like they'd been shipped in from a Pitbull music video.

When Isobel didn't respond, Violet stopped and pivoted. "What did I tell you about showing a little skin?"

Isobel looked down at her nightclub ensemble: black leggings and Joan of Arctic fur-lined boots paired with an Eddie Bauer parka over a black turtleneck. She called it her "French cat burglar" look. Not only did it throw off a sixties beatnik poet vibe and hug all the right places on her six-foot-tall frame, but it had the added benefit of protecting against a Chicago winter. She was nothing if not practical.

"This isn't really a good night to be looking for a man," she muttered mutinously.

"It's Valentine's Day. This place is filled with losers who couldn't get a date and now they're on the prowl for the leftovers."

"Like me?" Because she certainly didn't include Violet in the desperate-dateless-leftovers category. Her sister currently might be without an official boyfriend, but she was keeping a few members of the Rebels hockey team—the team they jointly owned and ran with their elder sister, Harper—on the hook. Not exactly principled, but Violet wasn't known for her scrupulous attention to the rules.

Vi grinned big. "Exactly like you!"

Who was Isobel kidding? Satan would be ice-skating to work before she got lucky, which suited her tonight because she really should be at home, replaying game videos in preparation for tomorrow: Her first coaching gig with the Rebels. So, all right, she was only a consultant, but it would lead to more. She knew it.

"It's a good thing we're on the list," Violet shouted over her shoulder as she elbowed her way through the frenzy with sharp jabs, "because there's no way we would have gotten in with you looking like South Pole explorer meets South Side gangbanger."

The list? Now that Isobel thought about it, they *had* skipped a considerable line along with the serious scrutiny of the club's security. Violet looked like she belonged here with her fabulous gold bustier, a black band masquerading as a skirt, and lashings of colorful ink adorning her gleaming olive skin. Really, she fit in anywhere that was cool and dangerous.

The two had only recently started hanging out when the requirements of their father's will threw the formerly estranged half sisters together to manage the team. Two years ago, Isobel hadn't even known of Violet Vasquez's existence, as dear old Dad had shoved the result of his one-night stand into the Chase family armoire. On Clifford's death five months ago, Violet had moved from Reno to Chicago, and she was largely responsible for relieving the tension that thickened the air whenever Isobel was in the same room as big sis Harper. Isobel theorized that since she grew up out of Cliff's shadow, Violet wasn't burdened by the Chase legacy. She had a way about her, a go-for-broke attitude, that Isobel envied.

"What list?" Isobel asked just as they reached a short stairway leading to a VIP area. "What's going on, Vi?"

"We're hanging with Cade and the guys."

Awesome! A night skirting ethical boundaries with pro hockey players who worked for her.

Violet was already skipping up the stairway littered

with bored supermodels, several of them wearing skimpy cropped tops that barely covered their tits. The poor women were either freezing to death or highly aroused, because their nipples popped like pucks against the thin fabric. The letters VESNA blazed from several surgically enhanced chests. Why did that word sound familiar?

A few more steps and it became clear that the line of women clinging like sex-starved limpets to the stair rail was an actual queue with a goal in mind. A mall line for Santa, perhaps, where a deviant Mr. Claus was about to have the time of his freakin' life. And here was Isobel blindly following Violet, who now waved at someone behind the velvet rope at the top of the steps.

Shit.

Isobel's heart sank to her not-gettin'-laid-tonight boots. She recognized the head elf pulling back the rope, though Alexei Medvedev was more crusty goblin than Christmas imp.

Vadim Petrov's right-hand man hadn't changed much in the eight years since she'd last seen him, his age still anywhere between forty and sixty. Following some ridiculous feudal custom, the man supposedly owed service in perpetuity to Vadim's bloodline. He served as cook, porter, alarm clock, and bodyguard, to name just a few of his jobs. No doubt he picked up his charge's dry cleaning, ushered women out of Vadim's bed in the early hours, and waxed his boy's scrotum for that silky, manscaped feel.

If Isobel had thought Alexei might have forgotten

her, she was quickly disabused of this notion when he let Violet through but placed his Russian solidity in Isobel's path. Seemed she was persona non grata again. They sized each other up, and Isobel was happy to say that she was still taller than him, her six feet besting Alexei by a good four inches. But he made up for it in squat, torpedo-shaped bulk. Plus, she was at a clear positioning disadvantage—he could easily push her down the stairs.

And he looked like nothing would please him more.

"What's up, Igor?" He'd *loved* it when she called him that in olden times.

Wondering why the holdup, Violet turned and grabbed her arm. "Hey, she's with me, *tipo*."

After a few seconds, Alexei stood back, his soulless, shark's eyes boring into Isobel. All he was missing was the two-fingered prong gesture *I'm watching you*. Fine, they understood each other.

Moving forward into the crowded room—huh, not so exclusive after all—Isobel felt her skin prickle with foreboding. As if it knew something she didn't.

She turned, and *whoosh!* Sure, she didn't need all that breath in her lungs anyway. Vadim Petrov sat on a chocolate velvet couch wearing a sharp suit, an icy stare, and a half-naked blonde.

The man had made a bargain with the devil, and the devil had yet to call in his marker. Undeniably beautiful, he sported mountain-high cheekbones that pronounced his descent from an aristocratic lineage, eyes as blue as Lake Michigan in spring, and full lips that miraculously softened the sharp angles of his face. Coal-black hair fell over his brow, its silkiness appearing as untouchably otherworld as its owner. And don't even get her started on his sculpted, tatted body—currently covered up, thank Gretzky—which he proudly flaunted on billboards as often as his numerous sponsorship deals demanded.

A few days ago, the Rebels had traded him in from Quebec. The plan was to use him on the left wing, but he wasn't quite game fit, owing to a recurring knee injury. This gave him plenty of time to indulge his other interests: clubbing and manwhoring.

For the briefest moment she wished she didn't look like a lank-haired, parka-sporting, clodhopper-wearing schlub the first time in years she'd been less than ten feet away from him. But then she shot titanium into her spine, cocked her hip à la fuck it, and sidled up to Violet.

Cade "Alamo" Burnett, one of the Rebels' defensemen, had just kissed Violet on the cheek and looked like he wanted to lean into Isobel, but seemed to change his mind at the last moment. *No problemo.* Isobel was all about boundaries.

"Hey, take off your coat, Iz," Vi said.

Isobel felt too warm, too cold, and mighty uncomfortable. "Not staying long."

"Izzz . . ."

"Oh, okay. Keep your bustier on." As she unzipped her parka, she was surprised to feel a tug. "Uh, that's mine."

"I know, I'm trying to—"

"Back off, lady."

After a few seconds struggling, she discovered that the woman behind her was actually a coat check person and not a parka thief.

Isobel really should not be allowed out in public.

She hoped Vadim wasn't watching— *Oh, who cares what he thinks?*

Apparently her eighteen-year-old self did, because that's what she'd reverted to. *That* loser's traitorous gaze couldn't help itself, and when it landed on the Russian again, Isobel was surprised to find him watching her with mild amusement. This was different. When he was nineteen, humor had been about as foreign to him as a PB&J sandwich.

Some guy who had "PR clown" written all over him was taking a photo of the blonde as she inched her hand inside Vadim's lapel, apparently needing the warmth only those muscles could provide. Two seconds later, the blonde was subbed out for a redhead, who appeared to have similar body heat problems. Santa, aka Vadim, whispered in her ear, probably inquiring if she'd been naughty or, you know, extra naughty.

The tabloids called him the Czar of Pleasure, a man as well known for his exploits in the bedroom as for those on the ice. Oh, Isobel's tell-all about Vadim's erotic talents would make for some *really* surprising reading.

Eyes bright with admiration, Cade looked around the VIP room plastered with signs for Vesna, which

Isobel now recalled was a high-end Russian vodka. "Man, I want a vodka deal."

"You'd be lucky if you got a deal fronting Budweiser Clydesdale piss, Alamo," came a slow drawl behind them.

Remy DuPre, the Rebels' center straight from the heart of the bayou, appeared bearing the most frou-frou drink Isobel had ever seen. Blue with a big chunk of pineapple in the center.

"Is that for Harper?" Isobel asked, knowing it wasn't, because her sister wouldn't be caught dead in a club with the players even if her boyfriend's presence gave her a good excuse. *Banging one of them is bad enough*, Harper was fond of saying. *I need to at least give the illusion of labor-management boundaries.*

Remy's blue eyes crinkled. "I'm just here to make sure these boys get home by curfew."

Isobel hid her smile. She liked how Remy had stepped up to the position of elder statesman since his arrival four months ago. She also liked how Remy was a calming influence on her older sister. He could have bailed on the Rebels when he had a shot at trading out, but didn't because he loved Harper.

A pang of envy bit into Isobel's heart, but she breathed it away. She wasn't looking for the love her sister had found with Remy, but she wouldn't say no to the obvious fireworks that lit up their bed. Not that anything like that would be happening in this god-awful club.

Excusing herself, she headed over to the bar set

off in an alcove, determined that this would be a one-drink-and-done kind of night. A plastic-encased menu listed the cocktail options: Vesna Driller, Vesna on the Beach, Vesna Slap 'n' Tickle . . . you get the idea.

The bartender, who was cute in a swipe-right kind of way, caught her eye.

"Hey," she said, pinning on her I'm-dateable-let's-practice smile. "So what's in the Vesna Bomber?"

"Vodka, grenadine, and passion fruit," she heard behind her in a tone that could freeze a Cossack's ball sac.

Here we go. She turned, the first thing that popped into her head skipping her filter and landing right on her tongue. "Sounds girly."

Okay, so no one would ever describe Vadim Petrov as "girly." Before her stood the most masculine streak of cells to ever grill Isobel's retinas, and she lived in a world teeming with machismo.

"Thought you hated vodka," she said.

"I do." A negligent wave of his hand said this was all beyond his control. Who was he, a mere multimillion-dollar spokesman, to counteract stereotypes about Russians?

The gesture might have been casual, but his stare was anything but. "I was sorry to hear about your father."

"Oh. Thanks." It still gnawed, less a sharp pain now, but a constant awareness of the void. Clifford Chase had been driven, difficult, and demanding. He'd expected great things from his favorite daughter, so her failure to make a career in the pros had strained their relationship.

She missed him like crazy.

Vadim had lost his own father about eighteen months ago. She opened her mouth to offer similar condolences, but they got stuck in her throat with all the other things she longed to say. He'd had a strained relationship with the elder Petrov, a billionaire businessman with rumored ties to the Russian mob, and a man who didn't want Vadim to play hockey in the United States. Better he expend his athletic energies for the glory of Mother Russia. Sergei Petrov got his wish—after Vadim's visit to Chicago all those years ago, his son enjoyed a star-making turn in the Kontinental Hockey League.

Isobel might've had something to do with that.

The silence sat up between them, the tension expanding. Vadim seemed to be expecting her to say something, so she happily obliged.

"How's your knee?"

Not that. His eyebrow raised slightly. "Improving."

Tiptoe around his ego. "There are some special drills you could do to help with your speed. Get you back to how you were preinjury."

"I'm sure the team will do what is necessary."

"Yes, we will."

Gotcha! That eyebrow became one with his hairline.

She cleared her throat. "Moretti has assigned me to give you personalized attention. We'll meet for an hour before each regular practice and work on your skating."

Now that injury had forced her out of the game, coaching was all she had left. This morning Dante Moretti, the newly hired Rebels general manager, had appointed her as a skating consultant with one charge: get Vadim Petrov into good enough shape so they could qualify for the play-offs in two months. She'd planned to drop this knowledge on the man himself after tomorrow's team practice, but hey, no time like the present.

Now she waited for his predictable explosion.

"There is nothing wrong with my skating," he grated.

"There's always room for improvement," she said with unreasonable cheer. Kill the boy with happy. "Right now, you're placing too much weight on your uninjured leg and it's thrown off your motion. We'll focus on—"

"Nothing. I can work with Roget." The regular skating coach.

"He doesn't have time to give you the extra attention you need. It's typical for teams to hire consultants, especially for players who are underperforming."

And there was that famous Russian scowl. Poor ol' Vad was a touch sensitive about his diminished capacity since that knee injury had sidelined him for half the season. Having battled a career-killing injury herself, she understood what he was going through. The doubts, the questioning. The fear. But, unlike her, he was in a position to get back to full strength as a pro. What she wouldn't give for a similar opportunity.

He snorted. "You are not just any consultant, though, are you, Isobel? You are a part owner of the team. You are Clifford Chase's legacy. And even after his death, you are getting your way."

She understood she'd have to get used to slings and arrows, accusations of using her father's name and her position as owner to get a coaching gig. But that last dig about getting her way? Said as if she had done that before.

"I know what I'm doing, Vadim."

"Do you?" He leaned in, using his height to intimidate. It sort of worked. "You can no longer play at the pro level, yet you insist on playing games. With me. And not for the first time. Once your selfishness screwed with my career."

"That's not what happened."

"Isn't it? Three years—" He cut off, his anger a cloud that practically stung her eyes. "All because you put me in your crosshairs, Isobel. Well, forgive me if I would rather not trust my professional future to you."

Her cheeks heated furiously. Of course he would see it that way. She had been young, immature, more sheltered than the average eighteen-year-old. All she knew was hockey. It was her life, and then Vadim had skated into it, and she'd seen something else. Her eyes had opened to beauty and passion and—hell, she'd been a teenage nightmare.

He stood close enough for her to view rings of blue fire around his irises and a smudge of pink lipstick tinting his jaw. It was hard being Vadim Petrov.

Regularly bombarded by photos of him in magazines and on billboards over the years, she wanted to
think it was easier to look at him objectively now. As
a perfectly formed machine of mass and muscle. As
a chiseled Renaissance sculpture that was cool to the
touch. She wanted to think it, but she remembered too
much about the last time she had been this close to
him.

Apologizing for how it all went down would make
things easier.

Well, not exactly *easier*.

They had to work together, put aside their differ-
ences for the sake of the team. But she didn't like his
assumptions about how she'd landed this job. Or
maybe she didn't like that she half agreed with him.

Doubts that she had right completely on her side
put her on the defensive. "These late nights at the
club will have to stop." She curved her gaze around his
broad shoulder to the ever-increasing line of women
waiting to sit on his lap. "You're going to need your
sleep for the extra practice you have to put in."

He didn't respond to that, but if he had, it was easy
to guess what he'd say. What every athlete would say.

I know my limits. I know what my body can take.

Athletes were consummate liars.

He leaned in again, smelling of fame, privilege, and
raw sex appeal. Discomfort at his proximity edged out
the hormonal sparks dancing through her body.

"Does Moretti know that we have history? That you
are the last person I wish to work with?"

Before she could respond, someone squealed, "Vadim!" A blond, skinny, buxom someone, who now wrapped herself around Vadim in a very possessive manner. "You said you'd be back with a dwinkie!"

A dwinkie?

Drawing back, Vadim circled the squealer's waist and pulled her into his hard body. "*Kotyonok*, I did not mean to be so long." He dropped a kiss on her lips, needing to bend considerably because she was just so darn petite! Not like big-boned Isobel, who could have eaten this chick and her five supermodel Playmates for a midmorning snack. A group of them stood off to the side, clearly waiting for the signal to start the orgy. And Vadim clearly wanted to give it, except he had to deal with the annoying six-foot fly in the sex ointment.

Why did the lumberjack hotties always go for twigs instead of branches? Did it make them feel more virile to screw a pocket-sized Barbie?

Yep, feeling like a schlub.

But he didn't need to know that. All he needed to know was that she had the power to return him to competitive ice. This was her best shot at making a difference and getting the Rebels to a coveted play-off spot. Vadim Petrov and his butt-hurt feelings would not stand in her way.

"Do you need to talk about it, Russian?"

She infused as much derision into the question as possible, so that the idea of "talking about it" made him sound a touch less than manly. Big, bad, brickhouse Russians didn't need to talk about the women who'd done them wrong.

"There is nothing to talk about," he uttered in that voice that used to send Siberian shivers down her back. Now? Nothing more than a Muscovian flurry.

"Excellent!" Superscary cheerful face. "Regular practice is tomorrow at ten, so I'll see you on the ice at 9 a.m. Don't be late."

Pretty happy with her exit line, she walked away.

Far too easy.

A brute hand curled around hers and pulled her to the other side of the bar, out of the sight line of most of the VIP room. She found her back against a wall— literally and figuratively—as 230 pounds of Slavic muscle loomed over her.

He still held her hand.

If she weren't so annoyed, she'd think it was kind of nice.

She yanked it away. "Who the hell do you think you are?"

"Who am I?" he boomed, and she prayed it was rhetorical. Unfortunately, no. "I am Vadim Petrov. Leading goal scorer for my first two years in the NHL. Winner of both the Kontinental and the Gagarin Cups. A man not to be trifled with. And you are, who, exactly? The daughter of a hockey great who was not so great when it came to running a team. The woman who can no longer play yet thinks she can offer 'tips' to me. To me! You may have pedigree, Isobel, but there is nothing I can learn from you."

This arrogant, douchewaffle piece of shit!

She straightened, pulling herself millimeters from the wall, which had the effect of putting her eye-to-eye with him. Or eye-to-chin. Close enough.

Too close.

He was breathing hard, and so was she, the lift of her breasts teasing, tantalizing brushes against his chest.

"One conversation and you're out of breath, Vaddy? We're going to need to work on your conditioning."

More of the dark and broody. More of the nipple pops against her sweater.

Stop being so Russian, Russian!

"My conditioning regimen is fine."

A glance over to the bar found "Dwinkie" biting her lip in concern, throwing nervous blinks at her gal pals, and possibly planning an extraction with SEAL Team: Boobs Are Our Weapons.

"Getting your exercise with puck bunnies and Vesna groupies doesn't count." Isobel slid her hand between their bodies and brushed his abs. Good God, hard as ice and hot as sin. "As I suspected, a bit flabby with all your time off. We'll take care of that with your recovery program."

He stepped back, as though burned by her touch, and she willed away the ping of hurt in her chest. At least she knew where they stood on *that* score.

"I will discuss this with Coach Calhoun and Moretti tomorrow."

"You do that, but do it early, because I'm still

expecting you in full gear at 9 a.m. And, Vadim? I'd suggest you quit with the trail of women looking to sit on your . . . knee. We don't want to weaken it or any other parts of your anatomy. Keep that up and you won't even have a shot at *Dancing with the Stars*."

Then with the reflexes that had once accorded her MVP status on the ice, she escaped his orbit and headed back into the crowd.

TWO

Isobel charged into Rebels HQ in Riverbrook, thirty miles north of downtown Chicago, on track for her father's office.

No. The office of Dante Moretti, the Rebels' new GM.

She was late, so she gave a quick wave of *yes yes I'm here* to his assistant and crashed through the door with her typical aplomb. Harper was already there, seated in one of the leather armchairs, which Isobel knew from personal experience were not as comfortable as they looked. In her hand was a coffee cup—not a mug, but a white porcelain cup on a saucer—which accessorized perfectly with her whole put-togetherness. Corn-silk-blond hair in a chignon, a houndstooth check sleeveless dress, black patent heels. Harper looked like she owned a pro hockey team.

They had never gelled, not for want of trying on Isobel's part. From her earliest memories, Isobel adored her older-by-six-years sister. So pretty, so blond, so petite. Popular with everyone. But the admiration wasn't reciprocated.

After Clifford Chase married Isobel's mother, Gerry, he had abandoned his daughter from his first marriage. Harper had taken that hurt and used it as a shield whenever Isobel tried to get close. She hadn't understood then why Harper pushed her away. Their father was a tough man to like, and while Isobel adored him, it had taken her a long time to acknowledge his faults. She now recognized the pain their father had caused. Six-year-old Harper, abandoned by Cliff, forced to live with her depressed, eternally blotto mother while Isobel enjoyed all his attention.

All of it.

Named after Lady Isobel Gathorne-Hardy, the daughter of Frederick Stanley, Sixteenth Earl of Derby and donor of the Stanley Cup, Isobel had lived her entire childhood burdened by her father's expectations. *Skate faster, Isobel. Shoot harder. You're my winningest girl.*

The past five months since his death had been turbulent, to say the least. Old wounds were ripped open and hastily sewn up, all so the Chase sisters could get through the next few months and make the play-offs. As for what would happen then, Isobel had no idea.

Whereas Harper looked like the model of an NHL franchise owner, Isobel most certainly did not. She'd awoken late and thrown on a tracksuit and sneakers, shoved her hair into a ponytail (with a rubber band from the junk drawer, because she couldn't find anything else), and raced to the Rebels' practice facility a few blocks over to meet with Vadim. That was an hour ago.

He hadn't shown.

She'd texted, called, and received nothing in response. But then she saw his man, Alexei, in the parking lot forty-five minutes later, which meant Vadim had turned up for the team's regular practice.

Needless to say, she was pissed. And now she was late.

Dante looked up, a tall white porcelain pot in his hand—it matched the cups, naturally—and acknowledged her entrance with, "Coffee, Isobel?"

"Yeah, sure, thanks."

Dante Moretti was an unlikely GM, all dark broodiness and Italian hotness, who Isobel assumed had exited the womb wearing a Michael Corleone scowl and a three-piece Armani suit. After handing off the coffee cup on a saucer (biscotti, too—nice), he sat one butt cheek on the desk, facing them. Strong thighs were lovingly hugged by pin-striped pants. Such a waste, and further proof that God was a man.

A former player, Dante was the first openly gay general manager of an American professional sports team. In the macho world of the NHL, his appointment as an assistant in Boston had made waves, and now his ascension to the top echelons as GM in Chicago had brought a tsunami of attention to the Rebels organization. They were already fielding a barrage of vitriol as a woman-owned team; adding a gay chief executive to the mix encouraged all manner of trolls to come out of the woodwork.

Bring it, haters.

"Am I to be fired?" he asked lightly.

"No," Harper said, all treacle. "We'll give you longer than two weeks, Dante."

"Well, that's a relief. You called this meeting, so perhaps it's time to tell me what's up."

The sisters shared a glance. They'd agreed that as the most experienced when it came to managing the team, Harper should lead this conversation. But now she looked as though her emotions were clogging her ability to speak. In the past few months, Harper had changed. She wasn't the ice queen of yore. The terms of their father's will had unveiled vulnerabilities she'd been hiding for years. Falling in love had softened her.

Seeing her sister's hesitation, Isobel stepped into the breach. "We weren't completely honest when we hired you, Dante."

He took a sip of his coffee and set it down on his desk. Then he moved the cup and saucer a foot away, perhaps in anticipation of his reaction to whatever they were about to say.

"Continue."

"You know about our father's will, about how the team was left to the three of us to jointly manage." If Dante thought it odd that the third in their sisterly triumvirate wasn't present, he didn't let on. Violet refused to attend any meeting or game unless she was contractually obliged to.

"It was all the media could talk about for three months," he said with unmistakable impatience.

"Well, there's more. A stipulation in the will says that if we don't make the play-offs this season"—*here goes nothing*—"the team will be sold off."

She had to give it to him. Not even a blink.

"Sold off to whom?"

"A consortium waiting in the wings. We'd get a semi-decent inheritance-slash-payoff, and the rest would go to Clifford's alma mater to set up a hockey scholarship." Isobel looked to Harper to verify that about covered it.

Harper smiled her thanks and said, "That's it in a nutshell. We thought about telling you before you came on board but didn't want to let the pressure sway your decision."

Dante's throaty growl was his first emotional reaction. "Oh, you didn't, did you?"

"Either you think the team has a shot or you don't," Isobel said, already on the defensive. "The team's ownership shouldn't make a difference."

Dante looked unconvinced, and rightly so. "Then why tell me now?"

"Because this isn't merely any old year," Harper said. "It's make or break for the family. Violet will probably sell off her portion to us at the end of the season, assuming we can afford it, but Isobel and I want to continue in ownership. This means everything to the two of us."

Isobel shot a look at Harper. She'd always assumed Harper would fight tooth and nail to become sole owner of the team. Since when had she considered that the two of them might jointly run operations?

Dante shook his head, a rueful smile creasing his handsome features. "So now I'm part of the inner circle." It sounded like he'd rather have been left outside in ignorant bliss. "Who else knows?"

Isobel turned to Harper. "Have you told Remy?"

"Last night. I didn't tell him sooner because . . . well, because."

Because she didn't want to use the will's stipulation to force him to stay with her. A month ago, Remy had a chance to trade out to a team with a better shot at making it to the postseason. Telling him about the "play-offs or bust" requirement would have muddled his decision, throwing pity for Harper's predicament into the mix. She would never trust that he'd remained because he loved her.

Dante nodded. "Anyone else in the org? Other players? I've noticed Violet is pretty close to some of them." His disapproval was obvious.

"She knows better," Isobel said quickly. "We don't want it getting out, and the players don't need the extra pressure. The only other person who knows is Kenneth Bailey." The Rebels' lawyer.

Dante pushed off from the desk and walked to the window.

With Dante's back to them, Isobel turned to Harper for a check-in on how she thought the conversation might be going. Harper's head was cocked as she blatantly ogled their GM.

Stop it, Isobel frowned.

You stop it, Harper frowned right back.

That made them both giggle, which drew Dante's querying look.

"Uh, sorry," she muttered. "Just nervous." *And concerned we might have a suit for sexual harassment as well as breach of contract on our hands.*

"I did wonder at some of your decisions before I came on board. They seemed rather rash."

Harper placed her coffee cup and saucer on the desk. "We needed to hit the ground running. Throwing everything at it and bringing on a veteran like Remy, particularly as the team was rudderless for a while, was the best strategy."

"St. James seems to be in better shape," Dante said, referring to their team captain, Bren, who was coming off a rehab stint for alcoholism that had left the team bereft of strong leadership for a while. "I'd have a case for saying this materially changes the terms of my contract."

"Or you could see it as the challenge it is," Isobel said. "Whatever happens, your contract is good for three years. Any new owner would have to buy it out, so you're not going to be disadvantaged financially."

"That's not really the point, is it, Isobel?"

No, it wasn't. If they didn't do well, and he was kicked to the curb by a new owner, it would be harder for him to move laterally to another organization. Not without a solid season behind him. They'd effectively tied his career to the fortunes of the team.

Welcome to the world of pro sports management.

"If you need time to think about it . . ." Harper trailed off.

As he viewed his surroundings, Isobel would have given her left tit to know what was going on inside that handsome head of his. She imagined him taking in the corner office, thrilling at his achievement in rising so far—and cursing the Chase sisters for throwing this wrench in the works.

After several interminable seconds, he faced them, his mouth set in determination. "Looks like I'm an honorary Chase for the next four months."

Phew!

They chitchatted about tomorrow's home game against Dallas, the tension of the earlier conversation dissipating with every minute they discussed this sport they each loved in a different way. As they made to leave, Dante called Isobel back. "Could I have a word?"

Harper smiled at them both, said her good-byes, and left.

Dante's demeanor was all business. "Why weren't you with Petrov this morning before the team practice? Too busy recovering from a Vesna hangover?"

Either the man had spies on the staff or he read TMZ on his way to work.

"He had a late night, so I let him sleep in," she lied. "Extra practice starts tomorrow." At his cutting look, she added, "Let me take care of Petrov in my way. I shouldn't have to tell you this, but athletes are sensitive and need careful handling. Russians, especially." *Vadim, especially.* "Pushing him will only make him dig his skates in."

Dante held her gaze for a long beat. "I know you want a full-time coaching job with a pro team, Isobel. With this team. We're making history here, but there's only so much change we can inflict on the team and fans in one year."

Sure, breaking glass ceilings all over the place was totally awesome, but Isobel had to wonder if she'd shot her own ambitions in the foot by agreeing to hire someone with so much on the line as their GM.

"In other words, the history-making quota for this year has been fulfilled?"

Dante smiled in sympathy. "In a manner of speaking. When I came on board, you knew my requirements. I understand that as one-third owner of the team, you're technically my boss, but I won't bow to internal pressure to make you a regular coach. However, if you can turn Petrov's game around, then that'd put you in pole position for a full-time gig next season." He sighed heavily. "If I'd been here in January, I wouldn't have brought him on. He's temperamental. Mercurial. But you and your sisters made that call—among others—and I have to work with it. Petrov's slowed down since his knee injury last year. He needs a lot of work to get him up to speed on the ice, and I think you can do it. This isn't a pity appointment, Isobel. It's a vital compromise."

She understood. She'd spent much of her life understanding.

Dante pulled out a pocket watch from his pin-striped vest. It should have screamed "pretentious," but instead it yelled "hot." The guy was really too much. "I want daily updates. I'll leave it to you to figure out a schedule that works around regular practice and games."

"Not to mention his numerous sponsorship commitments and nightclub appearances."

For the first time, Dante looked animated. "He'll certainly bring in a different kind of fan."

"Women with big . . . signs."

He chuckled. "What's a hockey game without glitter-covered marriage proposals and offers to incubate a star player's spawn held up against the Plexi? Some of his fans may be proof that evolution can go in reverse, but as long as they're putting their money where their über fandom is, then we'll take it."

Higher revenues meant more funds to spend on better players, which led to results and championships and butts in seats, thus feeding the hamster wheel of NHL success. She just hoped the Chase sisters would be around to see their hard work come to fruition.

"I can remake him a star on the ice as well as on billboards," she said.

"I know, Isobel. I have every faith in you."

If only the Russian felt the same way.

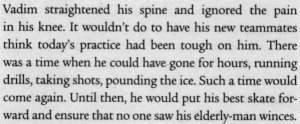

Vadim straightened his spine and ignored the pain in his knee. It wouldn't do to have his new teammates think today's practice had been tough on him. There was a time when he could have gone for hours, running drills, taking shots, pounding the ice. Such a time would come again. Until then, he would put his best skate forward and ensure that no one saw his elderly-man winces.

Twenty-seven years old and already in decline.

"Where y'at, man?"

Vadim looked up from his spot on the bench to find Remy DuPre, one of the Rebels' centers, looming over him. He cast a glance left, then right before answering with, "I am here. In the locker room."

DuPre laughed. "Sorry, Petrov, I meant how ya doin'? That's just how we say it back in my hometown. You were skating pretty hard out there."

Vadim assessed the man before him. Tall, but then most hockey players were. Thirty-five years old, but he held himself well for a man of his age. Most important was the fact that he was in a relationship with Harper Chase, the oldest of the Chase sisters. The headlines had died down during the last month, but Vadim had to wonder at the judgment of any man who would place himself in such a position with a woman. Sleeping with the woman who paid his salary and controlled his career? Not the most strategic of moves.

After a few days in Chicago, Vadim was still trying to work out the team dynamic. DuPre acted like the captain, though that official honor belonged to Bren St. James, a dour Scotsman who would give a gulag commander a run for his money. There didn't appear to be any tension between DuPre and St. James; their command of the team was close to co-rule.

"I'm fine," Vadim said, squaring his shoulders. "I expected the practice would go longer. That's how it was in Quebec."

"Oh yeah?" DuPre sat on the bench and started to unlace his skates. "Guess we decided to take it easy on ya, seein' as how it's your first week and all."

Easy? Sure they did. They were testing his limits, how far to push him, whether he needed special handling because he was fighting his way back to full fitness. This was good. Vadim didn't miss his old team, where in truth he was not used to the best of his abilities. When trading him in, Coach Calhoun had said they planned to use him on the left wing. Usually, right-handers such as Vadim were invariably placed on the right, but Coach and the team had recognized that his natural fit was his off side. Such intuition gave Vadim confidence that the Rebels knew what they were doing—at least in the coaching arena.

As for the rest of the Rebels organization . . . a team owned and run by women. Vadim had no problem with women running things, though he would prefer they did not fraternize off the ice, especially in his world of clubs and girls. He had invited his new teammates to the Vesna vodka PR event, as it was the sociable thing to do, and apparently Cade Burnett, the Texan defenseman, was friendly with Violet, the youngest Chase daughter. Vadim had known he would run into Isobel eventually, but he had not expected the judgment in her moss-colored eyes or the snark on her crimson lips. This was not the innocent adoration of before, a fresh virgin looking to be schooled in the ways of desire. This was . . . different.

Mostly, he had not expected his body's reaction to being so close to her after all these years. Theirs had been a teenage infatuation, a singular blend of uncontrollable hormones, fortunate proximity, and the knowledge that her father would not have approved. If it had not ended so abruptly, it would have fizzled quickly. Why, all these years later, would this woman—the source of such frustration, the one who had thwarted his career—make his body hard and greedy?

After last night's sparring at the club, he had left agitated and alone. That buzz he felt talking to Isobel had sizzled through his veins, keeping him awake and, much to his annoyance, horny. There was no good reason why Isobel Chase should turn him on in any way. Once, she tempted him, yes, but his tastes had changed.

He had not slept well, the pain in his knee bothersome. Not because he had allowed a few women to perch on it so he could fulfill his obligations to his sponsor! But at the end of the day, it liked to remind him of his failure. In the mornings, too. After slipping in and out of a restless sleep, he had hauled his body to the shower, hoping the steam would loosen it up. It took longer than he expected and delayed the start of his day.

Slight unease panged his chest at not showing up for Isobel's "special" practice session this morning. But if she thought he was blowing her off, it would not be the worst message to send. Five minutes in her presence, and she was sneaking under his skin again. Insidious, immature, infuriating Isobel. He was doing her a service, really. Any extended time with her would likely result in him throttling the minx.

His cell phone buzzed with a message from Mia.

Are you off IR yet?

Injury reserve. He ignored his sister's text. A mistake, as silence brought a torrent of questions.

Are you getting enough sleep?

Is the pain in your knee sharp or more like an ache?

Did you hook up with that blonde at the club last night? Or the skanky redhead? The TMZ footage was kind of grainy.

Chyort! His thumbs hovered over his phone in threat, though apparently not enough of one to make the messages stop.

Looks like they have cooties. All of them.

Then: *Czar of Pleasure. LOL.*

He groaned at the silly nickname. A woman had told a story to the gutter press about his prowess between the sheets, and a legend was born. He didn't recall this woman—if he had slept with a tenth of the women who claimed to have slept with him, he would probably be on his syphilitic deathbed—but he accepted the name because, why not?

"You're in demand, Petrov," Remy said with a grin as the texts continued to vomit onto his screen.

"My sister. She's a pain in my ass."

Remy looked sympathetic. "Got four of 'em myself. Worst affliction known to man."

Vadim wouldn't phrase it quite so dramatically. "She is young, and we don't know each other well. A recent connection." Not for the first time, the reason behind this sent his blood into a boil.

Remy rubbed the unshaven scruff on his chin. "Sounds complicated. I'm here to be your priest, should you need it."

Leon Shay, a left-winger like Vadim, strode out of the shower and into the locker room as naked as a babe. Not that Vadim minded—at this point, he'd seen more naked men than women—but there was something about the way Shay swaggered about with his swinging dick that bothered him. Territory marking, undoubtedly, given that Vadim was faster and had been brought in to shore up the left side. There was room for them both, but the better Vadim played, the less ice time Shay would get.

Which is probably why this ass placed a foot up on the bench with his cock at Vadim's eye level. On a derisive sniff, he swiped at his legs with a towel.

Catching Vadim's eye, Remy quirked his lips, affirming this was not Vadim's imagination. A minute later, Remy headed into the shower while Vadim answered his sister's text: *I am in practice. So should you be.*

"Gotta be careful around him," Shay said, pulling deodorant out of his gym bag.

Vadim arced his gaze over the locker room and, realizing that there was no one else here, peered up at Shay.

"Careful?"

"He's banging Harper Chase, so he may as well be spying on the team."

Ah. Looked like he had discovered the team's malcontent. Every locker room suffered one. Vadim waited for more on this rather entertaining brand of paranoia.

"Women running a hockey team." Shay shook his head at what he evidently thought was a great personal insult. "Just be careful what you say, because there's a direct line from here to Chase Manor."

Vadim found this both highly amusing and likely beneficial for future gamesmanship.

"If you refrain from treasonous statements, then you have nothing to worry about."

Shay stopped in the act of pulling his briefs on. "That's not how it works outside of Russia, Petrov. Here in the good ole US of A, we like to think our speech is not regulated or restricted in any way. And you know what else? Fuck me if Isobel Chase isn't angling for a coaching spot. Putting a fox in the henhouse, that's what that is."

"Are you saying this locker room is like a henhouse? Filled with *hens*?"

"It's a metaphor, Petrov. A metaphor for trouble."

Vadim pretended to consider this lesson in the English idiom. "*Da*. Trouble."

The team whiner regarded Vadim with suspicion, trying to determine if he was being made fun of. Vadim kept his expression perfectly vacant, not unlike a pose for one of his underwear photo shoots.

Encouraged by the silence, Shay continued his grumbling. "Women thinking they can run and coach men's hockey. And now a fag for a GM—"

He cut off as Cade Burnett strode into the locker room, wearing a towel and a wide grin. Vadim liked the cheerful Texan, who was having a good season.

"Petrov, trainer's ready for you," Burnett said.

About time. Vadim could have insisted his knee

injury required he go first for the postpractice rubdown, but unlike these soft Americans, he was fine with
waiting. Even if the stiffness in his knee would produce
the kind of pain he'd need his best poker face to endure.

As for what else he might need a poker face, Vadim
knew he'd have to watch Leon Shay carefully. Inside,
his blood boiled at the notion this man thought Isobel could not coach men's hockey. She was a champion! So perhaps Vadim had hinted as much to Isobel
herself last night, but her gender was not why he had
a problem with her as a coach. With their complicated
history, the present would become only more tangled if
they were to spend time together.

His life was already far too knotty to indulge her
ambition.

He stood, relieved that his knee elected not to
betray him at this moment.

Shay pointed at him. "Just remember what I said,
Petrov. Watch who you talk to."

Yes, Shay. Yes, I will.

Isobel headed toward the locker room at the Rebels' practice facility, determined to have it out with
the uncooperative Mr. Petrov. Turning a corner, she
bumped into a tower of unyielding muscle, fronted
by a snarl that had her almost recoiling. But that had
nothing on how Isobel's name on Leon Shay's lips
skeeved her the hell out.

"Miz Chase."

Yep, shower for one. Dry off. Then another.

"Shay."

This guy hadn't exactly welcomed the ownership changes at the top. He was built in the mold of her father, a man's man with distinct tendencies toward assholery. While Shay never came right out and complained, his position was clear: women should not be running hockey teams. Now he blocked her path, actually and figuratively.

"Got places to be," she said, and while she could have gone around him, she elected to wait until he moved around her. *Better keep that intimidation shit for the ice, dickhead.*

With one last sneer, he rounded her and walked away.

She shuddered. Make that shower a triple.

Pushing the locker room door ajar, she called out, "You guys decent?"

A rumble of male laughter answered, then Remy's voice sounded above the noise. "That's open to interpretation, but if you mean mostly covered up, then yeah."

She walked in, prepared for Remy's assurance to be a bunch of bull. In her years coaching the minors in Montreal, she'd seen a wealth of penis—long, short, fat, skinny, weirdly curved, and oddly shaded—so in-the-buff athletes no longer fazed her.

And would you lookie here? If it wasn't the very pleasant sight of Cade Burnett, towel-free and ass-out.

He turned slightly with a wicked grin, penis in profile. Not bad.

"Howdy, Isobel."

"Hey, Alamo." Reluctantly, she moved her gaze to points north. "Heard you fell on your pretty face during practice. You okay?"

"Yeah. St. James caught me with my helmet loose. Sometimes I forget he's an asshole."

She studied the growing bruise on his chin. "You're all assholes, but you're one of my favorite assholes."

"Bet you say that to all the good-lookin' Texans."

Such an outrageous flirt. "I'm looking for Petrov."

"In with the trainer," Remy said, the words muffled as he pulled a sweatshirt over his head.

She turned to leave, but didn't get far before she felt a hand touching her arm. Remy stood behind her, his expression sheepish.

"About this morning."

Yes. This morning. She was currently staying in a guest room at Harper's house, affectionately known as Chase Manor, in Lake Forest, a situation that was supposed to be only temporary. On her way to grab a cup of joe in the kitchen before the practice-that-never-was, she'd walked in on her sister and Remy in a pose she would need a lifetime supply of bleach to scrub from her retinas.

"I'm sorry about that," she said.

He looked horrified. "No, you shouldn't be sorry. Hell, that's your home, and usually Harper's over at mine. But I'd stopped by after the club last night, and well . . . you shouldn't have to tiptoe around your own house. To be honest"—he lowered his voice—"I'd rather we were living together at my place, but Harper wants to wait until the season is over. Less media attention."

"That's probably a good idea. Don't get me wrong, you guys are great together, but the next couple of months are going to need all our focus."

He rubbed his chin. "I s'pose." But he didn't sound like he agreed. Was he looking for her permission to push Harper on this? Humans with penises, so needy.

"Harper's crazy about you, DuPre. And I get to witness it in all its naked expression on our kitchen counters. Yay!"

Remy chuckled.

"We're heading to the Empty Net tomorrow night," Cade said as he rubbed a towel over his junk. "Gotta give Petrov a proper welcome. You in, Isobel?"

Fraternizing with the players deliberately and with Petrov specifically? Uh, no. Last night was an accident. Besides, she was fully aware of how in demand the players were by the opposite sex and just how willing they were to fulfill the supply side of the equation to any hockey groupie in range. A philanderer father and two cheating exes told her she did *not* need to witness that.

"Thanks, but I'm busy washing my hair." And with that, she headed out, steeling herself for a stern talk with their new left-winger.

She entered the trainer's room . . . and immediately wished she'd used the same MO as she had outside the locker room two minutes ago.

As in, should have knocked.

Sorry, Cade Burnett, your brief reign as King Perfect Butt is now over. A new ruler has ascended the throne.

Vadim Petrov took assology to a whole other level.

He lay stretched out, facedown, on the trainer's table, a towel draped over his back, leaving his lower half—*yes, ladies, the best half*—exposed. Two perfect globes sat up like melons. If melons could, uh, *sit up*.

Melons? Oh for Gretzky's sake, woman. Snap out of it.

Luckily, she had a few things going for her to aid in this snap-out effort.

1. She'd seen plenty of perfect hockey player ass. Dammit, she was a professional, and this was just another one.

2. Petrov's ass was old news. The guy had recently displayed it shamelessly in ESPN's *The Body Issue*, so the world and its Aunt Cecily knew every curve and contour.

3. Most important and most relevant to this situation, she'd actually touched/stroked/squeezed this particular ass years ago, and frankly, she wasn't looking to repeat.

Kelly Townsend, the team's head trainer, raised his chin and acknowledged her presence with a smile. Of all the Rebels' backroom staff, she liked Kelly the best, probably because he gave off a distinctly non-threatening vibe. In a boy band, he'd be the guy who brought flowers for your mom and didn't do any weird crotch-grabbing grinds during the song's instrumental bridge. A Brandon, not a Dylan.

"Kelly, how long do you need?"

"All done." Kelly smiled again, then opened his mouth to say something else. Instead, he turned to his patient. "Adductor feeling better, Vadim?"

A grunt from the Russian acknowledged it was. So that's why his towel was doing such a terrible job of covering up his ass. Isobel had thought it a bit much for a knee rubdown. With a nod, Kelly left the room.

Vadim sat up, unfairly pulling the towel over his groin so she missed the main attraction. Had he changed in the intervening years? If anything, he had to have grown bigger, which was terrifying, because the boy had rocked a manaconda at nineteen. Dicks didn't shrink with time, did they?

Note to self: Google "penis size changes with age." For science.

"We need to talk." As he futzed with the towel's perfect positioning—*get over yourself, Petrov, I don't care!*—she took a moment to note where else he might have changed. Definitely more tattoos. Some she recognized from before: that colorful babushka on his right forearm, the jaguar ready to pounce from his shoulder, symbols that held significance for him covering practically every inch of steely flesh. A new-to-her tat over his rib cage caught her attention. A set of skates in flames, Russian script entwined around it.

Then there were the abs. Jesus, you could grate Parm on those puppies. Peering up, he caught her burning stare, and his reaction was predictable.

Look all you want, but this is not for you.

Understood. She wouldn't break any mirrors, but

standing before him in Nike's spring collection ensemble, her dark brown hair in a ponytail, her face free of makeup, she looked nothing like the razor-thin models Vadim was regularly photographed with coming out of clubs.

There was no reason why that should have entered her head, except that once he had told her she was the most beautiful thing he'd ever laid eyes on. Not that she needed his compliments. Eighteen-year-old girls desperate to have their cherry popped by gorgeous Russians are usually all in.

Now his expression made it clear she had no impact on him whatsoever, which was fine because she was here to do a job. A sexless, no-chemistry, so-what-if-you-took-my-virginity job.

She started with an easy one. "How are you feeling today?"

"Fine."

"Oh, I thought maybe your knee was bothering you, and that was why you blew off practice."

Cue the Russian ice stare of doom.

"With me," she clarified.

"I don't need it. I can work with the regular coaching staff."

"We don't have time for that. Thursday is the start of six days on the road and the coaches will be with the team. You're on IR, so you'll be staying here and working on your skills—or were you planning to run drills by yourself?"

He remained as silent as the grave, his big hands

splayed on his towel-covered thighs. Everything about him strained taut. Muscles, body language, expression. But she didn't trust it to remain that way. Vadim's strength on the ice was his speed. No one transitioned quicker than him, a sleek cat that could uncoil and strike at any moment, just like that jaguar on his shoulder. She expected that was how it was now. Even at rest he was dangerous.

Speaking as a fellow athlete might be a better approach. "I know you're worried about getting back to full strength. I've been there—"

"And you had to give up."

Wow, that stung. She widened her eyes, fighting the tears pricking at her eyelids.

Since her injury two years ago during the inaugural National Women's Hockey League game, she'd lost all faith in her abilities. Sure, she had healed with a speed that amazed her doctors. They'd never seen anyone with a fractured skull recover so quickly. But they had been adamant about her competitive future—or lack thereof. A fall, a rough check against the boards, hell, a slip stepping out of the shower, and she might not wake up again.

Thirty-seven minutes. Her time on pro ice. Knowing you were all washed up by the age of twenty-five was sobering, to say the least.

Her father hadn't taken it well. Whereas any other parent would be trying to hold his kid back off the ice after she'd taken a skate blade to the head, Clifford had dismissed the doctors' concerns.

I played with a fractured femur once, Izzy. Every player knows what they can handle. Trust your heart as much as your body.

She'd tried, for him as much as for herself. Training with her team, the Buffalo Betties—who only allowed her to skate after she signed a waiver absolving them of all liability—she had suffered a hip injury two months in. Now it flared up when she pushed herself too hard, the pain a signal that she was no longer cut out for pro play.

Those who can't, coach.

Giving up her dream was the hardest thing she'd ever had to do. So nice of this Russian jerk to rub her face in it.

"Yes, I did have to give up. But I have plenty of experience teaching, and I've put together a plan to get you back on track."

She unearthed her iPad from her messenger bag and leaned against the massage table while it came to life. Damn, he smelled good. Why did the jerk have to smell so good?

She opened up her spreadsheet, each hour she planned to spend with him linked to a core set of skills they would focus on. Quickly, she whipped through the daily tasks: strength training, skating skills, knee exercises.

"I worked with two guys in Montreal last year and turned their recovery from a projected eight weeks to five."

"Linberg and Costigan," he murmured, close to her ear.

She drew back, surprised that one, they were so heart-stoppingly close, and two, he knew the players' names on the minor league team she had worked with.

"Right." She cleared her throat because he was staring at her now, all blue-eyed ferocity, his stance aggressive even though he was seated and hadn't moved a muscle.

"I will not need eight weeks, Isobel. Or five."

"No." She tore her gaze away and focused on the iPad. "I'm thinking more like two. Three max, if we work hard but are careful not to overdo it. My job is to get you back in the rink in time for the big push." The Rebels were at 28–20 win-loss right now with five losses in overtime. This left twenty-nine games in the regular season. "We need you in there for the last twenty games, Vadim."

Looking up again, she found his eyes magnetized to her, his focus burning holes into her soul. What was it about Russians that amplified the simplest look to the nth degree?

"The conventional wisdom is that you and your sisters are lucky to have done this well, considering."

"Considering we're women?"

"Considering you're coming off fifteen years of bad results. This year should be your rebuild, yet you have decided to trade aggressively and bring in players you would not normally acquire. Veterans at the end of their careers. Injured men who may spend the season on the bench. You are gambling, Isobel."

They were. At first she'd thought it was some cruel

joke her father was playing on Harper. Her older sister was supposed to inherit the team, and while Isobel felt invested in her father's legacy, she hadn't expected this role. Joint owner, on the spot, where her decisions affected whether the team stayed in the family or was sold off.

Isobel wondered if her father had wanted to give her purpose after her failed career. He had been so disappointed that she'd had to resort to coaching, not pleased at all that she had found a job in the minors. *Fucking Canada, Izzy?* Even now, she felt guilty that she had enjoyed the time outside his Eye of Sauron–like focus. But he had the last laugh when he drew her back into his orbit.

The requirements of the will stipulated that she had to attend every home game. Fine for Harper, and even for Violet, who didn't seem to mind uprooting her life in Reno. But for Isobel, something had to give. The tensions between coaching in Montreal and having to be on site for the Rebels in Chicago were too demanding. She had quit her coaching gig two months ago.

Part of it was to force Harper's hand. *Let me be a Rebels coach. Let's make this history you're always talking about.* But she realized that the job wasn't going to be handed to her.

She turned back to Vadim, his accusation that she was gambling still hanging between them.

"We want to make a big splash our first year out." He didn't need to know about the pressure they were under. All he needed to know was that she—and she alone—could get him back to the face-off circle.

"This is how I remember you. Striving to be the best. Living with no fear. Back then, nothing could get in your way. The Girl with the Blazing Skates."

That silly nickname he had given her would have sounded almost forgiving if that jibe about nothing getting in her way hadn't canceled it out. But he was right about one thing: there had been a time when fear was meaningless. She'd felt invulnerable. Unbreakable. And now? She was a frightened, scarred little girl begging the man who had made her a woman to give her a chance.

"It's a lot to ask, I know. Especially if you've never been coached by a woman before."

He appeared to consider what she said; the air between them thickened and charged. Maybe he had a point. Maybe their past history would impede the mission.

"Playing the woman card is not necessary, Isobel. I will submit to your will on the practice rink. You have two weeks to get me back on competitive ice."

THREE

Vadim stared at the egg white omelet in front of him, the same breakfast he ate every day during the season. "Perhaps you could mix it up one of these days," he said to the chef in Russian. "Add some cheese."

The chef, Alexei, regarded him with disdain, which should have been difficult for a man wearing an apron with the words Squeeze Me, I'm Delicious! But with Alexei, disdain was his resting face.

Vadim should have fired him years ago. A grown man did not need a minder. He'd only kept him around because Alexei had been so upset after the death of Vadim's father. The loyal retainer, assigned by the Petrov family to ensure Vadim's safety after a botched kidnapping attempt when he was eleven years old, had expressed no interest in leaving. Threats to Vadim these days, except from predatory women, were few and far between, yet Alexei remained.

He supposed it was good to have someone to run errands, a male assistant who did not simper with puppy dog eyes. If Alexei wanted to move on to another position, he could. For now, Vadim paid him as much as he was worth. He lived nearby in a smaller property and did not spend every waking moment with Vadim. Sometimes he was gone for entire weekends.

Then there was his primary use: he made an excellent mediator between Vadim and Victoria Wallace. Using his sister as a buffer smacked of cruelty, and that was where Alexei came in: screening his calls because Vadim refused to speak to his mother.

"You are sick of my cooking?" Alexei asked, his spatula raised ominously over the frying pan.

"Some variety wouldn't kill you."

Alexei gave nothing away, but that was par for the course. The two of them together were like Easter Island statues, yet Vadim suspected that after many years those strange monoliths understood one another.

"Something is bothering you," Alexei said, his attention back to the stove as he cooked scrambled eggs— with yolks, of course—for himself. "Is it the Chase girl?"

Vadim snorted. *The Chase girl.* Alexei was never afraid to let his feelings about Isobel be known.

"It's nothing." Their first practice together was in an hour, and he was oddly nervous. Around Isobel! He found himself wanting to please her, which was ridiculous. She needed to impress him. *Her* future in coaching was on the line.

"You remember what happened last time?" Alexei

asked. When Vadim didn't answer, Alexei carried on with uncharacteristic passion. "She ruined your career."

"And you accuse me of drama."

He was waving the spatula now, little pieces of egg landing on the counter like ice chips flying during a vigorous skate. "She drew you into her web, and your path to the American professional league was closed off. That was her fault."

Vadim had thought so once, but on reflection, he realized that Isobel was as much a pawn in all of this as Vadim was. Clifford Chase was protective, an alpha wolf shielding his cub. He had a vision for his daughter, and when he came across them that day, twined together in naked, postorgasmic abandon, he had seen what Isobel had not.

Vadim would have pursued this girl to the ends of the earth.

He wanted her beyond all reason, and he would have shocked and awed to make her his. A man like Clifford knew obsession when he saw it staring him in the face. With no sons, he had placed all his hopes and dreams in his daughter's tentative career. Nothing would stand in the way of Isobel's rise as the greatest female hockey player to grace a rink, especially not an infatuated Russian teenager.

Chase's tactics, while not sporting, had been understandable in his mission to push his daughter to glory.

Ensure that Vadim's visa was revoked.

Blackball him with the NHL commissioner.

Darken his name with Isobel.

I don't care if your father is Joseph Fucking Stalin, I will end you if you come near her again, Petrov. She's going to make history, but not if she has to play second fiddle to your career.

Of course he'd had help. Between Clifford Chase and Sergei Petrov, Vadim's own father, any chance he'd had with Isobel was destroyed.

The KHL was not such a bad training ground. The money was terrible compared to the NHL, but Vadim didn't need money. And Lord knew his father was pleased to have him close to home again, away from the potentially bad influence of Victoria Wallace, not that he'd heard from her. His own mother, only one time zone away in New York, and she made no effort to connect with the son she left behind when he was ten years old.

It was in the past—both his mother and Isobel. Five years ago, he had started his pro career in North America, his exile at an end. His life so far had been based in Canada, and while his forays into the States for away games placed temptation in his way, only once had he given in to his urge to see the Girl with the Blazing Skates.

It had ended disastrously.

He turned to Alexei, who was now shoveling what looked like a half dozen scrambled eggs onto a plate. Fucker. Now he placed his plate on the table and sat, knife and fork at the ready, a precursor to more "advice."

"You will let her control your destiny again. This is not the Petrov way."

Vadim pushed back his plate, annoyed because Alexei was right. Petrov men determined their own fates, and they certainly did not allow a woman to own them—on or off the ice.

"I will handle Isobel Chase," Vadim said with more assurance than he felt. "Now eat your eggs, you old fool."

"Again."

With one foot crossed over the other, Vadim rounded one of the face-off circles at the end of the rink, then continued in a figure eight around the other one. With each completed circuit, his anger bubbled beneath his usually calm surface. Finally he'd had enough, so he braked in a cloud of ice shavings.

"Again." Completely devoid of emotion, Isobel repeated the instruction.

He went again.

Boiled again.

Stopped again.

"A—"

"—gain?"

She blew out a breath. "I didn't tell you to stop, so that's all you're going to hear from me until I do tell you to stop."

"I know how to skate crossovers, Isobel. I've been skating since I was three years old."

She placed her iPad down on the bench and glided over to him. For a tall woman, she displayed remarkable grace and fluidity, but then those qualities had been the first things he'd noticed about her. Isobel Chase had remarkable talent, was a natural-born skater. Back then, he had tried to give her tips, only to discover that she needed nothing of the sort from him.

No, her needs had been more primal.

"How's your knee?"

Sore. "Fine."

"Then why aren't you bending it more? You can never have enough knee bend. Every part of your skating motion depends on getting lower."

She waved him off, so he backed up a few strides. Starting on her right foot, she circled the ice, staying close to the painted line, her knees bent perfectly as she brought her body low.

He could watch her all day.

"I do not have your center of gravity. I won't be getting that low."

"You used to bend your knee more."

She skated back over to the bench, and he was rather annoyed to find his gaze fixed on her ass in the snug confines of her tracksuit pants. Perfectly heart shaped, it made his fingers twitch in his gloves, so he was relieved when she retrieved the iPad and skated back. A couple of taps, and she pulled up a video from last season taken before the injury that had torn up his knee meniscus.

"See how low you're getting there?"

He leaned in to view the screen, the proximity allowing him to inhale her scent. Peppermint. Hibiscus. Bella.

Memories flooded his senses, making his mouth water and his cock hard. *Please, Vadim, I need you. So bad. Only you.*

Now the skate was on the other foot, because he needed *her* to get approved for play again. And here she was with her ridiculous instructions to bend his knee and "get lower." As if he could not figure that out for himself. He was a professional!

"Your skating stride is so much smoother here. Now you're overcompensating by leaning on your non-injured side."

"My knee is fine."

She made a sound—was that a growl? His cock certainly thought so.

"This isn't going to work if you lie to me. I don't want you to overdo it and risk reinjury."

"You worry about this little job you have been assigned. I will worry about my health."

She clutched the iPad to her chest. Her considerable rack, if he was being honest, and he was always honest with himself. She had not been so well endowed years ago. At that time, she was barely a woman, tall and strong, but with no curves to speak of. Now she had an ass he wanted to take a bite out of and breasts he wanted to suck deep and long.

Intolerable.

"This *little* job is the difference between you playing

and not. *Dancing with the Stars*, Vaddy baby. It's where all the washed-up pros end up."

Annoyed at his reaction to her, he skated away, throwing out over his shoulder, "I will be playing, Isobel. You will have no say in that. I spoke with Moretti—it is clear why you have this job."

Her brow crimped. Naturally, it was adorable. "Please. Enlighten me."

"He is new and no doubt under pressure to bow to the owners. You can write your own ticket."

"If that's the case, I'd just appoint myself as head coach and be done with it."

"You are also conscious of what the fans and media think, so you are starting small. Really, you could have called or texted, Isobel. Buying my contract seems like a lot of work to bring me back into your world."

"You weren't my first choice. But luckily your poor play this season meant Quebec was happy to offload you."

He ignored the brief stab. The last six months had been difficult. Isobel understood this, yet they could not resist these little cuts.

"I think you wanted to be closer to me. Just like before, right, Bella?"

A blush crept up her cheeks on hearing his endearment for her.

He would test her. Make her angry and emotional. Make her cry. Because angry, emotional crying was not the stuff of coaches. If she was serious about a career in the NHL, she would hear worse.

She would get him game fit. He would get her battle ready.

He continued to needle. "Yes, I think that must be it. It seems that the female owners of the Rebels would like to abuse their position and use the players for their personal pleasure. Your sister and Remy DuPre—that is interesting."

"Is it?"

"Harper may have duped a Rebel player into her bed, but please don't imagine you and I will be renewing our acquaintance in a similar manner."

That got her attention, at last. Her creamy skin blazed, her crimson mouth twitched, and even from a distance he could see those melted-shamrock eyes darken. She looked like she wanted to scream at him. Burst into tears. Slap his face.

Yes, Bella. Let us see if you can handle the barbs of every player, coach, and fan who will dismiss you. Let us see if you can handle me.

Fury powering her stride, she skated over, skidding to a halt mere inches from his face. As before, she was magnificent.

"You've found me out, Petrov."

"I have?"

"It's all an elaborate ruse. We bought your contract even though you really haven't been performing well this season. Let's face it, you've sucked donkey balls, Vadikins. But I convinced my sisters that I alone could bring you back to top condition. Make you a valuable asset to the team. I also made sure I'd be the only one working with you . . ." She leaned up on the tips of her blades, a balancing act that required great skill and remarkable ankle strength. Close enough that he could have slipped his tongue between her lips and tasted hers.

Her breath was a hot puff of temptation. "So we would have all this alone time."

With that fiery gaze, she held his own.

Unerring.

Unflinching.

Un*til* her mouth creased, and she broke into a laugh. He remembered that laugh. Just as before, it hit him right in the balls.

She used the edge of the iPad to poke him in the chest. "You thought I'd go to all this trouble to try to get into your hockey shorts, Petrov? I'm a team owner—I can have any of these Rebels boys with the snap of my fingers!" She chuckled, clearly enjoying herself. "Despite what that supersized ego of yours thinks, the only performance I want from you is on the ice. Maybe if you spent less time carousing—"

"Carousing?"

"Yes, it's nicer than calling you a club-hopping, vodka-sodden manwhore. Less of that and more effort on your day job, please. And don't worry yourself that I'm inter-ested in 'renewing our acquaintance.' I've had better lays with the Ukrainian delegation at the last Games."

He had to say he enjoyed this sharp-tongued, quick-witted version of Isobel. But not enough to admit it to her.

"There is nothing you can teach me."

"So sure, Russian."

"I am positive."

"We'll see." She skated back to the edge of the rink. "Again."

Damn that fuckwomble Russian!

Isobel kicked at a wastebasket in her tiny office—more like a converted closet in the Rebels' practice facility—and tried to take satisfaction in its contents spreading all over the floor. Kit Kat wrappers mostly. Her weakness. Better her weakness be a delicious chocolate snack than Vadim "Asshatski" Petrov.

Of course she'd encountered sexism in Montreal. But sexism in the minors was small potatoes compared to a major pro hockey team. Or maybe it was just Vadim's clear lack of faith in her.

No different from anyone else's.

Moretti was likely looking to off-load her so she wouldn't push for more. Harper had probably put him up to it. Just give her something—anything—so she'll feel useful.

She kicked at the wastebasket again even though she couldn't repeat the satisfying wrapper dump 'n' spread. It hit the door of her closet-office with a resounding clank.

The door sprang open with Violet on the other side. She took in the scene before her. "Petrov?"

"How'd you guess?" Isobel had filled Violet in on her new assignment but left out the salient fact that they knew each other—intimately—from back in the day. "He's not buying the shit I'm shoveling."

Vi waved it off. "Forget Petrov. Let's talk about your nonsex life. I've found this guy who I think is perfect for you."

"That's what you said about the guitar player. And the firefighter." How could Isobel not find a firefighter hot? Likely because he wasn't a sexy calendar-gracing one like those Dempsey guys who were briefly famous a couple of years ago. No, this firefighter looked like he spent more time on desk duty with his hand permanently lodged in a box of Krispy Kremes. "You also promised I'd feel sparks with the Board of Trade guy." But nothing. No chemistry. Not like—

Forget it. There might have been chemistry, but chemistry didn't guarantee shit.

"Starting today, I'm on a man embargo. I need to focus on work." She pulled up Vadim's gait analysis on her iPad. She needed to get through to him.

"Maybe you should take a page from the book of Harper. Do a player."

"Yeah, because that's the way to get the respect of my peers."

Violet shrugged. "Women have been using their feminine wiles to persuade the dumber sex to their way of thinking for centuries. Maybe the Russian needs more carrot and less stick."

"Been there and *nyet*."

Oops.

Violet's face dropped. "Been. There?" She waved to the rink as if that was where Vadim was right now. "*There* there?"

Isobel covered her face with her hands and peeked out through the cage of her fingers. "Not a word to Harper, 'kay?"

Violet made a *lips zipped* motion and waved for Isobel to continue.

"Years ago, he spent a few weeks training with the Rebels while he decided which team he should sign with. It was the summer before I went to college, and Dad had me train with them, too. He wanted to make sure I was tougher than beef jerky before I went to Harvard and—"

Her sister spiraled a finger of *move it along*.

"I—I might have had a crush on Vadim. Like a full-scale infatuation. You wouldn't know it to look at me now, but I was a bit more forward in those days. More confident. Basically, I threw myself at him."

Isobel had the world at her feet then. Hockey super-stardom was beckoning, and she'd applied her bloom-ing self-assurance to the all-important task of virginity divestiture.

Violet looked more sympathetic than surprised. "Nothing wrong with knowing what you want and going after it. And if anyone's worth fluffing the boobage and hiking the skirt for, it's a tasty piece like Petrov."

"That's what I thought. Of course I *might* have neglected to tell him I was *virgo intacta*. I was sort of desperate to get it out of the way before college and I wasn't looking for hearts and flowers, just—"

"Boom, boom, I'm a big girl now?"

"Yep. God, he was so hot, Vi." And somehow he'd become hotter, because the universe was a grade A bitch. "He was already getting so much attention from the press, the NHL, women, and he'd fix me with that Ruski stare and I was a goner. My dad loved him, too. The son he never had, and then—"

"You mean . . ." Violet's mouth dropped open. "The V-card punching, two-pump chump who ruined your life was Ivan the Doable?"

"I should never have said that." Her memory flashed back to one of the semiregular Awkward Sister Bonding sessions instituted by Harper when they started managing the team together. Alcohol might have been imbibed. Confidences might have been shared. "I was being overdramatic because you'd played far too much Stevie Nicks, plied me with several boxes of Girl Scouts Thin Mints, and poured two bottles of Pinot down my gullet. He didn't ruin my life. I built it up into this life-changing thing, and you know how you assume it'll be awesome because there's all this chemistry?"

Vi nodded her recognition.

"Well, nothing."

"Nothing? What are we talking about? A supreme case of vodka dick?"

"No, his equipment worked just fine. I expected fire-works, but it was uneventful. He was gone in sixty sec-onds and I was all, 'Is that it?'"

Shock enlivened Violet's features. "The Russian was a . . . cock-a-doodle-dud?"

"Right. Bad in bed. Terrible, actually." She covered her mouth, unable to believe what had emerged from it. Vadim Petrov, renowned ladies' man, NHL stud, the Czar of Pleasure, had no idea how to make a woman orgasm.

"It was over before I could say, 'Maybe if you rubbed it that way.'" So I pretended the earth moved and fig-ured the next time would be better. He just needed a little instruction, ya know? But then Dad caught us immediately after and went ballistic. He actually chased a naked Vadim out of the house with a hockey stick."

Violet doubled over. "You're kidding! The poor guy."

Yeah, the poor guy. And that was only the begin-ning of the crapstorm their father had rained down on him.

"So your first time sucked. Everyone's first time sucks. Believe me, no teenage kid has a clue what he's doing." Violet appeared determined to defend the czar. "He must have improved, because he can't seriously be getting that much tail and not know how to satisfy a woman."

"If your motto is one-and-done, then how would you ever know how terrible you are? He's probably left a trail of frustrated women from Moscow to Quebec."

How liberating to talk about it. For years, she'd blamed her inexperience, but she'd had sex since. Nothing to write home about, but orgasms had ensued—man-made orgasms that left both parties with the conclusion that yes, sexual congress as it's defined has occurred here.

"A crying shame." Violet shut the door and sat in the chair opposite with her feet up on the desk, which she knew Isobel did not condone. "A guy like that not knowing how to use the tools the gods gave him."

"What it tells me is that you can't judge a book and all that. There might be great chemistry, but it doesn't always work that way. Vadim and I were incompatible in the bedroom. I mean, he probably knocks the socks off everyone else, but when it comes to the 'tab A into slot B' business, we don't gel. To be honest, I don't care about that anymore. Sex is over-rated."

Her sister scoffed.

"I know you want to save me from a life of miserable solitude, but believe me when I tell you, I'm quite happy riding this life solo. Not everyone needs to be paired off." The words sounded hollow to her ears.

"Everyone needs sex."

"No, they don't. That's just what glossy magazines and crappy rom-coms have duped you into believing."

"I'm thinking that psychologists and sex therapists might have a word to say about it."

Witch doctors, the lot of 'em. "I have a fat vibrator,

access to online porn, and a filthy imagination. Tell me how a real-life boy can improve on that."

Violet shook her head in pity. "That infatuation you felt all those years ago for Petrov. Don't you remember how your heart fluttered and your skin flushed and lightness overtook every cell in your body?"

"Nope. I don't." What came later had squeezed it out of instant recall. Now all she remembered was embarrassment and worst of all, guilt. It was easier to pretend her reservations about Petrov related to the sex dramedy, but there was more.

Three years. All because you put me in your crosshairs, Isobel.

After he was chased from her house, he had texted, asking how she was. If he had hurt her. She told him she was fine, then she never heard from him again. A month later, she read that he'd signed a contract with the Kontinental Hockey League in Russia. But she knew Vadim had wanted to play in the NHL. It was all he'd ever talked about, and now he was the KHL's new star.

Score one for Clifford Chase.

No one had excited her on and off the ice the way the Russian had all those years ago. She was determined to have him. She was determined that he'd be the one to relieve her of her pesky virginity, consequences be damned.

Catch me if you can, Vadim.

She'd spent that summer driving Vadim wild. So strange to think there was a time when she had this power over him. Over any man, because whatever magic she once had, it was lost. And now the power she possessed was different, the power to make or break his career in the NHL.

He needed her help. And he needed to get over the past so they could get on with the future.

FOUR

Not many experiences compared to hanging in the bathroom stall at a local bar with sweats around your ankles, listening to a brood of chickies drool over the man who made you a woman and did a pretty crappy job of it.

"I can't believe he's even hotter close up."

"Gah, I know! Those cheekbones look like they were—"

Forged over hell's anvil? Carved by the devil's scimitar?

"Made for me to lick them!"

Or that.

The Empty Net was a local bar near the Rebels' arena in Riverbrook, so it was a natural watering hole for anyone associated with the team. The guys liked it because they didn't get hassled, though since the Rebels' fortunes had improved this season, a few more puck bunnies had wandered in from their hutches to visit. The energy was different tonight, for sure. Usually the ambient noise was AC/DC, pinball pings, and bro banter, but tonight's soundtrack was the clicking of heels, nails-on-a-chalkboard giggles, and "do you have a martini menu?"

Russian hockey royalty was in the house—and it had brought an entourage.

After leaving the bathroom and the gaggle busy adjusting their plumage for maximum impact, Isobel plopped down onto one of the bar stools farthest away from where Vadim and the rest of the team had set up court. None of them had spotted her, and she preferred to keep it that way. She didn't usually spend much time here, but the team's head trainer, Kelly Townsend, had sent her a text asking if she could meet up.

Before she could order a drink, her phone screen lit up with a smiling face: Jen Grady, her former roomie at Harvard and now the captain of the Montreal Mavens. They caught up every few weeks.

"Hey, Jenny-Benny, what's up?"

"Not much. How's the noggin?"

"Oh, still attached." Isobel moved on quickly, as she always did whenever her injury came up. "I expect you must be busy getting ready for Worlds." The Women's World Hockey Championship was starting in a couple of weeks. Her heart clamped at the thought of how she was excluded.

"Yeah, drills till I can drill no more. So a little birdie told me you're goin' at it with Petrov."

"What?"

"You're his personal coach. Nice work if you can get it, girl."

Her gaze wandered to the other side of the bar.

If the woman wearing a vagina-length skirt—uh, in February—would only move a smidge . . .

"Yeah, well, he's a Russian pain in my ass who doesn't appreciate when I'm trying to kick his."

"Hey, don't kick that perfect ass too hard. We've all seen *The Body Issue*."

Apparently, Vadim Petrov's flawless melons were destined to haunt her like the Ghost of Mistakes Past. "Airbrushed, my friend. Let me list his faults."

"Don't! I'd rather live in ignorant, Petrov-is-perfect bliss." She coughed slightly, changing the tone. "So Lindhoff was asking about you."

Stefan Lindhoff was the assistant coach for Team USA during Sochi and had just been appointed as head coach for the next Games in Pyeongchang, one year out.

"He was wondering if you were going to try out for the Games," Jen said. "Said he left a couple of messages for you."

He had, and she'd ignored them. "It's been so busy here with the team and my love life. You wouldn't believe how much action I'm not getting."

Jen laughed dutifully. "Look, I know the doctors told you to take it easy. You went through an unbelievably hard time after your injury, but did you ever think that maybe you have more competitive play left in you? Coach will likely use Worlds to fill most of the spots, but they're still holding tryouts in Plymouth in a month. Coach wants to see you there. *I* want to see you there. If you think you're ready, of course."

Ready? It was one thing to skate demonstration cross-overs for unappreciative pros. Getting back out there in the hurly-burly of battle was another thing entirely.

"Okay, okay, I'll give him a call. Find out if he's really interested or if you're just projecting."

"You wound me, bitch." Then, softer: "Think about it, Iz. We have silver, but let's go for gold. One last shot."

On ending the call, Isobel considered Jen's words. She'd assumed her playing career was over, but apparently a little flattery and the idea she might be wanted were powerful incentives. God only knew she wasn't wanted by Vadim Petrov.

Tina, one of the Empty Net bartenders, caught her eye. Beer would aid in her decision-making process.

"Hey, T, how about a Blue Moon IPA?"

"I got that," she heard behind her.

Kelly sat on the seat beside her, smelling freshly showered and wearing a blue button-down shirt tucked into dark wash jeans. His light brown hair was slicked back with hair product.

"Oh, hey!" Isobel said, discombobulated at how well he cleaned up. She'd never seen him in anything but sweats. "You don't have to do that."

"Why? Because you're paying my salary?"

"No." *Yes.* "Because I—" She stopped. Restarted. "I was going to make some feminist case for buying my own drinks."

"You can buy the next round," he said. "I'm all for feminism where alcohol is concerned."

"Fair 'nough."

He ordered the same and waited until the glass was set before him, then raised it and clinked against hers. "To the Rebels."

She murmured her agreement and took a sip. "So what's on your mind?"

His brow crimped. Crap, that had sounded rude, jumping right into the fray like that. Small talk was so not her forte.

"Well, I figured with you coaching Petrov, it might be good to draw up a plan so we're all on the same page about his program."

Warmth infused Isobel. So far, the Rebels' coaching staff had been cool toward her, understandable given her ownership credentials. But she'd been a well-respected coach before she was a franchise owner, and that was where her heart lay. Or at least where it had landed.

One last shot, Iz.

"That'd be great."

For the next thirty minutes they chatted about the player on the other side of the bar. It might seem odd, but really they were discussing him as an asset. A mass of muscles and tendons and bones. All his value lay in ensuring that his body and mind were in tip-top condition.

So color Isobel surprised when halfway through the second round—which she had bought—Kelly let loose this gem: "Would you like to have dinner with me sometime?"

A mouthful of beer went down the wrong way, and Kelly had to clap her on the back while she recovered.

"Not terribly encouraging," he said.

"Sorry, it was just—did you ask me out on a date?" She thought about his hair product, his button-down shirt, and how nice he smelled. "Is *this* a date?"

He held up his hands. "No! I'd never try to pull a fast one like that."

She gave him the once-over.

"I mean . . . I put on a nice shirt. Best foot forward and all."

"Wish I'd gotten the memo," she muttered, feeling extra unsexy in her sweats.

"I've been watching you." The hands went up again. "Not in a creepy way, but I've noticed you since you arrived a few months ago. I can see you're in a tough position, wanting to have more say in the coaching, but not wanting to step on any toes. I really admire you, Isobel, and all you've accomplished."

More flattery. Don't let anyone ever tell you it wasn't the ultimate aphrodisiac. Hell, she could see why Petrov banged every woman who told him "you're the best, Vadim! The absolute best!"

"You'd like to have dinner with me?"

"Sure, why not?"

Slightly less than a resounding vote of confidence, but he was the first guy to show a genuine interest in her in forever. Didn't couples meet at work all the time? Couples, you know, those people who shared similar interests, strove for common goals, had things to talk about at the end of their day. And he'd initiated it, so it wouldn't look like she was using her boss persona to force an employee into dating her. It might be weird, but it also might be . . . perfect!

Was she attracted to him? Almost as tall as her, he had nice normal hair and warm hazel eyes and he was clearly in shape. Not the bull shoulders of—*do not go there*—the athlete type she was used to meeting, but still toned and strong. His smile didn't give her flutters exactly, but that kind of attraction was so overrated.

She allowed herself to go there after all. She had thought sex would be awesome with the Czar of Pleasure, and look how that worked out. Fireworks happened to other people. She wanted a guy she could talk to.

"Yes, let's do dinner." And then she laughed coquettishly to affirm her interest.

He smiled. In response, her heart gave a little jump. Nothing earth-shattering, but enough to know she wasn't completely denying herself the hearts-aflutter experience. She was sure of it.

Standing, he kissed her on the cheek. "See you at work tomorrow?"

"Sure."

"I've got to go, but this has been really . . ."

"Nice?"

"Yeah." He cocked his head thoughtfully. "Nice."

Vadim wished he hadn't come out tonight.

Sure, the company was pleasant enough. The players were an enjoyable bunch, not afraid to poke fun or rake him across the coals, especially about his attractiveness to the opposite sex. Several women had positioned themselves kitty-corner to their table, throwing seductive glances his way. He had wondered aloud to his teammates why they didn't approach, and Erik Jorgenson, their Swedish goalie, said that they rarely did. That in fact very few women frequented this bar at all.

Vadim didn't understand this. Hockey players were considered gods in Canada—there were hockey fans, and then there were French Canadian hockey fans—and all of Vadim's non-ice time in Quebec had been spent holding women at arm's length. It was tiring, but a necessary part of the job. Sometimes his arm slipped and let one or two through. These were the perks. They worked hard on the ice so they could play harder off it.

"Looks like word's out that the Czar of Pleasure is here," Cade said.

This again. If he was feeling more like himself, he would have raised his head and given one of the women—the pretty blonde with the high-pitched giggle and the rack that didn't grow naturally—the nod to join them. But he was not feeling like himself. He was feeling irritated, and it was because of Isobel Chase.

Insidious Isobel, yet again sneaking into his marrow. He refused to admit she might have a point about how his injury had affected his motion. Even if she did have a point—which she did not—how was he supposed to focus on skating drills when she was gliding around in those pants, stretched taut over her delicious curves? Coaches should not have heart-shaped asses! She had grown into her body, for sure. Now she was the complete package: grace, strength, sexiness, and a smart mouth he found infuriatingly attractive.

And she expected him *not* to be distracted by these things.

"Why don't you give them the look?" Erik blew his fair hair out of his eyes and nudged Vadim, gesturing at the women huddled like a she-wolf pack at the bar.

"The look?"

"Yeah, the one from your underwear commercial," Cade said. He lifted his chin and squinted while doing something odd with his lips.

"What's that?"

"The look, dude. Like Zoolander but infused with Siberian charm."

"*Dúrak*," Vadim muttered. Idiot.

Ford Callaghan, the Rebels' right-winger, who looked like a Viking, laughed. "Alamo, I think you just got insulted in Ruski."

The amiable Texan held up his fingers and started a count, then stopped in the middle of his left hand. "That's eight languages now. Gotta love the internationalism of the National Hockey League."

Everyone laughed, even Vadim, who admired a man who didn't easily take offense.

Leon Shay approached the table, a bottle of beer in his hand. "Ladies," he said as he took a seat. His eyes met Vadim's, and something like a challenge passed between them. Interesting.

"Well, would you look at that." Cade shifted his gaze to the bar, inviting them all to follow. "Looks like Little Miss Coach has got herself a boyfriend."

Little Miss what? Isobel sat at the far end of the bar in the shadows. Vadim had not seen her walk in, but now he realized there was another entrance on the other side. How long had she been here? And what was this nonsense about a new boyfriend? It was only Kelly, the trainer.

A laugh fluttered from her direction, soft, cock teasing, and instantly recognizable. Isobel laughed like that when she was flirting.

Vadim's chest contracted, catching up with the conclusion his balls had already made.

"They are just work colleagues."

"No, something's going on there," Cade said. "She's doing the lean."

"The lean?"

Cade inclined his head until he was mere inches from Vadim's nose. "The lean, my friend."

Vadim returned to looking at Isobel doing the lean. And laughing. Then Kelly leaned in—*everyone was leaning*—to kiss her. Only on the cheek, but that was surely unnecessary between work colleagues.

"Perhaps they are just friends." *They are not just friends.*

"Nah, Kelly wants her," Ford confirmed. All eyes turned to assess the bearer of this new piece of information. "He does. He asked me if she was dating anyone."

Shay took a slug of his beer. "Well, if she wants

on the coaching staff, fucking her way in is as good a strategy as any."

The tightness in Vadim's chest increased, and his hand white-knuckled the beer bottle. The others remained quiet, undoubtedly used to Shay's grousing. Vadim was not yet used to it, so he asked, "What does that mean?"

Shay rocked the neck of his bottle between his thumb and forefinger. "It's no secret she wants a coaching position. She's a team owner, so I suppose she could just appoint herself, but that looks shady. Having an in with the backroom boys is a better play. The long game."

"Or maybe she just likes him," Ford said, grit in his tone. Vadim decided he liked Ford very much. "You've been sniping about the ownership since old man Chase died, Shay. You have to admit things have turned around since his daughters took over."

Shay made a noise of disgust. "Are you kidding me? What did they do? Made a few decent trades." He tipped his bottle in deference to Ford, who'd been acquired five months ago, the start of the Rebels' turn-around. But Remy DuPre's trade was the true catalyst. Since his arrival, the team had steadily risen to fourth place in the division. A play-off spot was within reach.

"So they spent money in the right place," Shay grunted. "Christ, if there's anything a woman's good at, it's spending money. But if they think landing us with a female coach is going to get us to the play-offs, then they must be overdosing on fuckin' estrogen."

No one was inclined to disagree.

Vadim's chest felt like a band of hot steel was cinching it. He could not allow this commentary to go unchecked. "Isobel Chase is an excellent skating coach. I am honored to be working with her."

All eyes flew to him. Perhaps he had overstated it, but when English is not your first language, the results were often more dramatic than intended.

A few taut moments passed while everyone at the table chose a position.

"They have a female gold-medalist ice skater working with the players in Boston," Cade muttered. "Said it's really improved their reaction times."

Ford shrugged. "Yeah, it's pretty common these days."

"As consultants," Shay spat out. "For people who need the extra attention."

The table's temperature, which had previously been thawing, once more plunged toward the Arctic. That dig was meant for Vadim, but he would leave it for now. One day, Shay would be injured and would need the extra attention. *Bog dal, bog vzyal.* God gives, God takes away.

However, Shay, as well as being a nasty piece of work, was also one of those people who didn't know to quit while he was ahead, as his next statement proved.

"If she can't get in by fucking a trainer, I expect she'll find a way with a player. Right, Petrov?"

Kelly had left the bar, and Isobel was now standing. Perhaps they had some arrangement to leave separately. Vadim didn't think that was a good idea, not if everyone knew of her ambitions to become a Rebels' coach. Not if everyone thought she would spread her legs to do it.

He would speak to her, but first, Vadim had to deal with this piece of garbage, Leon Shay. The moment ticked over, while out of the corner of his eye, Vadim watched Isobel heading toward the exit at the far end of the bar. She wore the same tight black pants of temptation as earlier—no wonder Kelly was all over her!

Satisfied she was out of earshot, he turned to Shay. "What did you say?"

He knew exactly what he'd said, or at minimum, what he had implied. He would give the man one chance to make amends.

Shay was enjoying himself, his eyes sparkling with malevolence, his mouth twitching with the bullshit on the tip of his tongue. "She's got multiple plays here. But maybe her easiest option would be to bang it out with the new Russian star. Worked for her sister and DuPre."

This was exactly the scenario Vadim had teased Isobel about during practice. His intention had been to see how far he could push her, to toughen her up, but damned if he'd sit still and listen to this asshole malign her motives.

"And why would you assume that would happen?"

Shay looked him right in the eye. "Because you fucked her years ago."

FIVE

In the immediate wake of this revelation, a curious stillness descended over the table. Time stalled. Breath stopped. As if Vadim's response was the only thing keeping the world itself from tipping over off its axis into outright hostilities. These men didn't know him well, but even they must recognize that Shay was two seconds away from a skull-meets-beer-bottle situation.

"You know this because?"

"Straight from the horse's mouth, Petrov."

His stomach dropped to the planked floor. Isobel had shared this? That did not square with what he knew of her.

"You two are buddies now?" Ford asked incredulously.

Shay laughed, clearly pleased to have the table's focus. He was a little man who needed attention and who would take it whatever way he could. Every fury-fueled cell in Vadim's body was currently engaged in not ripping out Shay's lungs.

"Nah, I was passing by her office and overheard

her spilling the beans to Violet." He leaned in, an ugly snarl on his lips. "You popped that cherry and left her hanging, man. Don't they teach you how to satisfy ladies in Siberia? Or are they all too toasted on vodka to care?"

Vadim grabbed Shay's shirt, a fistful that—judging by the man's squeal—also included chest hair, and yanked him over the table. The shatter of glass provided a semisatisfying exclamation point, but true gratification would only come when Leon Shay was blinking at the last beats of his bloody heart as it lay on the floor outside his chest.

Unfortunately this pleasurable state of affairs would have to wait, as four hands restrained him to the point that he had to release his hold on Shay. A few seconds more, and Vadim was removed from Shay's orbit and hauled toward the bar.

Cade held up a hand to the concerned bartender. "No trouble, we'll pay for any damage."

On Vadim's other side, Erik let him go but ensured that his goaltender body mass kept Vadim close. He said, "We're cool, yes?"

"No, we are not."

"Think you might want to amend that statement," Cade said.

"Why?"

"Because we like drinkin' here, budski."

They both stared at him, waiting for an answer.

He gave them the only one he could. "Shay and I need to talk."

Cade grinned, all Texan ease. "Sure ya do. And we all need to avoid the tabloids and a night in lockup. Let's think about how you might want to approach this, Vadster."

Erik, as serious as Cade was lighthearted, nodded. "Think, Vadim."

Vadim glanced over at the table, where a member of the bar staff was picking up the broken glass. Ford helped her, then raised an eyebrow in Vadim's direction. Shay sat with arms folded over his chest, looking unfazed at the chaos he had created.

"I think I would like to beat him into an early grave."

Cade winced. "Keep your passion for the game, Petrov, which you won't be playin' if you don't cool your jets. So, let's see where we're at. Is it true?"

"Is what true?"

"You and Isobel?"

Vadim growled. "This is no one's business."

The stares of his teammates continued.

Chyort! "Once, eight years ago, when we were teens, she and I—"

"Hold off on the details there. Now I'm guessin' you don't want this information out there in the ether, and as for Isobel—"

"Who is telling the world," Vadim finished for him.

"Her sister," Erik said.

With a big hand on Vadim's shoulder, Cade turned him so he was no longer facing the table or Shay's ugly face.

"You got any sisters, Vad?"

He thought of Mia. Beautiful, perfect Mia, who was equally as infuriating as Isobel Chase. "Yes, I have one. She's difficult."

"I'll bet. So I'm guessing this sister of yours probably isn't telling you all her deep, dark secrets, but it's different when it's sister-on-sister."

Erik made a weird noise.

"Ah, hell, that's not what I meant, Swede. Now, when a girl speaks to her sister, that's like she's writing a 'dear diary' entry. She's not telling the world. She's telling her best friend, or somethin' close to it. So I wouldn't equate a sisterly confidence with a post on her Facebook page. Now, she probably should have kept this girly chat for a bottle of vino and a pillow fight back at Chase Manor instead of sharing the deets in a drafty old office in the basement of Rebels HQ—"

Vadim turned, ready to tear Shay fifty new assholes, only to have Erik block his path as if Shay stood in the goalmouth. These D-men were impossible.

"But she didn't," Cade continued. "And if you do what you want to do to Shay, believe me when I say this will no longer be between a few buds in a bar, but it'll be spreadin' faster than a prairie wildfire with a tailwind. And while this will probably have very little impact on your day-to-day, you being the Czar of Pleasure and all, it won't look so good for Isobel, especially considering the current situation vis-à-vis her employment aspirations."

Vadim considered this, plucking the essentials from Cade's circuitous reasoning. "She'll be slut shamed."

Cade finger pointed in the manner of a pistol. "Bingo, budski. Now I don't know Isobel all that well, but I do know her sister Violet. She's the kinda girl who could brush that off with a fuck-you-haters, but she's not the Chase sister trying to get a foothold coaching men's professional hockey. You want to make that harder on Isobel or you want to calm the fuck down and figure out a plan?"

Vadim was forced to admit the Texan was right. Rumors about a past—or current—relationship with a hockey player she was coaching would not make Isobel look good. Instinctively, he knew he could trust Cade and Erik. Ford, too.

That left Shay.

"I will be calm," Vadim said in his fake-calmest voice.

The Swede asked, "Really?"

"Yes, I will be as calm as the Caspian Sea on a clear summer day."

Cade looked to Erik for a translation and, satisfied with what he found there, took a few steps back. "After you."

They returned to the table and sat again. The drinks had been replaced, the broken glass cleared away. No evidence remained of the burst of violence from a few moments ago, except for the tingle of tension tainting the air.

Shay smirked. "All right there, Petrov?"

Inside his chest, Vadim's organs were playing musical chairs. He was unsure what would happen when the music stopped.

"I said—"

"I heard what you said."

Shay's lip curl was downright ugly. "Oh, I see. You're gonna wait until you get me alone. Maybe jump me in the showers."

He didn't sound scared, although he should. He really should.

"Actually, what I have to say to you would be best with witnesses. This way, there will be no misunderstanding. Yes, it is true I was with Isobel a long time ago when we were teenagers. That's in the past. Today we have a professional relationship. She is a coach. A good coach." He rested his forearm on the table and moved closer. He preferred to look a man in the eye before he threatened to terminate his life. "Do you keep your skate blades sharpened, Shay?"

Confused by the change of subject, Shay huffed out a cough of acknowledgment.

"That is good. It will certainly make things easier. If I hear that you have spread this information or that you are talking trash about Isobel, first, I will take your skates and strangle you to semiunconsciousness with the laces. Then I will use the blades to slice off your balls. If your blades are not sharp enough, this will be more painful than it needs to be."

The entire table had stilled, the only movement a sheen of sweat breaking out at the side of Shay's temple.

Vadim sat back, satisfied. "Another round, my friends?"

Shay stood quickly, his thighs banging the table. "I'm out. Calling it a night." He glanced around, perhaps waiting for his teammates to urge him to stay. No one did. "We good, Petrov?"

"That is up to you, Shay."

With one nod, he slithered out like the snake he was.

A moment of stunned shock passed. Then another.

"Gentlemen, why so serious?" Vadim asked when the silence became awkward.

Cade shook his head. "That's some twisted imagination you got there, Petrov."

"I am Russian. We do not fuck around when it comes to revenge fantasies."

This set them off into noisy laughter. Nothing like the threatened castration of an asshole to bond a group.

Another round of drinks was ordered, and Erik and Cade picked up an earlier conversation about whether a vampire or a robot would win in a fight. The important issues of the day. This gave Vadim time to brood on what Shay had said, specifically the words he had used.

"What does it mean to leave a woman hanging?"

The D-men stopped talking, shared a glance, and then looked at Ford.

"Callaghan?" Cade asked casually.

"Context?" Ford replied, equally casually.

"It's what Shay said," Vadim said. "That I left Isobel 'hanging.' Then something about women toasted on vodka in Siberia."

Ford nodded slowly, as if he didn't quite understand but time might help him get there.

"Burnett, that sounds like a southernism," he said. "Care to explain?"

Cade nodded. Then nodded again, this time rubbing his chin. "Don't know about a southernism. But by my understanding, it's when a woman doesn't quite . . ."

Vadim wasn't mistaken in thinking everyone leaned in slightly. In fact, the entire bar appeared to have quieted, all waiting for the answer to this vital question.

"Um . . . complete the act."

Vadim frowned. "Complete the act?"

"The sex act," Cade said with the assurance of a medical professional.

Vadim arced his gaze over the table. No one could quite meet his eyes.

He remembered his time with Isobel, if not with blistering clarity, with a certain nostalgia, despite what came afterward. She had been soft and warm and . . . wet? Yes, wet. Of course she was. Passion dictated their hurry, but that was to be expected. Their foreplay was daily, on the ice, with Isobel flirting and laughing.

Just like she had with Kelly earlier.

He recalled her soft moans, her begging words. *Please, Vadim. I need you, Vadim.* Then the sharp cry she tried to hide. Not pleasure, but pain. So brave, his

Bella. Surprise had halted his thrusts, but she clung tighter, urging him to continue because she was a tough girl. A fighter, a future champion. And while he'd been annoyed that she didn't share with him the crucial fact of her virginity, he was already too far gone.

Beyond knowing.

Fuck.

"Are you saying that Isobel didn't come?"

Ford grabbed his shoulder. "Keep it down, man. Who's to say what happened exactly?"

Except the people who were there. Some women were quiet. Vadim had screwed partners who lay there like dead frogs, expecting him to do all the work. Assuming that sheer nakedness and beautifully sculpted curves were a substitute for sexual chemistry.

They were not.

But Isobel was a willing participant, arching her body into him, rubbing her breasts against his chest, moaning her encouragement. True, she did not tell him to do specific things to ensure her pleasure, but it was her first time and she was young, just eighteen, and he wouldn't have expected it. That was his job.

His. Job.

"If that's what she said to her sister, perhaps it's something that happens to her always . . ." He trailed off, not wanting to voice his worst fear.

"Yeah maybe," Ford offered, not unkindly.

"More likely, you failed in your manly duty," Erik said.

Cade elbowed the Swede, who raised his palms to the air. "Well, that's what it sounds like."

That *was* what it sounded like. He had failed to bring Isobel to orgasm. During her first sexual experience with a man, he had not satisfied her.

Ford patted his arm, and Vadim decided he didn't like him so much after all. "I wouldn't pay attention to anything Shay says. He probably made that up."

Perhaps, but it was a rather specific detail.

Vadim searched the faces of the men before him. "Do you think he made that up?"

An unmistakable delay was followed by nods and murmurs of acquiescence.

Shay must have made it up. The alternative was not possible.

Not with the Czar of Pleasure.

SIX

With more pep to his step than the destination deserved or his night could attest to, Vadim walked into the trainers' room an hour earlier than usual for his remedial lessons with Isobel. The Rebels' captain, Bren St. James, lay on the table, getting his shoulder examined by one of the team doctors and Kelly.

Vadim had not slept well. He would say he had slept terribly, and not even Alexei's warm milk concoction was enough to send him back to sleep. (Alexei believed warm milk and brandy solved everything.) All night, Vadim had replayed that one night with Isobel, but eight years had morphed it beyond recognition.

The sex was amazing.

The sex was adequate.

She had screamed his name over and over.

Because she was in pain.

In her eyes, he had seen desire and trust and honesty.

The mind could play the cruelest tricks.

Again he sent that mind back to the day he had finally slipped inside Isobel's body after weeks of burning for her: a late afternoon in July, the air thick and sultry, the trees lining the driveway to Clifford Chase's house green and bright.

I curl in on myself, hunching my shoulders lower while waiting to be admitted. Another furtive glance over my shoulder tells the same story as the first five furtive glances: no one is watching me.

The big oak door opens. My chest opens right up with it.

Bella.

Her dark chestnut hair is down and curled over her shoulders, and she wears makeup—smoky gray lines around her green eyes and slashes of pink on her cheeks and lips. I've never seen her in makeup before. It makes her look older than her eighteen years, and I suppose I should be grateful, because as mature as she is on the ice, she appears young off it.

"Vad!" She grabs my hand and drags me inside; then her arms circle my waist as she presses her body to mine. Her supple breasts push up inside her low-cut top, which is pink and has sparkles on it. Her hips are covered in tight black pants that stop halfway down her calves. Her feet are bare. It's weird to see her in anything but hockey gear or sweats.

I smell it immediately. "Have you been drinking, Bella?"

A small giggle escapes her. "Just one." More likely two or three. "To steady my nerves."

I smile. "Why would you be nervous, Bella? I am just a friend visiting another friend." But I push my erection into her fabric-covered heat all the same.

"You're more than a friend, Vadim."

Yes, there's nothing very friendly about my feelings toward her.

"I shouldn't be here if you are drunk," I say, thinking it through and not enjoying the conclusion.

"I'm not drunk," she insists, and her words aren't slurred—or not slurred enough—so I allow my desire to muffle any negative thoughts. I've waited too long to let a couple of drinks stand in the way. After a month of flirting and touching—and let's face it, her skating rings around me, an incredible turn-on—I will finally have her.

But I don't want to rush her because this girl is special. Every time I see her, my heart skips beats and my dick throbs painfully to make up for it. Either way, it produces problems for my circulation, making my brain a blood-free zone.

I'm a dizzy fool when it comes to Isobel Chase.

"Want a drink first?" she asks. "I have vodka."

"I don't like vodka."

"But you're Russian!"

"The only thing I want to drink, Bella, is you."

A very pretty blush blooms underneath her makeup. "Oh wow, you sure know how to fire up a girl."

"Yes. Yes, I do." And then I take her mouth boldly, only gentling at her gasp. Take it slow, Vad. We've kissed once before in the locker room at the rink, but it was quick, our worry about being caught by her father keeping our passion at a simmer.

"We're alone?" I whisper against her mouth, though I know she wouldn't ask me here unless we are.

She nods, eyes glazed over with both lust and trust, then she takes my hand and leads me toward the stairs.

Again I hesitate. I want to get it right. Treat her right. "Perhaps we should watch TV?"

She steps in close, her hand cupping my raging erection. "Does this want to watch TV?"

No, it does not. It wants out and in, where the "in" will be the sweetest oblivion. With her soft hand stroking my dick, I know I would be an idiot to turn down this opportunity. This beautiful, bright-eyed blitzkrieg of a girl wants me, has made it clear from the moment we met in every heated look and flirty comment.

The Girl with the Blazing Skates has this boy on the ropes.

His mind whiplashed back to the present. One of the trainers—Ted—was calling him over to the table.

What did the past matter? Once there was a boy, infatuated with a girl, desperate to have her. Too desperate, it would seem, for he hadn't taken care of her in the way a woman, especially a virgin, should be cared for. In the years since, there was no doubt as to his prowess. Women spoke to newspapers about it, for God's sake.

No lover left his bed wanting. All of them received the Vadim Petrov deluxe orgasm treatment (perhaps he should slip *that* to the newspapers). If he were to make the mistake of favoring Isobel Chase once more, she would be left in no doubt as to what had occurred. The best orgasm of her life!

"How're you feeling today, Vadim?" Ted asked.

Furious. "A little stiff. It is often this way in the morning."

Ted nodded as Vadim assumed the position: track bottoms pulled down to shorts, and on his back on the table. This gave Vadim a chance to assess Kelly, who was still working on St. James's shoulder.

Vadim aimed for cool objectivity as he glanced sidelong at the man. Open and easygoing, Kelly possessed an all-American guilelessness that immediately aroused Vadim's suspicion, not because he doubted Kelly's motives for asking out Isobel, but because Vadim understood them all too well.

He was what one would call "a good guy."

This disgusted Vadim. Isobel would be bored to tears with this man in her bed. He probably would ask for permission to kiss her, to touch her, to go down on her. Theirs would be a relationship filled with "you first; no, you; no, you." So much respect for each other that there would be no allowances made for the demands of true lust.

This was the man she wished to allow access to her body? He would not know what to do with her.

Just as you did not know all those years ago.

The door opened and a dark ponytailed head curved around it. Isobel's green eyes alighted on Vadim and dismissed him before moving on to Kelly and staying put.

Vadim's blood raged at the notion that Kelly Townsend was more deserving of Isobel's attention.

"I'll come back," she said to Kelly, as if picking up in the middle of a conversation.

Kelly stepped away from the trainer's table just as Bren St. James sat up, the rubdown finished. "We're done here. What can I do you for?"

Isobel smiled with a lot more warmth than this worm deserved. "It's not important. It's just . . ." She hesitated and swung her gaze to Vadim, who made no secret of the fact that he was listening. He held that green-eyed gaze with challenge.

Her brows formed a V in plain annoyance. "Later."

Kelly nodded, apparently pleased with that. *Later*. When they would discuss important things. Like dates. Or orgasms.

Ted asked Vadim about the adductor muscle that had been bothering him, and the distraction meant that Vadim missed Isobel's exit. Had she shared a longing look with Kelly before she left? Were they now communicating without words?

Vadim was not enjoying this. Not at all.

But maybe Isobel had nothing to do with the cloud hanging over him. He preferred to attribute his mood to the phone call he had received an hour ago from Mia. She wanted to meet up with him at the next away game in New York, which meant the pressure was on once again. Would his body be ready for play? Would his mind be ready for Victoria Wallace?

Yes, that was the reason for his irritation. Not Isobel Chase.

~

Mr. Siberia was a total joy this morning.

Of course, that conclusion would assume that degrees of joy were possible with the Cat's Meow from Moscow. (Violet's latest nickname, even though Vadim wasn't from Moscow and the rhyme sucked.) Isobel put Vadim's chilly demeanor this morning at a 9.5 on a scale of one to ten—"seriously pissed off, speech impossible"—but the scale didn't even go below an eight, which was "annoyed with a chance of Russian swearing."

Ever since he'd unloaded that glare when she popped her head into the trainers' room, he'd been acting as if someone had cut out the crotches in his designer suits. Now they were running sprint drills from the center line to the blue zone. At first he seemed to be working through it, but with each rep, he'd up the growl quotient at her as he skated by.

Kind of sexy, but that was neither here nor there.

Isobel didn't have time for sexy, growly, bad-tempered Russians playing havoc with her hormones, not when she might be headed out on a dinner date with a mere mortal who was just her speed. She hadn't had a chance to touch base with Kelly, but she'd gone home last night after their chat feeling more hopeful than she had in a while.

Kelly Townsend might be the one.

Nice and harmless, a guy she could talk to. What better basis on which to build a relationship? Lust as the foundation might work for other people, but not for her. The proof was muttering to himself on every skate-by.

"Want to talk about it, Russian?"

He stopped, spat a curse at the ice, and then continued with the drills.

Fair enough. She wasn't here to be his sounding

board. Lord knew she understood what he was going through, but everyone had to deal with injuries in their own way and on their own timetable. Isobel would focus on Vadim's skating and leave whatever was happening between the ears to the team's shrink.

After ten more minutes of semidecent skating and Olympic-quality cantankerousness, she called a halt and took a seat on the bench rinkside. As she entered notes into her iPad, she became aware that he had skated over, cleared the rink barrier, and now stood before her. In skates, he loomed close to six feet seven, everything about him supersized.

She peered up. Damn, he was pretty, even when grumpy. "How does the knee feel?"

"Good. Best it's felt in a while."

Surprised at his even tone, she studied him more closely now, looking beyond the superficial perfection. She'd assumed his temper tantrum was related to his uncooperative body.

"That's great. But if you're pretending it's better to get me to sign off on you quicker . . ."

He sat on the bench beside her, pressing his muscular thigh against hers, its heat a bulwark against the chilly rink. There was plenty of room on the bench. He didn't need to sit so close or flaunt such a balls-out pose. She could have pulled away, but manspreading was just one of the many crosses women had to bear, and she refused to let him think this bothered her. Because it didn't. It was just a thigh. A pillar-thick, incredibly massive, heat-conducting thigh.

"Believe it or not, Isobel, I'm a team player. If I wasn't ready, I would say so."

Sure you would. "You looked good out there today. You didn't tire like the first time we did this."

He stared at her, into her. There'd been a lot of that intimidating staring back in the day, and she was quite immune *thankyouverymuch*—oh, who was she kidding? Vadim Petrov in thermonuclear glare mode was enough to make her melt.

Lust. Not a good foundation.

His lips were moving, but she missed what came out of them, or rather her muddled brain couldn't quite compute what came out. She rewound the last two seconds. She could have sworn—"What did you say?"

"Are you dating Kelly?"

He must have spotted her in the Empty Net and jumped to the right conclusion. "And this is your business because?"

"I don't think it's a good idea."

"You don't think—you don't think—" Sputtering, she knew she sounded like a loon, but how was she supposed to respond?

Turned out she didn't have to, because Mr. Nosy Parkov was still spouting unsolicited opinions. "Your position is precarious."

"What position is that?"

"As a team owner who is female and trying to obtain a job on the coaching staff."

Right, *that* position. "What have you heard?" Was someone else gossiping about what they'd seen in the bar? Kelly shouldn't have kissed her cheek. Damn.

"The fact you might be using him to gain favor with the coaching staff was remarked upon." He shrugged as if this was nonsense, but he felt it his solemn duty to keep her informed.

Now she was the one growling. She thought back to who else was sitting with Vadim last night. Callaghan, Burnett, Jorgenson, and . . . Shay.

"Did Shay remark upon it?"

"He did, and while no one agreed with him explicitly, the seed was sown."

Her cheeks burned. To have her motives categorized so malevolently was both embarrassing and disheartening.

"So how's the seed, Vadim? Has it sprouted yet? Has it grown into a tree in here?" She poked at his chest, angry with herself, with him, and with the high school gossips who wanted to rip down something before it had even started.

He grasped her hand and placed it flat against his chest. Oh my. His heart pounded, violent, vehement kicks under her fingertips. Those drills must have taken more out of him than he'd let on.

"I make up my own mind. If you think that a relationship with Kelly is more important than this gossip, then ignore it. They are only words. But . . ." He trailed off.

She felt her body angle closer. "But?"

He was still holding her hand, burning his heat

and know-it-all assholery into every receptive little cell. "Will he satisfy you, Isobel?" His darkening gaze wavered between her lips and her eyes. "Will he understand what makes your pulse race, your blood surge, your body crave more?"

Pulse. Blood. Body. Crave. More.

His lips hovered an inch from her mouth, and beneath her hand still wrapped in his warm, sandpaper-rough one, she felt all that Russian passion. *Th-thunk. Th-thunk.* She felt it downloading into her blood, rewiring her neurons, rebooting her dormant libido. Her body didn't just crave—it demanded. Gratification. Satisfaction. To be filled and used. Her breasts swelled. Hot, slippery dampness pooled between her thighs. She squeezed her core to get some much-needed relief.

It only made the craving worse.

Or maybe it made the craving better.

His eyes were dark discs of night, the blue impossible to discern, and she knew two things.

He's going to kiss me

and

I'm going to let him.

Wait, he was not kissing. He was speaking. She thought she might have said "What?" but it came out as "Whuu-aaa?"

"So, is it more important?"

"Is—is what more important?"

He hoisted an eyebrow. "A relationship with Kelly. Is it more important than gossip?"

Screech. Kelly. That's who they were talking about

while she imagined this big, broody Russian fulfilling the fantasies her vibrator couldn't. She drew back, blinking away the lust fog she'd become lost in.

Did she want people thinking she'd earned a coaching spot because she was dating the head trainer? Begging him over pillow talk to put a good word in for her? It wasn't as if Kelly had any true power here; the decision would be down to Coach Calhoun and GM Moretti. The test was how she worked with Petrov. There were no shortcuts.

She peered at Vadim, who waited patiently. Or she would have thought that if he hadn't squeezed her hand a smidge. Was that her imagination?

"I don't know."

"There is your answer." He released her and picked up the stick he had leaned against the bench. Then he stood and headed toward the exit to the tunnel, leaving her a growly, confused, horny mess.

SEVEN

Isobel looked out over the crowd of eager faces in her U-12s group, each masked behind a visor. The Hockey for Everyone foundation was a charity that focused on inspiring interest in the sport in disadvantaged youth. Hockey wasn't cheap, between the club dues, the gear, and the money to fund trips to play other teams. Getting kids involved at a young age without shifting a considerable burden to their parents was what this was all about. Isobel gave her time to the foundation as a consultant and came in and coached once a week at the hockey club in Bridgeport on Chicago's South Side.

It sure was nice to hang with pupils who cared for her opinion.

Once baseball season started, she'd likely lose them to warmer weather, but giving them a chance to do something that fostered physical exercise, teamwork, and competitive spirit was worth any amount of her time.

"Today we're going to work on penalty shots. Miguel, you good with starting in goal?"

The bright-eyed twelve-year-old skated a couple of

feet forward. With the extra padding of goalie gear, he was practically swimming in it, but he'd stood out when she first started with the group. Small for his age, he'd picked up skating like a natural and knew all about net coverage from every angle.

"Yes, Coach Chase."

She liked the sound of that. "Now head on over to the goal. Marcus?" She sought one of her other goalies, a kid who had hated the idea of being a goaltender when he started. When she'd explained that the goalie was the most important player, he came around. "Marcus, after ten shots on goal, you'll switch out with Miguel. The rest of you will line up and hit the puck after I drop it on the line."

"Even the defenders?" This question came from Jessica, one of three girls in the club. Isobel was hopeful they could recruit more, but for now Jess, Natasha, and Gabriella were representing the girls.

"Yep, even the defenders. You never know when you'll have a shot, so you need to practice as well."

Isobel skated to the line while the kids formed a line a few feet back. Once Miguel was set up in goal, she dropped the first puck and skated out of the way. Natasha glided up and gave it a tap. Too weak, and Miguel had no problem deflecting it. During the first round of fifteen shots—the number of kids in class today—Isobel watched, noting each player's attempt and how it might improve. On the second round, she offered observations. Harder. Aim for the five-hole. Try a feint.

By the time twenty minutes of penalty drills were over, each of them had scored at least twice. It did her heart good to see the joy on their faces as that puck slid below the tender's body.

"Okay, that was great, guys. Everyone help with picking up the pucks and then go hit the locker rooms."

As Isobel gathered pucks, Gabby skated over with Natasha. They nudged each other, clearly building up to say something.

"What's up, ladies?"

"We were wondering . . ." Natasha started, and looked to Gabby for help.

"Do you know Vadim Petrov?" Gabby blushed, and then launched into giggles, which set Natasha off into her own gigglefest.

"Yeah, I do. In fact, I'm giving him a few lessons right now."

"You're his coach?" Gabby's eyes widened in admiration, and Isobel felt a little warm bathing in it. "Is he as cute close up as he is in the underwear commercials?"

More cute. A hundred times more cute. Not only that, but every time I'm with him, I revert to your age. Since when did twelve-year-olds have crushes on dangerous, unsuitable men like Vadim Petrov?

"Sorry to burst your bubble, guys, but a lot of that is airbrushing. In fact, he's got wrinkles. Pimples, too."

The girls' faces crumpled in disappointment. *Get used to it, ladies. Men will do nothing but.* A couple of the boys hovered nearby, listening in, and now Jordan, one of her centers, skated closer.

"So he's okay with a woman coach?" There was a touch of challenge in it.

"Well, Jordan, he's okay with a coach. I don't think the fact I'm a woman has anything to do with it."

"Do you think he might be able to visit?" Gabby asked, her eyes bright with visions of hot, albeit wrinkled and pimpled, Russians. "It'd be great to have a real hockey player showing us some stuff."

Chopped liver right here, apparently.

"I'll see what I can do. Now off you go, your parents will be waiting."

The kids skated off, bubbling with excitement that a "real" player might make an appearance. *Le sigh.* She sat on the bench, trying not to resent Vadim or Moretti or her injury, thinking about what the hell she was doing with her life. A few minutes passed and a new group of kids came on the ice, the thirteen- to fourteen-year-olds in the bantam class. She looked up as a big set of thighs entered her field of vision.

"Hey, Isobel."

"Hey, Jax. How's it going?"

"Not bad." The older kids' coach, Jackson Callaghan, brother of Rebels right-winger Ford, once had a promising career laid out before him. A car crash over ten years ago ended his dream, but in the last few months he'd taken over as the head coach for the junior club. "How's my dickhead of a brother doing?"

"Pretty good. Holding the first line together."

Jax gave a subtle chin nod to the bench beside her. She displayed her palm, and he took a seat.

"So, other than running a pro hockey team and teaching Petrov how *not* to be a Russian asshole, what are you up to these days?"

She laughed. She didn't know Jax all that well, but she liked his blunt approach.

"Just assessing all my options. Jobs. Men. Sandwiches."

"Oh yeah? Got some good stuff in the works?"

"Chicken and cheddar from Potbelly's. Then I'm thinking college coaching or back to the minors."

He nodded, then jerked upright and shouted out to a couple of boys on the far side of the rink. "No checking during warm-up!" The troublemakers parted and headed back into innocuous figure eights.

Jax sat again. "How's the fund-raiser coming along?"

In a few weeks, they would host a glitzy gala to funnel more money into the Hockey for Everyone coffers. They chatted a little about it, but Isobel's mind was still stuck on her various career dilemmas. "Do you mind if I ask you a question?"

"Sure."

"If you had a chance to play pro, even if it was just one night, would you take it?"

"Without hesitation."

"Even if it meant you risked reinjury or worse?"

"I'd skate toward that faster than my kids inhale Gino's deep-dish." He cocked his head. "You got another shot, Isobel?"

"Maybe."

He stood and did a quick pirouette on his skates to face her. "What did Gretzky say? You miss a hundred percent of the shots you never take."

Yep, that's what he'd said. The Great One could always be relied upon to steer a girl true.

Vadim held the phone up to his ear, determined to listen closely and read between the lines.

"Hello," a sleepy, sexy voice said. A little Gallic irritation in it, too.

"Bonjour, kotyonok. You are still asleep?"

"Vadim," she replied in that French purr he had adored for a week while Marceline was in Quebec for business late last year. "It's 6 a.m. in Paris. Of course I'm still asleep."

He heard her fumble and then the telltale click and expelling of smoke. She had hid her habit in Quebec, but there had always been that faint trace in her hair, on her clothes. Not like Isobel, who smelled like flowers.

He shook his head, conscious of his mission.

"I hope this isn't a bad time." He didn't really care, but that was her cue for her to remove herself to privacy if she had someone in her bed.

"It is never a bad time for you, Vadim. I have a flight to London in four hours, which should give us plenty of time to—"

"Not today, kotyonok," he said with a grimace. "I am calling to ask you something. It is . . . delicate."

"*Mon Dieu*, you have some disease!"

"No, not at all." He always used condoms. Perhaps that was it. Perhaps a woman—Isobel—did not get the full impact because he was encased in rubber. Or perhaps he was grasping at straws.

There was nothing for it but to spit it out.

"When we were together, did you come?"

A slight hesitancy. "Did I—what?"

"Orgasm, Marceline. I believed you did, but I wanted to be sure."

Silence.

"Marceline?"

"*Oui*, Vadim, I am still here." Her voice was now tinged with Continental amusement. "I am trying to understand. Are you writing a memoir?"

He sighed. This was the reaction of the two women he had already called tonight. Everyone wanted to understand his rationale. Was it not a perfectly valid query?

"No. I am just doing some research . . . on behalf of a friend."

"Hmm."

He hurried on. "I have my own techniques and I wondered if there was something you liked that I could tell him." Nothing had ever sounded more stupid exiting his mouth.

He heard her sharp intake of breath as she dragged on the cigarette. "Vadim, *our* time together was wonderful. But sometimes a woman is too tired and it makes things easier, *non*?"

"Makes what easier?"

"The male hurt feelings. Their egos, so fragile."

She talked about men as if he wasn't a member of this sensitive species who needed to be shielded from realities. He could interpret this as an insult or as a sneaky French way of giving him the information he wanted. Knowing Marceline, it was both.

"And when a woman is tired?" he prompted.

"Or not in the mood or feeling pressured to perform for any number of reasons, she must decide if her lover's sulking is something she wants to endure."

Vadim's head pounded. He wished he hadn't called. He wished he hadn't heard a word about that conversation from Shay. He wished he'd never slept with Iso—no, he didn't wish that. Of all the things he wished for, that was not one of them.

"So you would fake an orgasm to avoid a man's pouting."

She laughed, low and cruel.

"I have, but not with you, Vadim. We had a wonderful time together in Quebec, *n'est-ce pas*? I will be in Chicago for business soon. Perhaps we can get together?"

"Sure." His mind was trying to wrap itself around what she had just said. Why tell him the secret thoughts of women and orgasms if this didn't apply to him? Was she speaking in hypotheticals or trying to hint that his sexual skills were subpar? Yet she wanted to see him again—and he knew she wouldn't be visiting so he could act as tour guide around the Windy City.

On balance, he had to conclude that he'd delivered the orgasms she was looking for. Vadim Petrov didn't have a problem. Other men had problems—and some women, too, if Marceline's catalog of excuses on behalf of the sisterhood was to be believed.

"I should let you get ready for your flight, Marceline. Au revoir, kotyonok, and merci."

He ended the call, assured that he had absolutely nothing to worry about.

EIGHT

Isobel couldn't take her eyes off the perfect breasts being shoved in her face. Similarly, the body attached to those breasts was a work of art. Gilded skin, curves in all the right places, a hint of glitter over the décolletage.

"You havin' fun, hun?" the perfect specimen asked, and there it was—that revealing bobble of an Adam's apple.

Isobel nodded dumbly, placed a dollar bill in the performer's G-string, and watched the hip swivel that took her away to a table of rowdy bachelorettes.

She turned to Harper, who was eyeing the proceedings at the Kit Kat Lounge and Supper Club, Chicago's premier drag bar, over her martini glass. "I'm not sure if I should be jealous of that body or think seriously about my sexual orientation."

"No reason why you can't be both," her older sister mused. "She's hot."

Violet popped a truffle fry into her mouth and groaned. "Too. Good. But y'know, if you're leaning that way it might make things easier—or explain a lot."

Lesbianism would really be the simplest solution. Women were a lot less needy.

Harper asked, "So how's Gerry?"

Isobel made a face at Harper, who responded with, "Just asking."

Violet looked puzzled. "What am I missing?"

"All allusions to lesbianism come with the obligatory ask after my mom's health." Isobel leaned in and cupped her hand over her mouth. "Because my mom's a lesbian."

"I didn't know that!" Violet threw a look of giddy glee at Harper. "But I thought she was remarried to some guy called Danny and playing golf in Scottsdale."

"Dani is a woman. When my parents divorced five years ago, she finally came out."

Harper chuckled evilly. "Cliff was pissed."

More than pissed. The notion that the gold-medal-winning ice skater he left Harper's mom for faked her way—in every possible way—through her marriage had made him livid with rage. What did the man expect when he'd chosen his second wife like a man chooses a breeding mare? Ice-skating pedigree. Check. Childbearing hips. Check. The rest. Who cares?

As for why her mother had not only hidden who she was but also married a brute NHL enforcer—and wrecked another home in the process—Isobel had never really obtained a satisfactory answer.

I had sponsorships, Izzy, expectations of my sexuality because of my career in ice-skating. And your father was very persuasive . . .

God save us from alpha dickheads who could make women "forget" they were lesbians. Isobel was determined she wouldn't make her mother's mistakes. Not that she was hiding who she was, but she wanted control over her life. And that included both her professional life *and* her sex life.

She was still mulling over Vadim's "warning" about getting involved with Kelly. What business was it of his—of any of the team—whom she dated? And while he half seduced her with all that Russian ferocity at this morning's practice? The nerve of this jerk.

Affirming the soundness of her internal process, Chaka Khan's "I'm Every Woman" came on, sending the bachelorettes at the next table into a frenzy.

"So I have a hypothetical."

Harper raised an eyebrow. "Go on."

"Let's imagine there's this guy who on paper looks like he could check all the boxes. Good-looking, common interests, easy to talk to, and best of all—"

"Hung like a horse?" Violet offered.

"Interested in me."

Harper and Vi looked suspicious, wondering about the catch.

"There doesn't seem to be any problem—"

"Except . . ." Harper did her eyebrow thing again. Tomes were communicated.

"Being with him might start people gossiping."

Violet pointed. "You sneaky cur! Is some bangin' hockey player trying to get in your sweatpants?"

"No. This is hypothetical. There's this guy I sort of like—not a player!" She glared at Harper, who was giving off her patented *Harper Does Not Approve* look. Hypocrisy levels through the roof. "But it might look like I'm using him to get ahead in my career."

Harper sucked down a mouthful of martini. "Would you be?"

It had never occurred to her until Vadim Petrov had opened his big, sexy mouth.

"No. I actually like him."

"This guy"—Violet squinted—"it's not Moretti, is it? Because he's playin' golf with your momma, if you know what I mean."

"I know that, but *daaamn*, right?"

A moment of silence was offered for the female tragedy that was Dante Moretti's homosexuality.

Vi continued. "So this guy could be the one. The one who meets all your requirements. Tall, built, looks good in a suit."

"That sounds sort of shallow," Isobel mumbled, though those were the specs she'd listed during a previous sister-bonding session. They also happened to fit a certain Russian to a T.

Not thinking of him.

"So he's perfect on paper," Harper said thoughtfully, "but you're looking for excuses to sabotage it before you've even given it a chance."

Isobel nodded with the enthusiasm of a very happy basset hound. "Basically!"

Over the sound of their laughter, Harper's phone

rang and a smile lit up her face. "Speaking of out-of-bounds players, I'm going to take this somewhere quieter."

Watching while Harper moved out of earshot, Violet popped another truffle fry into her mouth and chewed slowly.

"You and Kelly would make beautiful babies, *chica*."

Isobel's cheeks warmed. "Let me guess. That gossip Cade Burnett."

"You were spotted in the Empty Net weaving your tangled web."

"Which I didn't even know I was weaving until Kelly asked me out to dinner."

Violet grinned, her smile so like their father's that Isobel's chest tightened.

"And you said?"

"Sure! Let's do that sometime!" Her fake cheer gave way to worry. "But now that the old biddies are gossiping, I don't want anyone thinking I'm using Kelly to get entrenched with the backroom staff."

Violet scrunched up her face. "Why would you even think that? Did someone say something? Because Cade didn't mention it."

Her heart skipped a beat. "No, not at all."

Violet visibly relaxed. "Oh, that reminds me. Tina at the Empty Net said there was a bit of a kerfuffle in the bar a couple of nights ago."

"Kerfuffle?"

"Yeah. Vadim and Shay."

She sat up straight. "What happened?"

"She said Vadim and Shay almost came to blows. Erik and Cade had to talk him down."

"That's not like him. He's very concerned about his beautiful face."

Violet laughed. "If I looked as hot as the Russian, I'd be worried about it getting punched, too. Cade said it was just a bit of territorialism over the left wing. Weird, right?"

Yeah. Weird. This must have happened the same night the boys were gossiping about Isobel's "sleeping her way to success" career strategy. What was going on here?

Violet was tapping into her phone. "So, what can you tell me about Petrov? Dick-tabase-worthy or no?"

Her sister maintained a very inappropriate Tumblr dedicated to dick pics and GIFs. Isobel wondered how many of the Rebels she'd managed to inventory and how much they should set aside for the inevitable lawsuit.

"It was years ago, and I don't remember much." *Timber!*

"Have you seen his underwear ad?" Violet shoved the phone up close in Isobel's face, leaving her no choice but to take it so Vadim's package wasn't melting her face Indiana Jones style. She examined where Violet had zoomed in, right on the mouthwatering ridge pressing against the thin cotton.

Her sister pointed at the image. "Left curve. Nice girth. And looks like they had a fluffer on set for the shoot."

"I doubt it."

Violet snatched the phone away before Isobel could embarrass herself. "So, you do remember! I'm tellin' ya, if the Russian wasn't a walking example of false advertising with the no-no on the oh-oh, I'd be telling you to hit that till you can hit it no more."

"We have rules."

Violet was momentarily distracted by a Beyoncé impersonator, who looked far too good in a sparkly leotard as she belted out "Single Ladies."

She turned back to Isobel. "You're taking your cue from Harper 'I bought him, I own him, I'm fucking him' Chase? There's this cavalcade of hot-assed muscle at your fingertips. Why the hell shouldn't you be taking advantage of the perks of team ownership?"

"Like you and Cade?"

She smiled regally, which immediately made Isobel suspicious. While Vi had a lot going for her, regal wasn't really in her wheelhouse. "The Texan has a zillion problems that not even someone as amazing as me can solve. I'm looking for something a bit more compelling. A fixer-upper."

Like a certain brooder of a captain with a Scottish accent, a six-month AA chip, and more baggage than could fit in the hold of a 747. Everyone had noticed Violet teasing Bren St. James and how he glared at her like she was something on the sole of his shoe. Isobel couldn't help thinking Vi was setting herself up for heartbreak, though. Men were incapable of fundamental change—she'd witnessed it with her father, a philanderer who never saw a puck bunny he didn't want to pet.

Hockey player was just another synonym for *cheater*.

"Look, I'm going to say something here," Isobel said. "About dating hockey players."

Violet groaned. "This again."

"This isn't just because of us being team owners and how it's an ethical minefield, though it is. I would tell you this even if that wasn't the case. Hockey players have the toughest schedules in all of professional sports. Half the season they're on the road during the coldest months of the year, which means they're usually looking for a warm body."

Her sister grinned and raised a hand. "I volunteer as tribute."

Isobel remained serious. "The problem is when your feelings go beyond that. You'll end up falling for one, but his schedule won't change. Now you're a wife and/or girlfriend, hanging out with the other WAGs, all of you feeding this vicious cycle of 'what's he doing in Denver?' or 'the game was over thirty minutes ago, why isn't he answering his phone?' I've hung with minor league players for the last two years, and even those little shits are playing away. I dated two guys in college who, yep, you guessed it, cheated on me. That's how my father met my mom, Vi. At an away game in Philly while he was married to Harper's mom."

"That's how he met mine, Iz."

Isobel's heart sank to the floor. Of course, Violet

would know that. She was the result of a one-night stand in Vegas.

"Sorry, I didn't mean to imply your conception wasn't a beautiful thing."

Violet was all mock affront. "How dare you? The heavens opened in chorus as soon as Cliffie's sperm top-shelfed right into my mom's egg!"

That set them both off into giggles. Isobel had tried to encourage Vi to talk about how she felt on the subject of deadbeat dads, but the girl always deflected with humor.

Violet grasped Isobel's hand. "You know how I said this was the year of the V, in all the ways that can be taken? I'm not combing the Rebels' classifieds looking for open WAG positions. I just want to have a good time."

Isobel squeezed her sister's hand back. Violet was a breast cancer survivor, something she'd only recently shared with them, and she was grabbing life by the reconstructed tits. It was admirable, and while Isobel had had her own brush with mortality on the ice a couple of years ago, she had handled it differently. Turned inward and lost all her confidence. She didn't feel like that girl who had her whole life spread out before her like a success buffet.

Silver, Izzy? Clifford's voice boomed in her head, and she tried to filter out the tinge of disappointment in his tone. *Next time, you'll get gold.*

Those who can't, coach.

Or perhaps, those who can't, figure out a way to get back on the ice and win for Team USA.

No, a man wasn't the answer, not even a cute, non-threatening trainer. Why not take a page from the Book of Violet and make this *her* year?

Not to get some, but to get some piece of herself back.

NINE

"Isobel, wait up."

Isobel turned to find Kelly walking quickly to catch up with her in the parking lot after her practice session with Vadim. Almost a week since that night in the Empty Net, and she'd been avoiding Mr. Nice Guy. Which made her quite the dick.

Vadim's "advice" had riddled her with doubt. She knew she wasn't using Kelly to get ahead in the organization. Kelly knew it. Hell, he wouldn't have asked her out if he thought her motives were suspect, would he?

"I thought maybe we could set up that dinner." He smiled, and goshdarnit was he handsome. Vi was right. The spawn of their union would be gorgeous. Nice, clean, all-American genes with not a scrap of Slavic imperiousness in sight.

Not thinking of him.

"Right. Dinner."

He frowned, and on Kelly, that looked more like a query laced with optimism. It was like his face couldn't express negativity. She saw potential here, but not while her job prospects were up in the air. It wouldn't be a rejection, more like a postponement.

"I'm thinking this might not be the best time. The next two months are crucial for the team"—more crucial than he could possibly know—"and I want to focus on the play-offs. We'd still see each other—"

"At work," he said.

"Yes, and we can get to know each other better that way before we take it to the next level." By which time she'd be sure of the next steps in both her professional life and her personal one.

Of course, he was completely within his rights to say *Screw you, I don't want to do this on your timetable,* but she hoped he'd be patient. If he was anything like the man she thought he was, he would be patient.

"No problem, Isobel." He leaned in and kissed her on the cheek. Such a gentleman. This care is what she'd been missing. Kelly was the one. She was certain of it.

But first she would call Coach Lindhoff and tell him she wanted one more shot.

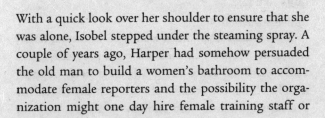

With a quick look over her shoulder to ensure that she was alone, Isobel stepped under the steaming spray. A couple of years ago, Harper had somehow persuaded the old man to build a women's bathroom to accommodate female reporters and the possibility the organization might one day hire female training staff or

PTs. But that consideration didn't extend to bathing facilities for humans with breasts.

Which was why Isobel was taking a shower in the players' locker room.

She fisted the tile, leaning in to take the weight off her legs and, consequently, her hip, which had been acting up.

That's what happens when you push too hard, Chase.

But she had no choice. Watching Vadim skate was no substitute for a hard session on the ice. All this time on her iPad planning other people's careers had left her soft. So she might have gone overboard tonight, because her hip was screaming at her like an old woman whose canasta partner was screwing up.

She found it much easier to skate drills and push beyond her limits when there was no one around. Lenny, the head of security, was cool with opening up the practice rink for her—cupcakes from Benison's were the key. This afternoon, Coach Lindhoff had been thrilled to hear from her and had invited her to train with the team ahead of Worlds. She'd declined, citing Rebels' obligations, but in reality, the true reason for her reluctance to take Lindhoff up on his offer was not quite so noble.

You're a pussy, Iz.

There you are, Dad! She'd wondered where her father had gone. Probably ducked out for a pastrami sub in Hell's cafeteria. Since his death, he'd been popping into her brain for occasional visits, usually to tell her she wasn't working hard enough or injuries were for the weak or coaching was the domain of those who had nothing left to prove.

Tonight she'd put some extra mustard on every glide, bitching at her muscles to work hard and knowing they'd be bitching at her right back later. Like now. But that was okay. Her father expected nothing less. Leave everything on the ice, even during a practice. No distractions, especially boys. Champions don't have personal lives.

What he meant was *female* champions don't have personal lives, because her father had certainly put the *person* in his own personal life. Where the person was Cliff Chase, the center of the universe.

He had worried about her going to Harvard, so far from home. So open to temptation. After finding her in bed with Vadim, he'd removed the Russian from her orbit. Better not to run the risk that hormonal Isobel would choose her heart over hockey. Every night at college, he'd called, ostensibly to see how she was, but really to ensure that she wasn't out at some bar, making unsuitable friends, meeting horny boys, risking everything he had worked for. *Practice, games, study.* These were all that mattered.

Isobel wasn't the only one whose dreams were destroyed when she took that blade to the skull thirty-seven minutes into her first professional hockey game.

Her last professional hockey game.

Each of the sisters had received a letter from their father at the reading of the will—a last note from beyond the grave. She didn't know the contents of her sisters' notes, but she had her own letter memorized by heart.

> *Dear Isobel,*
>
> *From the moment I saw you in your mother's arms, I knew you would be the one to carry on my legacy. You've made me so happy already, and while your injury might have set you back, I know this isn't the end. Sharing the team with your sisters might not seem like a way back to glory, but your competitive spirit will lift the Rebels up—and you with it. Don't give up, my winningest girl.*
>
> *Love, Dad*

Sure, Cliff. No pressure.

On the subject of pressure, the hot water felt so good. Chase Manor's five bathrooms had decent showers, but nothing beat the pulsing power massaging her skin and bones and marrow right this minute. Determined to stay until she pruned or the water ran cold, she jumped when the lights went out.

Had someone thrown the master switch? Lenny knew she was here, so that seemed unlikely.

In pitch darkness, she blinked and tried to adjust to the midnight blackness. Crap, this was all she needed. She stepped out, fumbling for the towel on the hook, and immediately knew:

She wasn't alone.

Her heart thumped rabbit kicks. A shuffling sound answered it, sending her ninja reflexes into hyperdrive. With no hesitation, she shoved the heel of her hand forward and up, screamed something that should have sounded like "Fuck you!" but instead came out as "Fooooo!" and was immensely gratified to register a connection with the asshole who was trying to creep up on her in the dark.

Vadim doubled over like a sack of beets, clutching his throat. Vainly, he tried to speak before she kicked the living shit out of him and finished the job. His eyes watered. His throat throbbed. If that's what she could do with a single heel chop, he shuddered to think how close he had come to having his genetic line end tonight.

"Iso—Iso . . ." The word would not form.

"Vadim? Oh my God, Vadim!" She fell to her knees beside him, her hand searching and curving around the back of his neck. "I had no idea that was you. I just sensed danger and self-preservation kicked in."

He held up the hand of forgiveness, not that she could see it in the dark. What had he been thinking? That he had heard the pitter-patter of water and wanted to give whoever was here a heads-up so they wouldn't react like Isobel had just reacted. Then the lights went out and . . .

As suddenly as it had happened, the lights came on again.

"Must have been a power outage," Isobel said.

He turned over so he was in a sitting position. Somehow that made it easier to swallow and his eyes weren't so watery. He was glad of this, because the sight before him should not be blurred in any way.

A naked Isobel.

Unfortunately, her position hunkered before him meant he did not have as good a view as he would have liked. The valley of her breasts was inviting, the soft mounds almost begging him to plump them up with his hands, but her knees hid what he knew to be beautifully pink nipples. Unless they had changed. Perhaps they were darker now, would harden perfectly, even taste different, when he swirled them with his tongue and sucked them into his greedy mouth.

How could he be turned on right now?

"Just take deep breaths," she said, her hand rubbing his neck softly. Oddly, it reminded him of his mother and how she would soothe him when he lost a game. His father had rarely attended, but his mother had never missed him playing, right up until the day before she left.

This was not where his brain should be going.

"You'll be fine in a couple of minutes, Vadim."

Spoken from the depths of experience. How many men had she disabled in this manner?

"I didn't mean to scare you," he croaked out.

"Well, you did."

"You've done that before?"

"A woman living alone has to be forearmed, even in Canada where the muggers are polite. Do you think you're okay to stand now?"

He shook his head at such a ridiculous question. He was absolutely fine. He went to stand, but she placed a hand on his arm.

"I should grab a towel first."

"I do not need a towel."

She arched an eyebrow. "For me, durák."

Did she just call him an idiot in his native language?

"Yep. I just did," she said, reading his mind. "Now turn your head. No peeking."

Out of respect, he did as he was told, wishing he had eyes in the back of his head.

"Okay, you can get up now. If you're able." She tightened the towel around her breasts, tucking it in to secure it.

He stood, shaking off her helpful hands. Embarrassment had evicted shock.

"I was coming to warn you." His voice sounded rusty.

"Warn me? About Russian behemoths skulking around the shower room?"

"Yes," he said, not understanding *behemoths* but assuming it was an insult. Most everything from this woman's mouth was. "It is a particular problem in this professional hockey player locker room."

Guilt flashed across her features. "I'm sorry. I should have known it was someone connected with the organization. Someone who wouldn't hurt me."

"No, you reacted correctly. It's better to punch first, beg forgiveness later."

She grabbed another towel and wrapped it around her head. "What are you doing here, Vadim?"

"I could ask you the same thing. In fact, I'm fairly certain I have more reason to be here than you."

"It's after eleven at night, and we're both here. Anyone would think that's pretty fishy."

He rubbed his chin, feeling Machiavellian. "Yes, they would."

Evidently annoyed with his evasiveness, she skirted him, a twitch to her hips, while he took a long, hard look at how her ass moved with the terry fabric. An ass he had already acknowledged to be sublime, but really it was her legs he had always enjoyed the most. Long, tanned, and toned. Legs that had carried her to glory. He would enjoy nothing more than seeing them wrapped around his hips.

This line of thinking was ridiculous, considering the warning bells he had rung in her ear about dating Kelly. But he did not wish to date her. He merely wished to fuck his sexy coach.

That's when something struck him. Too busy losing himself in the glorious thought of burying himself between Isobel's thighs, he had failed to see that the twitch in her hips was not readily attributed to a sexy swivel, but . . . for the love of God, she was hurting.

"Isobel, why are you walking that way?"

She stopped and threw a glance over her shoulder. "What way?"

"Like you have been injured."

"It's nothing." She continued to the outer locker room.

He followed and found her standing with hands on hips staring at his gym bag and the skates lying beside it.

Her lips thinned. "You're here to skate?"

"I need to get back to my full speed." With the team on the road for a few away games, now was the perfect time to improve his strength and skills absent prying eyes.

"You shouldn't be skating without supervision. You'll push yourself too hard. Kelly won't be happy when he finds out."

"Kelly? Why are you so concerned with what Kelly thinks?"

She squinted at him. "We're a team here. We're all concerned *as a team* when one of our assets is engaging in behavior that could curtail his recovery."

Yes, an asset. That's all he was to her. He let that go for now, as any further inquiry would make him more furious. "You are trying to change the subject. I asked why you're walking like a wizened old grandmother."

"Just a long day. But thanks for the lovely comparison."

He knew she'd had a hip injury in her quest to return to professional-level play. He didn't need to have gone through that himself to understand how devastating it must have been for her. Isobel had always been a fierce competitor. To lose what defines you must be tough, and he resolved to be gentler with her.

"Bella, I—"

"Don't call me that," she snapped.

"Okay, *Is-o-bel*." He said it low and rough so she understood that it did not matter which name he used, his intentions when saying it were the same. "Can I not be concerned when I see you hurting? If anyone understands that, it's me."

She looked like she wanted to disagree, but the words wouldn't come, likely because she knew he was right. Only athletes understood other athletes.

"I was out on the rink, putting in my time," she said quietly. "And I know you're going to wonder why a coach would do that."

"You want to be able to keep up during our practices. You're worried I will surpass you and think you have nothing left to teach me."

"Not exactly. I need to feel I'm at this top level, even if I can't compete on that stage anymore." She looked away in the direction of the rink.

The only stage that mattered.

There was more to this, but he didn't press. "We understand each other, Isobel. But skating to the point of pain will not help. When we meet for practice tomorrow, what use will you be to me?"

Her lips curved. "I could say the same about you. No skating without me or another coach present, Vadim. I—*we* can't risk you overdoing it, not when you're so close to making the roster."

"I am?"

"Of course you are. We're so close"—as she spoke he moved in, gratified at the slight bulge in her graceful neck when she swallowed—"to making the play-offs, but we need that extra push. You're what we need."

But was he *what* she *needed?*

"No skating tonight, Russian. Come in thirty minutes early tomorrow, and we'll get to work."

"Da."

"Now, I need to get dressed, so if you don't mind . . ."

"I will wait outside."

"You don't have to do that."

That was the other thing that niggled at him. She was here solo. Naked. Wet. Anything could have happened to her, including seduction by a hard-as-a-puck Russian.

"I will walk you to your car. It is not safe for you to be here alone."

That made her smile. "Ask your Adam's apple how safe I am."

"Yes, you are tough, Isobel, the toughest woman in all of Chicago. I will still be waiting outside."

Five minutes later, she emerged, carrying her coat and a gym bag, her hair still damp and down around her shoulders. A slight curl was starting in it, a kink he remembered wrapping around his fist as he had plunged inside her.

They walked to her car, the silence barely masking the whirligig of thoughts in his brain. The five-minute wait had given him time to think. To brood. To plan.

She stopped at her car, unlocked the trunk, and loaded her bag inside. Her green eyes held his, those tilting eyelashes fluttering wide.

"So, see you tomorrow?"

He needed to know. It was a thrumming imperative, and he could no longer go without an answer.

"Isobel, when we were together, did I make you come?"

TEN

Isobel froze, not quite sure she'd heard that right. Perhaps it was a problem with Russian-English translation. In Vadim's pretty head, maybe "come" meant "enrage you" or "drive you bonkers." Or perhaps he was still reeling from being throat-chopped by his female coach and former teen crush.

Because he couldn't possibly be asking *that*.

"Excuse me?"

"Must I repeat it?"

"Uh, yes. You must."

"I have reason to believe that you may not have"—he paused, and that hesitation gave her hope that he'd realized his error and was self-correcting—"completed the sex act."

The sex act? "You mean, did I come with *you*?"

He looked exasperated. "Is that not what I said?"

"Yes, but is that what you meant?" Her cheeks were heating, but not quite enough to counteract the March wind chill. "Vadim, it's cold and late and—"

He leaned around, his body covering her with that

mountain of pure-carved muscle, and opened the door of her Camry. "Get in." Then, leaving his gym bag on the icy ground, he walked around to the passenger side, opened that door, and climbed in. He pushed the seat back, but he was so tall that his legs remained bent.

Brain in disarray, heart struggling to catch up to her muddled thoughts, she got in, started the engine, and turned up the heat.

"This might take a while," she muttered, hyper-aware of his hulking presence in her car and still reeling from his question, the one she was hoping he'd just forget. She glanced over to find Vadim rocking his usual sexy-serious self.

Good grief, she was going to have to discuss this.

"Now." She turned to him, a touch of schoolmarm in her tone, ready to make allowances for English being his second language, or maybe it was his fourth or fifth. Vaguely, she recalled he spoke French, Spanish, and German. "What makes you think I didn't, uh, do what you said I didn't do?" Other than the fact it was true and any guy who wasn't completely focused on his own pleasure would be able to figure it out. "Have you been thinking about it? Or maybe you knew all along?"

"So it is true." He looked crestfallen, or as crestfallen as a stoic Russian could get.

"Well, yes, why would you ask if you didn't think it was a possibility? Where is this coming from, Vadim?"

He grunted something in Russian. Hell and damn,

she was going to have to massage the poor guy's fragile ego. "Listen, I hear that happens a lot when it's a first time."

"It does not happen to the women I'm with," he said with just the right amount of imperiousness. *And we're off.*

"Are you saying *I'm* the problem?"

"Have you had this issue with other men?"

"That's none of your damn business!"

"Are you a lesbian?" Unfazed by the scowl that ridiculousness deserved, he continued to probe. "Do you fantasize about women?"

"Do you fantasize about yourself?"

That amused him. "I am at the center of all my fantasies, yes."

Of course he was. The man was sex on skates. "Vadim, what the hell has inspired this word vomit? Did you have a little 'problem' with one of your club bimbos, and it's brought on a bout of dick gazing?"

"I may have overheard you discussing your first time with your sister."

Her heart fell through the floor of her car. "You were eavesdropping on my private conversation?"

"It was loud enough to inform the entire arena!" Said as if *he* was the wounded party. "Was this just standard locker room talk? Were you merely venting because you were annoyed with me after our practice?"

"You think I'd make that up?"

"Women can be very vengeful."

"All right, listen, oh mighty Petrov. You might be

living in your own paranoid Shakespeare fantasy where the women who are not out to fuck you are out to get you, but believe me when I say I wouldn't lie about something like that. You sucked in bed!"

All of Chicagoland might have heard that one.

This outburst didn't shock him. Instead, the shock was all on her side because of what he said next.

"I'm sorry."

"You're what, now?"

"I'm sorry."

With a shaky hand, she turned down the heat on the dash. It was pumping out at full blast now, and she was feeling far too toasty.

They were clearly at cross-purposes, his true meaning lost in the snarky back-and-forth. "Sorry that you called me a lesbian?"

"I did not call you a lesbian. I asked if you were one while I gathered evidence."

That was some mighty fine hairsplitting, but she let it slide.

"I'm sorry because I failed you during your first sexual experience, Bella. I should have made it better for you."

His regret seemed genuine. She knew she was supposed to love seeing this arrogant man brought down a peg and filled with remorse, but she didn't like it. Not at all.

However, she secretly loved that he called her Bella.

"Well, I didn't tell you I was a virgin. You didn't have all the facts, so—"

He held up a hand. "No, I didn't, but that is no excuse. I was young and horny and excited because I wanted you more than anything. It was a time in our lives when anything seemed possible, yes? We were healthy, strong, and hot for each other, but I didn't take the time to discover how to please you. Any decent man would have done that. Perhaps I thought there would be more time to do so." He looked out the window, pain in the set of his beautiful mouth.

"Vadim, about what happened. After." *My father, your exile.*

"Let us not rehash the past." He returned his gaze to her. "Everything occurs for a reason. We end up where we are supposed to be."

True, but that didn't mean she couldn't be sorry that her father had banished him and put a stutter step in his promising career. Also, there was a finality about his words. They couldn't go back to those halcyon days of teenage infatuation and lust. They were all grown up, burdened with responsibilities.

"Vadim, some of the things I said before when I was talking to Violet . . ."

"About the quality of my lovemaking?"

Did he have to talk like a dissolute duke? No one should be able to say "lovemaking" with a straight face and make it sound so . . . sexy.

"Right. That. Well, I was pissed at your attitude that day in the rink, and it made me petty."

"Bringing the Ukrainians into it was a low blow, Isobel."

She rolled her lips in. *Must not laugh. Must not laugh.*

"You've always been so touchy about your neighbors."

"So you have not slept with the Ukrainian delegation at the Games?"

"Not the *entire* delegation." She grinned, and Lord love a duck, he grinned right back at her. Dangerous heat bloomed all over her body. Maybe she should flip to the AC, because any more Smiles of Devastation from the Russian and she would melt into the seat.

"I—I probably should get going. So, see you for practice tomorrow?"

He merely held her gaze. "Isobel, I am not nineteen years old anymore."

Didn't she know it. "Got that."

"In the last eight years, I have worked on improving myself. I am a better skater, and no one can beat me in a face-off. I know more about wine than any self-respecting hockey player should. I recognize designers on red carpets." He leaned in, his breath warm even in the heated car. "I have improved in all areas."

She swallowed. "I'm sure all your girlfriends appreciate it. Especially the designers thing."

His shrug was that of a man who considered himself woefully underappreciated.

"I would like to apologize. Properly."

Her lungs went on hiatus. He couldn't mean what she thought he meant. "Apology accepted," she said cheerfully, though it came out chipmunk style. Alvin would be so proud.

"You choose to act clueless about what I mean?"

"Are you offering to apologize with your penis?"

"It is my most improved area." He said it with such sincerity that she laughed, but immediately turned serious again because this was not a laughing matter.

"We tried it, and it didn't work, Vadim. In fact, I'd say it was disastrous."

"You're overstating the situation. It wasn't that bad."

She practically dislocated her eyeballs trying not to roll them. "Famous last lines in the history of seduction."

"We were kids. Neither of us knew what we were doing. I can guarantee we will not have the same problem."

"Vadim, you know I can't get involved with you. Even if I wanted to, which I don't, it's a terrible idea."

"So you like Kelly?"

"No comment."

"You do like him. Perhaps you are thinking this will be a good match for you. I suppose he is . . . nice."

That was *her* word for Kelly, and Vadim had no right to use it, especially when he made it sound like dog food.

"As if you're qualified to know that."

"I can recognize nice. It is very easy for a man to spot what he is not."

"You're not nice?"

He laughed mirthlessly. "Would you like to argue this point with me?"

"I'm sure all your girlfriends think you're nice."
Don't defend the man from himself!

"They think I am attractive, rich, and . . ." He
paused and shrugged. "That is it. That is what they
think."

"How sad for you," she said sarcastically. Though
she did think it sad if that was truly what he believed.

"So we are agreed. You are looking for nice."

"Most everyone is, Vadim. No one wants a creep."

He inclined his head until it almost touched hers.
"The opposite of nice does not have to be a bad thing.
Not when it comes to certain areas. Sex, for example."

"You can never stray long from that subject, can
you?"

"Men think of it often, yes. I am just a slave to my
gender. My offer is still open, you know."

Oxygen was at a premium. He was far too close.
"What offer?"

"To apologize. With my cock."

Oh, she got it now. There was no apology on the
table. This was purely Vadim Petrov trying to prove
he was top dog, the man who could make a woman's
panties drop with a smile and a wink.

"You raging dingus! You're not interested in 'my
disappointment' or in making up for that first terrible
time. All you care about is that there are women living
in this universe who didn't go off into the stratosphere
when your dick made its debut inside their vaginas."

"Only one woman, Isobel."

She scoffed. "So sure."

"I know."

"You didn't know back then. You just assumed tectonic plates shifted because, like all men, you imagine you're the epicenter of the orgasm earthquake. As long as *you* feel the earth move, to hell with everyone else."

Nothing but aristocratic hauteur from him now. "I am trying to be nice—"

"Nice? You just said you only recognize nice because you're the opposite!"

He curled a hand around her neck, his touch shockingly sensual. "Then I shall be the opposite. I shall be very, very bad, Isobel."

She wanted to say something about how "bad" wasn't the opposite of "nice," but this wasn't an appropriate time for an English lesson. Her pulse stuttered, then gathered strength, a relentless pounding of *yes, yes, yes.* He must have heard it because, the next second, his lips crashed into hers, taking control as if it was his right.

But she knew better, didn't she? She knew that Vadim Petrov was all smoke and mirrors, style without substance, a man whose only focus was his own pleasure.

Boy could he kiss, though.

This wasn't your standard teenage fumbling. This was a man who knew exactly what to do with his mouth. *Probably all that practice over the years,* she thought bitterly.

The bitterness melted in the face of a wildfire consuming her body. Pure, white-hot need. Maybe the owner of the lips didn't matter. Maybe it was just a joining together of body parts that worked in this never-to-be-repeated moment.

He halted, his expression impossible to read in the shadows.

"It is bad, yes?" His breathing was labored.

"Terrible," she murmured. "Again."

She expected him to say something cutting, but he surprised her.

He did as he was told.

He didn't taste like the boy she remembered. She thought she'd committed everything about that experience to her soul, both the bad and the good, yet Vadim's mouth was different now. He was different.

This kiss . . .

. . . different.

Spicy and sweet, authoritative yet testing. It cracked open something. Not inhibition, because that had never been her problem, but reticence. With other men, she would hold back, waiting for the sparks to fly. If it didn't ignite within a few seconds, she was already moving on, steeling herself for the disappointment that would come later.

Vadim's kiss blew her wariness away. If it was this good, then the rest . . . No, that was not going to happen.

He was an employee, a coworker, a tabloid man-whore, sort of a dick, and the guy who took her virginity and did a piss-poor job of it. If none of these reasons were enough to put a halt to this nonsense, then she was in deep freakin' doo-doo.

"Well?" he asked, though there was no missing

the blink back to reality of his eyelids. He was just as affected as she.

"You want a score?" she panted. "Seven point four. The French judge marked you down. Too much tongue."

This appeared to delight him, delight coming in the form of a lift at the corner of his decadent mouth. "It seems we both have lessons to learn. Again."

In a flash, he had pulled her across into his lap—okay, she may have helped because this couldn't *not* continue. Strangely, the snark fired her up. That hadn't been their thing before, but maybe his time in North America had improved his personality.

She liked this version of Vadim. She liked it very much.

She also liked his positioning of her core over his erection. His hands kneading her ample ass to bring her closer was another check in the "like" column. And, additionally, helping her improved opinion of him was his mouth back on hers, sucking, testing, exploring.

"Again," he murmured.

"Again," she sighed right back into his mouth.

Again.

Rubbing her center against him was divine.

His hands everywhere were divine.

That mouth . . . oh, God, that mouth was ten steps above divine.

And then that mouth was speaking Russian, rough, sexy, sweet nothings that drove her wild. Forced out all common sense. His mouth trailed her jaw, delivering little nips and hot licks to her neck.

"*Bella*"—something in Russian—"*Bella*"—more Russian—"*Bella*." As if one language was inadequate to express how she affected him.

She heard the scrape of her track jacket zipper, felt tingles as he applied openmouthed kisses to newly exposed skin. Her nipples were on fire, sensitive and needy. *Can't stand this. Going to die.* She ripped her bra strap off her shoulder and freed one aching breast.

"Suck me," she begged, and then his mouth closed over her tit and suckled hard. His moan on tasting her sounded like he was in pain, but she didn't care; all she cared about was this mindless grasp at pleasure.

The insistent pulse thrumming through her body beat louder, stronger, showing no sign of stopping and heading for the one place she'd never visited with this man. She rolled her hips and hiked her suggestive rubs into a dirty grind. He was huge against her, toting this hard, hot instrument of pleasure that stroked her just right.

Still not enough.

"Please," she begged as she rode him harder. Faster. Dirtier.

"Da, da, da," he said. *Yes, yes, yes.*

No. A loud noise shook her out of the madness. Though the window was steamed up Titanic style, she could make out the shape of a face. Lenny, the facility's head of security, jumped back.

"Ms. Chase! Shit, sorry. I thought you might be—uh,

sorry about that," he called out, his voice receding as he was already double timing back toward the facility.

Shocked back into reality, her heart in a mad clatter, she placed a hand on Vadim's shoulder to leverage herself back. His mouth made a popping sound as it dragged off her breast. Oh. God. She scrambled out of his lap, which meant she had to avoid several "sticks" poking her on the way back to the driver's seat. Vadim's penis, the gearshift . . .

Was she out of her mind, making out in the parking lot of the Rebels' practice facility? So the players—except the one she had just dry humped in the passenger seat of her Camry—were out of town, but security was here.

She'd need to double the number of cupcakes she brought next time.

"We're going to forget about that," she said while she shoved her breast back into her bra, the abrasion of her nipple still deliciously sensitive.

He touched his lips, then licked as if savoring her taste. "Are we, Bella?"

"Don't call me that. It's 'Isobel' or 'Coach.' That's all there is." She slashed a hand through the air. "I know you think you've got something to prove because of what happened last time, but it won't be at the expense of your recovery. Your bruised ego will have to take a backseat to getting you on the ice."

"You think this is what that kiss was about? My need to prove something?"

"Of course it was. That's all any man's kiss is

about." *And that was a damn sight more than a kiss, mister.* She pointed at the door. "Out."

He placed a hand on the handle, a slight curve to his lips that said *This ain't over.*

Oh, but it was. It had to be.

He climbed out, which took a while because he was tall and the car was small. Once outside, he held the door open, letting all the heat escape.

Unfortunately, her embarrassment chose to stay right here.

"I will see you for practice tomorrow, Bella. Do not be late."

With the grin of a wolf, he closed the door too quickly to hear her unbelievably witty response of, "Shut the hell up."

ELEVEN

At 8 p.m., Vadim walked into the bar at the team hotel in New York, feeling light of heart. This was new to him because 1) Russians did not suffer joy gladly and 2) the last year had been hell on his body, his spirit, and his sanity.

Tomorrow he would play.

This morning, a summons to Coach Calhoun's office had ended with this good news. Isobel had been there, too, nodding her head seriously while Coach yammered on about a testing phase and the need for Vadim to prove himself. And Vadim could only think of Isobel, how her tits tasted, and her soft moans as she straddled him.

Have I proved myself worthy yet, Bella?

For the past week, they had continued with their practices. Isobel wanted their relationship to be all business, and he was trying to respect those boundaries. He understood that she was under scrutiny by everyone, especially the other players. But that did not mean he couldn't dream. Fantasize.

For the next hour, he would set his dirty dreams aside and bond with his teammates over alcohol.

On Vadim's entry, Cade waved from the corner where he was sitting with Ford, Erik, Violet Vasquez, and Kelly, the trainer. Vadim raised a hand back, but instead of going over, he stopped in front of another booth. It was occupied, but Vadim figured the more mature conversation of the team's elder statesmen was preferable to sitting with his rival for Isobel's bed.

"Well, if it ain't our brand-new left-winger," Remy said with a big grin. "Take a load off and rest up that knee before it starts givin' you trouble, Petrov."

Amused, or as amused as someone with Russian DNA could be, Vadim sat in the booth beside Bren St. James, who nodded his approval. Fans claimed he resembled Khal Drogo in *Game of Thrones*—Vadim didn't really see it. More unusual was the fact that St. James was a Brit in the NHL.

"Captain," Vadim offered with a wry salute. "Another round, gentlemen?"

A waitress appeared in a flash. "Hi, there, handsome."

"Hello. Fat Tire, please, and whatever these guys are drinking."

"No vodka for you?" Remy asked.

"We don't carry Vesna," the waitress answered before Vadim could comment. She dipped close, displaying stellar cleavage that would normally have sparked his interest. Unfortunately his mind was stuck in a compact-size car with steamed-up windows as Isobel Chase ground her strong, fuck-me-baby body on his dick.

The waitress continued to speak while Vadim's mind strayed to a more pleasurable place. "But I can bring you a shot of Grey Goose. Mother's milk for you guys, huh?"

Vadim had never been a fan of vodka, even though he was the face of one of its high-end brands. "I'd better not risk it. Eyes everywhere," which made Remy laugh.

"You ready?" Bren asked Vadim as the waitress swayed off. Where Remy was easygoing and talkative, Bren was stoic. He spoke little, but when he did it usually carried a lot of weight, as it should with a team leader.

Vadim had been practicing on off days with the crew, but it was no replacement for actual game play. At two months since he had seen time on the ice, he was more than ready.

"It's been too long."

They both nodded. Veterans understood that injuries could do more than make a man itchy to get out there. They had a habit of destroying confidence and of making a player second-guess everything.

Like Isobel. Her vulnerability when she talked about her need to stay at the highest level even though she could no longer play professionally was a skate blade to his heart. Some were never the same after an injury.

Vadim had no intention of being the same. He would be better.

The waitress returned with two beers and a soda.

Remy took a slug of his beer. "So how's working with Isobel going?"

Tread carefully. Just as there were eyes everywhere, the ears were also ubiquitous.

"It is what it is."

Remy mouthed *wow* at Bren, who looked amused. "Quite the endorsement, Vad."

"No one likes the fate of their playing time decided by—"

"A woman?" Bren offered.

"Someone so young," Vadim countered. That Isobel was an excellent skater was undeniable, but no man enjoyed losing control. He especially did not enjoy how both his mind and his body rioted in her presence. Perhaps the female-in-charge element bothered him more than he cared to admit.

Or perhaps he wanted to fuck his hot coach until he lost all reason.

"I will feel better when I play."

Remy nodded. "She must have done something right."

"That's pretty magnanimous of you," Bren said to Remy.

Vadim's hackles were immediately raised. *He* could criticize, but he refused to tolerate it in others. "You do not like Isobel?"

Remy rubbed his chin. "She doesn't like me. Well, that's not exactly right. It's more that she doesn't approve of me and Harper."

"Thought she shoved Harper into fessin' up about you being the one and all that," Bren said.

"Yeah, but more for Harper's mental health. Something had to give and Isobel recognized that Harper's go-it-alone thing was messing with her mind. I'd say Isobel would prefer Harper was with anyone but a player, but as that's not happening, she has to live with her sister's choice. Harper says it's more because Isobel thinks hockey players are predisposed to cheat."

"Well, old man Chase wasn't exactly the best role model," Bren said. "Fucked his way through every hotel bar in North America. I'm only surprised there aren't more little Chases popping out of the Clifford gene pool."

"I think there can be only one Violet." Remy shot Vadim a sly glance before adding, "Yeah, you're never going to see Isobel gettin' involved with the players. As for Violet, I don't think she has any such scruples."

For a moment, Vadim thought this mischievous look in his direction was because Remy suspected that Vadim and Isobel had crossed a line, but then he realized that this was aimed at their captain. Had he thought Bren St. James looked dark before? A new storm front descended over his grave features.

"Burnett can't handle her," he said, and there was a finality about his statement that caught Vadim's interest. Bren and Violet? Talk about complete opposites.

On cue, a loud laugh trilled from the other side of the bar. If Vadim didn't know this belonged to Violet, their captain's white-knuckling of the edge of the table would have made this clear. Bren muttered something under his breath that sounded like, "Fuck."

"Why not ask her out?"

Remy held up a hand. "Sorry, Petrov, but the world's not ready for these kids to bang it out. We're all gonna need to invest in Kevlar first."

Bren glared at Remy. "Remind me why I choose to spend time with you, DuPre."

"Who else is gonna put up with your moods, *mon ami*?"

The Scot shook his head, a half smile on his lips. As fascinating as this was, Vadim was eager to get back to Isobel, particularly Isobel's self-imposed embargo on fraternization with the players.

"Apparently Isobel is interested in Kelly," he said, testing the temperature of the table and the validity of the theory.

Remy considered this. "I heard it's the other way around, but she's not opposed. Coach and trainer? Sounds like a match made in heaven."

Perhaps, on paper. Perhaps, one that would not offend whoever was offended by inappropriate hook-ups between team owners and players.

It was also what Isobel had said she wanted—once.

But there was a world of difference between saying and doing. And last week in the steamed-up confines of her ridiculous clown car, the doing told Vadim all he needed to know. Her mouth on his was the miracle he'd been missing for eight years.

Fury coursed through him at how he'd screwed up.

He had ruined her first sexual experience in his haste to get his rocks off. Nineteen-year-olds had a lot to learn about pleasing a woman, but surely he could have gone gentler with her. Listened to her body. Anticipated her needs. And now, that disaster lay between them like a peak that had to be scaled.

But he couldn't. He had to stay on his side of the mountain. He had to stay away from her so she would not lose respect from the world for her coaching skills.

An hour later, the small groups were dispersing, and while it was at least three hours to the team's midnight curfew, it was clear that the night was ending. Vadim didn't mind, as Mia had texted to say she was in an Uber and on her way.

He stood, so did Remy and Bren. "*Do zavtra*, gentlemen." Until tomorrow.

As he turned, someone bumped against his shoulder, though *bumped* was generous. If Vadim wasn't 229 pounds of rock-solid muscle, he might have taken a step back.

Leon Shay stood before him with Kazinsky, one of the defensemen. They must have just come in, because their cheeks were ruddy and a dusting of snow covered their jackets. Shay's eyes were cloudy. Unfocused. The man was drunk or close to it.

"Petrov, I hear you're starting tomorrow."

"It is what I am paid to do. It will be good to be back." Even if it was at the expense of Shay in the starting lineup. At half strength, Vadim was ten times the player Shay would ever be. Coach had made the right decision.

"So who'd you blow to get back on the roster?"

"Come on, man, don't start this." Kazinsky, evidently the wiser or more sober of the two, put a hand on his tipsy friend's arm.

Don't start what? Vadim looked from Shay to Kaz. The defender dropped his gaze in embarrassment.

Had Vadim not told Shay what would happen if he spread gossip about Isobel? He glanced down at Shay's running shoes, the laces now grubby from the snow-slushed Manhattan streets. Not idly, Vadim wondered if those laces would break when he wrapped them around Shay's thick, stupid neck.

Meeting Shay's unfocused gaze, Vadim spoke in a quiet, reasonable voice, though every cell in his body itched to do battle. "Perhaps we should speak outside."

Shay leaned in unsteadily, his breath stinking of whiskey. "So you can hit me and finish the hatchet job you started when you were traded in? And here I was thinking that Isobel Chase was going to spread her legs to get her dream job. Looks like you're the one who needs to whore yourself out, you Russian prick."

"*Poshol ti*, you fucking *kozyol*—"

"Okay, that's enough." Bren stepped in and wedged his body between Shay and Vadim. "Both of you, off to your rooms. It's too late for this shite."

A crowd had gathered, a mix of hotel patrons, the few remaining Rebels players, and Kelly. Bren stepped back, hands raised, seeking calm, and Kazinsky followed suit. Shay remained, his brain clearly in some sort of hamster wheel of confusion. Vadim would not hit a man who'd had too much to drink.

But that didn't mean he couldn't get the last word in. Not sporting, perhaps, but Leon Shay wasn't the type of man who understood these subtleties.

Vadim's agent often urged him to protect his face with the same zeal he used to cultivate his skill on the ice. A famous photographer had once called Vadim's bone structure flawless, and while he was usually opposed to inflicting damage on such perfection, sometimes one had to choose the lesser of two evils.

"I am sure if you work hard, Shay, you will have your place back on the first line."

Shay may have been drunk, but he was lucid enough to understand a veiled insult when he heard it. True, Vadim would never strike a drunk, but he would accept the first blow—and ensure this durák saw no ice time for the rest of the season.

So when that sloppy fist met Vadim's jaw, he accepted it in the way a Russian accepts the sharp bite of wind coming off the Ural mountain range. With fortitude and the knowledge that he may not win this battle, but the war had turned in his favor.

TWELVE

Isobel ran into Harper as her older sister was leaving Dante's room.

"What happened?" she demanded. Harper's text message had merely said: *Shay and Petrov are off the roster. Fight in hotel bar.*

Harper sighed. "Dante and I walked into the bar on the tail end of an argument. Bren and Remy were pulling the two of them apart, and then it was full-scale omertà." Mob code of silence. "As far as we can tell, no one filmed it, though there were a few civilians in the vicinity."

Isobel knotted her hands into fists. "We know Shay's a loudmouthed blowhard. He probably started this. Whatever *this* is." She looked over Harper's shoulder at Dante's closed door. "I need to talk to Dante. He can't suspend Petrov, not after all the work he put in. We need him on the ice."

Harper grimaced. "Our GM wants to set an example. Zero tolerance. And neither of us holds out much hope of this not getting out and back to the commissioner."

The NHL loved the fights on the ice—the big ratings

proved it—but anything that might tarnish the rep of the league outside of the officially approved violence was a big no-no.

"This is total bullshit, Harper. Vadim has to play."

Blood boiling, Isobel moved forward, their GM her goal, only to have her sister grip her elbow and steer her away toward the elevator. That petite stature hid the strength of an Amazon.

"Let's see how it looks tomorrow," Harper said. "If no footage goes up overnight on TMZ, then we'll have a better case for getting him reinstated."

Isobel had to concede that Harper might have a point. She'd always been savvy about tricky situations like these. "What did Remy say happened?"

"That it was just a spat over who was playing on the first line tomorrow."

"And you believe that?"

Harper shrugged.

"For God's sake, Harper, what's the point of having a hockey player boyfriend if he can't give you the inside track?"

"You know how they are, the bro code and all that. And to be honest, I'd rather Remy kept those relationships intact. The team has to know that everything team related goes in the man vault and that Remy won't be spilling the beans during nightly pillow talk. Of course, I have my suspicions. Knowing how Shay feels about women running the team, I'm guessing he probably made some crack about you, and Vadim came to your defense."

Isobel could feel her face flushing. Sure she wanted to know the origins of their fight, but not if it meant finding out *she* was the reason. "That's ridiculous. Vadim would never risk his place on the team over a dumb insult to me. It means everything to him to be back in play."

Harper pressed the elevator button. "Sometimes men don't always think about what's best for them." A not-unsubtle reference to Remy's uncharacteristic pounding of an opposing team's player during a game less than two months ago. All in defense of his woman when the bighearted Cajun found out this piece-of-shit player had once hit Harper.

"Are you going to tell me what's going on with you and Petrov?"

Isobel crossed her arms. Uncrossed them because that looked defensive. Then recrossed them because she should have stuck with her first instinct.

"There's nothing going on."

"How well did you know him before?"

Blessedly, the elevator arrived and opened, but alas, no occupants appeared to postpone this awkward conversation.

"Not that well." Which was true. "Dad wanted me to practice with the team before I headed to college, and he was there that summer for a few weeks."

"And?" They stepped inside, and Isobel pressed the button for the next floor, where they were both staying.

"And nothing. I went to Harvard. He signed a contract with the KHL." *After he popped my cherry and dear old Dad made sure he couldn't work in the USA.* "And now he's here. On the team. And should be playing."

They got off at their floor and walked toward their rooms. Harper's door came first.

"Isobel, a man defending you is very seductive. Believe me, I understand."

"You don't even know that's what it is."

Harper looked pitying. "Remy didn't say it, but he didn't *not* say it, either. And your defense of Vadim seems to be more than just the defense of a coach."

Isobel's heart knocked around her chest, checking in for visits with all the other organs. Harper's holier-than-thou attitude was really too much. "It's okay for you to get involved with a player, but the rest of us have to act like saints?"

Agh, shut it! She didn't want to get involved with Vadim. She didn't—hell, she had no idea what she wanted.

Wrong. Right this second, she wanted him to explain why he had put everything he—*they*—had worked for in jeopardy. It wasn't the first time, either. There was that near fight with Shay in the Empty Net two weeks ago, which Harper and Dante obviously didn't know about. Omertà, indeed.

"It's different for you, Isobel," Harper said with compassion, which made Isobel fidget. "Your position is more precarious because the coaches have such a big say in who gets to play. If you want to be taken seriously in this business, as a *coach* in this business, don't get involved with Petrov."

She shoved her key card into the door lock. "I'll see you tomorrow. Let's pray that your player's fists aren't all over the news."

With that, she closed the door behind her, leaving a fuming Isobel on the other side. Only she wasn't entirely sure whom she was mad at.

Isobel marched down the hallway of the Hyatt's sixteenth floor until she reached the door at the end. Fist up, she pulled her punch at the last moment, letting her knuckles fall with a light rap instead of a hard knock. Discretion was required. Come to think of it, why the hell was Vadim on this floor anyway? The rest of the team and staff were on eleven and twelve.

She didn't have time to dwell on that because a chorus of yapping barks greeted her knock before the door was opened by a dark-haired beauty dressed as a schoolgirl.

Or what a horny businessman might imagine as his schoolgirl fantasy. The pleated skirt of her Catholic school uniform showed way more skin than the nuns could possibly allow, and she may as well have abandoned her striped tie for all the actual tying it was doing.

Isobel flicked a glance at the door number again.

"I think I have the wrong—"

The woman squealed really, really loudly. She lunged for Isobel and with a surprisingly strong grip, dragged her into the room.

"You're Isobel Chase!"

"Uh, yep. That's me."

She slammed the door shut. "I'm a huge fan!"

"Of what?"

"Of you!" She shook her head in disbelief. *Right there with ya.*

The woman opened her mouth again and Isobel braced for more exclamation points, but whatever she was about to say was replaced by ferocious barking. A toast-colored Pomeranian stepped between them, protecting his owner. Pretty funny, really. Poms always thought they were much larger than their actual size, and this one obviously considered himself to be a Great Dane.

"Gordie Howe! Isobel's not a threat." The woman bent and picked up the dog, named after one of the most successful hockey players to ever grace the ice. Calling a cute, yappy pom after Gordie was its own sort of genius.

Before Isobel could comment, the greeter was back to talking Isobel's ear off.

"Oh my God, that goal you scored to knock out Mother Russia in the semifinals in Sochi—wow!" She leaned in, secrets in a pair of mischievous blue eyes.

"Yeah. Traitor. That's me."

Isobel pinned on a smile. After all, isn't that what you do when a crazy person likes you? Confused because Loco Chick was (a) dressed like a schoolgirl, (b) speaking in an American accent, yet (c) referring to Mother Russia, Isobel was at a loss as to how to proceed.

Oh right. "Is Vadim around?"

A voice boomed from far away—super far away, actually, because Isobel now noticed they were in a very luxurious suite. Vadim Petrov might be a vodka-fronting, underwear-hawking, hockey-playing superstar, but the Rebels org was sure as shit not paying for this upgrade.

"Mia!" Followed by a stream of Russian that sounded angry, but then streams of Russian invariably sounded angry. Except when they included hot, sexy panting against a woman's very receptive ear.

He emerged, wearing low-slung black sweatpants, a hot glower, and nothing else. As if she wasn't already pissed enough at him.

He held a phone away from his ear. "Why are you still here, Mia? Alexei is expecting you down in the lobby." On seeing Isobel, his frown deepened. "Ah, I am in trouble."

"Damn straight, Russian."

He said something to the young woman in his native tongue.

She rolled her eyes. "English, bro. You know I don't understand that BS."

Bro? He'd never mentioned a sister, and there was nothing in his files, but Isobel saw the resemblance now. Aristocratic cheekbones, startling blue eyes, and a runway model–tall frame. God help the men of New York.

His sister—Mia—divided a look between them, revealing one more way they were alike: a stubborn set to her chin. "I'd like to stay and talk to Isobel."

"It's eleven o'clock at night, and you have school tomorrow. Now say good-bye." With another unintelligible mutter into his phone, he hung up.

"I'm Mia, by the way," his sister, who Isobel was now realizing was an actual schoolgirl, said to Isobel. "Mia Wa—" With a nervous lip bite, she shot a glance at Vadim. On seeing his mouth hitch in a half smile and the decline of his head in a regal nod, she turned back to Isobel, her chin raised in—pride? "Mia Wallace. It's so great to meet you. Honestly."

Isobel's body prickled with awareness. That name— why did she know it?

"Wait. Mia Wallace? *Hockey phenom* Mia Wallace?"

A blush suffused her features, making her appear younger, and she smiled shyly. "I play." Her bashful glance slid to her brother. "Nowhere near as good as Vadim, of course."

Everyone in hockey had heard of Mia Wallace, touted as the next big thing. She was the full package, already being scouted by NCAA (though that was technically against the rules because she was too young at sixteen), the women's league, and companies for big sponsorships. She also had a backstory the media loved: a cancer diagnosis from which she'd rebounded just over a year ago. This girl was one tough cookie.

Mia squeezed Isobel's arm. "We are *so* excited Vadim's going to be playing again. He said he has you to thank."

"He did, did he?"

"Oh yeah. He's your biggest fan. After me."

Vadim's scowl pronounced him to be most definitely *not* Isobel's biggest fan. "Mia, Alexei is waiting."

"'Kay, I'll see you at the game tomorrow."

Oh dear. That sounded like she didn't know about his suspension. Maybe Isobel could soften the blow a little. "If you're going to the game, you could hang in the visitors' box with us. If you'd like."

The girl looked like every wish she'd ever had was coming true tonight. "Really? Vadim, can I?"

"If Isobel has invited you, of course you can. But only if you leave now and get some sleep. Your mother—" He snatched back the words. "Time to go, Mia."

Placing the dog down, the girl rolled her eyes and threw her arms around Vadim's neck, murmuring something that melted the ice in his eyes. Then Mia gave Isobel the same treatment. Not knowing what to do with this hug from a stranger, Isobel patted the girl on the shoulder, all while Vadim stared at the two of them intently.

"Say bye-bye, Gordie Howe!" Mia picked up the dog.

"Good-bye and good riddance, little-dog-with-big-shits," Vadim deadpanned.

Mia laughed her head off. "I'll text you tomorrow, bro! See ya, Isobel!" And then she was gone, with the puppy yapping the exit music.

Isobel couldn't help her smile. "So that's where all the Petrov personality ended up."

Pride ruled his expression. "She is . . . spirited."

"She adores you, and the feeling's obviously mutual."

Vadim threaded his arms over his chest. "This is relatively new for us. We only connected a short time ago."

There was a story here. "I've heard of her, but I didn't know she was related to you."

"Neither did I," he said bitterly. "My mother chose not to notify my father that he had another child. She moved to New York after she left us and only informed me of Mia's existence after he died eighteen months ago."

Wow, that sucked—and it clearly still stung Vadim. Pain radiated off him in waves. But she knew him well enough to recognize her pity would go unappreciated, so she skirted the edges of the problem. "I'm surprised her connection to you hasn't gotten out."

"It is for her protection. With her talent and youth, she is under a lot of pressure. If the media knows of her relationship to me, it may affect her performance. I think that you, of all people, understand this."

She did. Because she was the daughter of an NHL legend, the media had been relentless about her future from the moment she hit puberty and started skating rings around grown men. To be honest, the real pressure had come from her father, and she had to admit there were times when she would have gladly gone incognito. A few weeks without the Chase name would have done wonders for her sanity as a teenager.

"Should I be concerned why my coach is visiting me in my hotel room late at night?"

"You know why I'm here, Vadim. What the hell were you thinking? A fight? In public? With Shay?"

Through her outburst, he stood stock-still in
those erotically thin sweats that shaped everything
and somehow drew more attention to his assets
than if he'd been naked. The trim waist, narrow
hips, muscular thighs. Yeah, yeah, she'd deliberately skipped over that all-important area, because
if she gave it a moment's thought, she was going to
get trapped in his dick-sand. But thinking about *not*
going there was the one thing guaranteed to turn her
eyes into magnets. Perhaps a quick glance to prove
her mettle . . .

No fair! The drape of the cotton was like a perfect
kiss to that intriguing bulge. Was that a cock at rest or
was something more interesting going on there?

She refocused. *This is not why you are here. You are here
because all the work you put in was for nothing.*

While the energy between them zip-zap-zinged,
Vadim watched her carefully. He seemed to be holding himself at bay, that jaguar on his shoulder a fit-
ting proxy, his fists on his hips in the least casual
arms akimbo she'd ever seen. Every muscle in his body
strained, and not for the first time, Isobel wondered
what it would be like to have this fully mature beast—
not the callow youth of before—take her hard.

"You've been cut from tomorrow's game. Maybe
more games."

"It was worth it."

He had *not* just said that. She threw up her hands,
glad to have another outlet for the inappropriate lust
rippling through every nerve ending.

"You'd better tell me what started this, because I swear to God, Vadim—"

"What? You'll tickle it out of me?"

She blinked. What a weird, funny, distinctly un-Vadim thing to say.

"Don't get cute with me!"

He sighed, back to his default setting of all drama. "Isobel, you should leave now. We both know that we do not do well together in small spaces."

She cast a theatrical look around the room. "Looks like you've got a big enough space right now. Big enough for your giant ego and your dumb muscles and your huge dick!" *Don't talk about his dick. His big, beautiful . . .* "You'd better not be expecting the team to pay for this."

He moved toward her, bringing with him that giant ego and dumb muscles and huge, ahem—she stepped back until her butt met the door.

He placed a hand on the frame beside her cheek. "It would be best if you leave."

"Not until I get an explanation. I can't go to Coach and Moretti to get you reinstated without all the facts."

"I was involved in a fight. I am out of the game. Those are the facts."

"Just like that? No way. We've worked damn hard to get you fit for play, and I sure as hell am not going to accept this. Start at the beginning."

"The beginning, Bella?" Ruefulness and amusement crossbred on his face. "As is so often the case, it began with a girl. The most fearless girl I have ever met. Skates like the wind, shoots like a sniper, swears like a Russian sailor."

"Sounds like fucking trouble."

And that sounded like fucking flirting. *Stop flirting with your player.*

Before he could make some flirty comment back— though flirting wasn't really in Vadim's wheelhouse— she tried to refocus on why she was here. Not because of his chest, or those tattoos, or that freshly show-ered man scent now tearing down every brick in her walls.

She thought of Harper's warning. *If you want to be taken seriously in this business, as a* coach *in this business, don't get involved with Petrov.*

Discuss "coach" things. "What did Shay say to set you off?"

"What makes you think he said anything? Perhaps I started it."

"I don't believe that."

He looked thoughtful. "I told him he would get his place back on the line if he worked hard."

She sighed, relieved.

"After he accused me of sleeping my way onto the roster."

She pushed back against his oh-my-God-those-pecs-are-unreal chest, needing space to haul air into her lungs. "He accused you of *what*?"

"It means nothing. If my personal coach were a man, Shay would think of some other insult. Because you are a woman, this is the best the fool can come up with."

"So you were defending my honor?"

"Actually, Isobel, I was defending my own." His mouth lifted in a self-deprecating curve, and it broke something open inside of her. Something she hadn't realized was better busted than cobbled together. "But the defense of yours was a natural by-product."

Oh, this guy. She knew what he was doing. Trying to put her off so she wouldn't feel all gooey that he'd come to her defense. It wasn't working. Her internal organs were a liquefied mess.

As for her vagina? She may as well just get it stamped Property of Vadim Petrov.

"What about the first fight, Vadim? At the Empty Net a few weeks ago? Were you defending your honor then?"

A storm swept across his face. "What do you know of this?"

"Just that you had to be restrained from punching him out. What the hell is going on with you two?"

"As I said, he is a man with idiotic opinions."

Agreed. "I don't like you getting into fights, not when we're so close." She meant close to putting him back to where he belonged: on the ice before a crowd of twenty thousand screaming fans. But the words hung between them, as heavy as the sexual tension she was drowning in.

Close enough to touch, to kiss, to feel.

Everything.

And that's what she wanted. Her sister's caution tried to sound its harsh siren again, but it was overridden by something else Harper had said:

A man defending you is very seductive.

It was, and it wasn't something Isobel was used to. Not needing anyone was how she'd been raised. Isobel had spent her life following her father's blueprint.

Your gender is meaningless. You're as strong as any man on the ice. You don't need to rely on anyone for a damn thing, especially boys. They'll only get in your way.

Being groomed for independence was all well and good, but sometimes riding this train solo could be so, so lonely. The solace of Vadim standing up for her, of being there for her even though she hadn't asked for it, crashed through her.

The physical evidence of his chivalry was darkening with every passing moment. She reached out to touch the bruise on his jaw. "Gotta take care of this pretty face, Russian."

"I would rather carry this badge." He leaned into her hand, accepting her comfort. His eyes closed briefly on a gentle sigh, then reopened so fast she wondered if she'd imagined the moment. "This is dangerous, Isobel. If someone saw you come in here, it would not be good."

"I'm just a coach going down on my player like a ton of bricks."

"Going down? My English is not perfect, but I believe the phrase is 'coming down.'" His mouth dropped to her lips, and his eyelids fell to half-mast.

Meanwhile, something else was rising to full mast. "Or maybe you mean what you said?"

She tried that on for size in her head. *I'm just a coach going down on my player.* It sounded so wrong, just right, and everything in between.

He was practically on top of her now, his erection pressed against her belly. Yet his words still tried to contradict the biological imperative that had both their bodies in its grip.

"Bella, if you don't leave now—"

She kissed him before he could finish that ridiculous sentence.

THIRTEEN

Isobel Chase was kissing him.

He refused to kiss her back.

Rude, perhaps, but really he was thinking of her honor. In her position, she was particularly susceptible to accusations—witness Shay running off his mouth—and Vadim didn't want to risk that. All he'd ever wanted was to protect her.

So he would not kiss her.

Tell that to his cock, which refused to play along.

Move to plan B. As long as he did not part his lips or grab her hips or give her any encouragement whatso—*damn.*

Somehow, during his oh-so-logical thought process on how to defend this woman's honor, he had pinned her against the door. His body covered hers, his hands cupped her perfect heart-shaped ass, and his mouth devoured her like she was his last meal.

Yes, incredibly honorable.

There was always plan C. Just a few seconds. He

would enjoy the heat of her mouth and the feel of her curves, then send her on her way. This he could handle. As long as she did not part her legs—*fuck*.

Her thighs fell open and the welcome of her still-covered pussy engulfed his still-covered erection. Her leg hitched up to give him better access, and his hips shoved forward of their own accord. She was moaning now, soft, desperate sounds into his mouth. Their tongues tangled, the taste of her all he had missed and everything he could not have.

Not going to last, not going to last.

He jerked away and put a few necessary feet between them. This huge suite was suddenly too small.

"What's wrong?" she panted, her eyes maddened with desire.

"This can't happen, Isobel." He waved between them. "I won't have you be the subject of gossip."

She was breathing hard, the rise and fall of her breasts mesmerizing him. All it would take was the hook of his little finger on the ring of her tracksuit zipper. He could pull it down slowly, reveal all that milky flesh. Taste her once more . . .

"I'm already the subject of gossip, Vadim. I may as well be hung for a sheep as a lamb."

"I don't understand that."

"It means if I'm going to do the time, I may as well do the crime. Unless you don't want this."

He looked down at his cock, jutting true north, screaming at him to take what was his.

"I think there is little doubt I want this."

"That's just biology, Vadim. Cocks aren't really known for their great decision making."

"Mine is more discriminating than most." He moved closer to her, but kept a safe distance. "Never doubt that I want you, Isobel. But I also know you're trying to build your career as a coach and that it wouldn't look good if it emerged that something happened between us."

If she knew that they were already the subject of gossip because of her own indiscreet chatter, she would be furious. He would have to be strong enough for both of them.

He stepped away, his hard-on pulsing in protest. *Quit your whine! You will fuck my fist later.*

"This is for your own protection, Isobel."

She nodded. "Okay. I suppose I should thank you for being the sensible one here, seeing as how my hormones are incapable of seeing reason."

She should, but he suspected she would not. He wasn't buying this for a second.

"I understand that you're trying to protect me, but the way I see it, you're really trying to protect yourself. I get it. After our first and only time together, your fear is understandable."

"My fear?"

Turning her back on him, she placed a hand on the doorknob. "That you can't make me come."

The door opened.

The door shut.

That last action might have had something to do with him closing the gap and slamming the door so hard the frame shook.

"Do you really think I'll fall for this?"

She didn't turn, which was good, because if he looked into those emerald-fired eyes, he would be lost. His chest settled against her back. Her ass, while not touching him, was mere millimeters away from his erection.

"Fall for what?"

"This challenge to make up for what happened between us before." His chin dipped, his lips glanced across her ear, drawing a shiver from her. "Do you think calling me chicken is the way into my bed?"

It is. It so fucking is.

"Not at all." Her body shifted, testing the bounds of the space between them. The lightest brush against his cock triggered his groan. "I mean, I can tell your discriminating cock is raring to go, and I've no doubt you can perform on your end, but you have to admit a tiny bit of doubt, Vadim."

"Any doubts I had were wiped away by your moans when you ground your body on my dick last week."

On a lusty sigh, she fell back against his chest, aligning her curves with every welcoming slot on his body. *Prekrasno.* Perfect. Her ass against his groin fit like the final puzzle piece.

"I didn't even make it home," she murmured. "I had to pull over to the side of the road and finish all by myself."

Chyort voz'mi! He gripped her arm and turned her, expecting humor and challenge. He got that, and so much more. Excitement and desire, but also vulnerability.

How could her face express so much when his mouth could express nothing at all?

"Do you doubt my ability to satisfy you, woman?"

She had the nerve to hesitate. "I'm pretty turned on right now, but I was last time as well. Eight years ago. Then"—she made a thumbs-down gesture—"*nyet*. Don't worry, V. Some people aren't sexually compatible. On the surface it looks like all the boxes are checked, but when the cock is locked, the key doesn't turn."

His heart thundered in his chest. His cock demanded vindication. He could not believe he was falling for her bait, yet every goading word was working to draw him in. "The key will turn, Isobel."

"Yes, well, I'm sure it will." She gave his bicep a squeeze, then patted it—all condescension. "Just not for us."

He curled a hand around her neck and pressed his lips to hers. No kiss yet, because she didn't deserve it.

"You little brat. I will show you how the key turns. The key will turn all night!" Furious at what she had driven him to, he stepped back and jerked his hand away from his body.

"Get in the bedroom. Now."

Isobel could not believe Vadim had fallen for that.

Sure, she knew that intellectually he was completely

aware of her game to get him on board. Really, she was annoyed that he was using the "protecting her honor" excuse to unilaterally decide this, but knowing Vadim the way she did, arguing this point would only entrench him.

Honor was big with Russians, and with Vadim in particular.

She wanted him and she would have him. Just for tonight, though. After all, a man like Vadim Petrov wasn't for keeps.

She sat on the bed, yanking off her Joan of Arctic boots while Vadim paced. Back and forth, forth and back, looking up every few seconds to check her progress. Socks off. Another look. Hoodie was history. Another look. Ten seconds between glances, which meant he was—oh, God—counting off in his head.

She was down to leggings and a tank top.

"Are you going to wear a rut in the carpet, Russian, or a rut in me?"

He stopped, and stabbing his fingers through his hair, spoke with immense effort. "Remove all your clothes immediately."

"*You* remove them."

She swore his erection poked higher in his sweatpants.

"Isobel," he warned.

"What's wrong, Vadim? Are you afraid you might get overexcited if you peel off my top and get a bra strap sighting? If your fingers graze my skin, will we start to see little Vadim"—she pointed at not-so-little Vadim, now straining to punch through the thin fabric—"weeping his cockhead off? Worried you'll blow before you can get me there?"

"Yes."

Oh.

She'd been teasing him—mercilessly, she now realized—and he was actually concerned. *Nice going, dummy.*

He continued. "I am currently running my stats from every season starting five years ago."

"What are you up to?"

"Third year in the NHL. My best season to date."

With a teasing lick of her lips, she accessed her memory banks. "Thirty-eight goals, 64 assists, 19.5 shooting percentage, 8 game-winning beauties."

He halted the pacing and faced her with hands on hips, his expression one of lust battling disbelief.

"Did I just turn you on even more, Russian?"

"Yes!"

She winked. *Evil, thy name is Isobel Chase.*

Apparently this was the last straw. "Why are you torturing me? Do you not realize that if I touch you too soon, I cannot be responsible? It will be fast, brutal, lacking in finesse. This time, I promise to make it right for you."

His admission of vulnerability floored her. To have this power over someone as self-contained as Vadim was both heady and humbling. As for the "fast and brutal" comment? Slippery warmth gushed between her thighs.

No more games. She gripped the hem of her tank and ripped it off over her head, her nipples tightening against her bra at the blue-fire flare of appreciation in his eyes. Then she stood, turned, and peeled off her leggings.

She might have paused a second just as they cleared her ass. Evil was a good look on her, and let's face it, she had a pretty great ass. His groan filled the room like a prayer.

Still with her back to him, she finished the strip, and was now left in a black satin bra with red bows and a matching high-cut bikini from Addison Williams's *Beautiful* collection—Isobel loved the complete, but still sexy, coverage of the pieces designed for full-figured women.

By the sounds she was hearing behind her, she guessed Vadim loved it, too.

Kneeling one leg on the bed, she looked over his shoulder to find him—oh yeah—stroking his erection through his sweatpants. The man was a walking god, all sculpted muscle, his body inked to highlight every ridge and plane to perfection. The spot between her thighs got warmer. Wetter.

"You wear this when you are coaching and tempting me with your black pants?"

She had tempted him in her unsexy sweats? "Sometimes. I like to feel sexy."

"They are—you are—" He placed a hand on her hip, and she sensed both reverence and restraint, but also a heat that burned through everything. "I will make it good for you, I promise."

He sounded so sincere—too sincere—and something tugged in her chest. A curl of regret.

She opened her mouth to respond, but got distracted when he hooked his fingers in the side of her panties and teased them off in a slow, torturous descent. And if it was this bad for her, it had to be killing him. In this position, she felt more exposed than if she had been facing him.

Leaving her panties at her knees, he traced a hand along the ladder of her spine, then circled her hip to clamp that same hand over the juncture of her thighs. *Yes.* Moving her ponytail aside, he nuzzled her neck and applied whisper-soft kisses to her heated skin. Just like in her car, her hips scouted ahead for pleasure, rocking and rolling. Seeking the hardness of his cock behind her, the grind of his fingers between her legs.

One of those magic digits parted her in a delicious swipe. That stroke shot erotic lightning to every extremity. "You are so wet, Bella."

She leaned into his touch, needing more, demanding more, and this girl got her wish when he rubbed harder. Impossibly good. She moaned, encouraging him to take control.

Gripping her hip, he turned her over and pushed her back on the bed. Her panties didn't last, and Vadim lay down beside her, still wearing sweatpants, his erection poking against her thigh. She reached for it, and he swatted her away.

"Not yet, Bella. Let me love you properly first."

Love? Surely, just a translation hiccup. "Oh—okay."

His fingers returned to their holy work. "I want to see your eyes."

In case she faked it, maybe? Now *she* was starting to doubt. What if she'd placed too much pressure on him, which placed too much pressure on her, and she felt a need to rush them to a conclusion just so they could move past this?

"I know what you're thinking, Bella." Those crystalline blue eyes held hers captive, his expression grave.

"I doubt it."

"You're thinking that there is a lot of pressure here." He applied a different sort of pressure with one finger, then two inside her. She accommodated the stretch by arching into the exquisite pleasure.

"There—there is. And I'm worried I've set us up to fail."

His mouth descended onto hers, kissing away the worries, the doubts, the past. There was a very excellent chance she was going to come with Vadim Petrov for the first time.

"Tell me what feels good, sexy girl."

"What you're doing is fine."

"Fine?"

"Good. So good." It was, but maybe if he . . .

"Be honest, Bella. Do you need my mouth on your breasts, my tongue in your pussy? Do you need it slow or fast? Hard or soft?"

She inhaled a couple of sharp breaths. His list of all the awesome gifts he could deliver opened her up. "My clit. Go slow. Build to it. Not too fast." The words gasped from her in staccato bursts, her honesty feeling almost as good as his fingers now moving to accommodate her request.

"Like this?"

"More like"—she placed his fingers on either side of that sensitive bundle of nerves and guided him to a steady stroke—"this. Avoid my clit until I'm all fired up."

He smiled, the most beautiful thing she'd ever seen. "Let us get you all fired up, Bella."

Having this alpha warrior following her instructions was surreal. And the sensations he was producing down below were proof that honesty was the best policy. The sexiest policy.

Throughout he watched her with an intensity that should have terrified her, like a prehistoric caveman seeing a woman for the first time. But this was Vadim, the most intense man she'd ever met. Even as a boy he'd rocked her with his fierceness, and now it was amplified in the man.

"How you have changed, Bella."

"I—I have?"

"Before you were beautiful. Now you are stunning."

Her hips rolled against his hand, the heat in her belly intensifying and then banking as he moved away from where she needed him most. Each retreat only built the next wave of sensation higher.

No orgasm yet, but this was undoubtedly the best sex she'd ever had. He was listening, and nothing was sexier than a guy who paid attention.

Now, she thought, and before she could say it, *now* was happening. A soft yet sizzling touch, and all that pressure overflowed. She came hard and long, with Vadim's fierce gaze proudly assessing her.

He should be proud. The boy had done good.

"That—" She tried to catch her breath. "Was better."

"It seems I can be taught more than how to improve my skating motion."

Intense Vadim was a total stud. Funny Vadim was a threat to her heart.

She swallowed, disliking the path of her thoughts. *Lust. Not a good foundation.* "So, what are you waiting for? Time to get naked."

"I am giving you time to recover," he said, taking his forefinger, still wet with her, and sucking it into his mouth. He moaned, deep and low, as if he'd never tasted anything more satisfying. "I think I just blew your mind."

Cocky Vadim? Yeah, he was pretty hot, too.

She gripped his erection through the fabric. Hard as those pecs, it had to be ready to blow. "You've been very patient."

He uncurled her fingers. "I will have to be patient for longer. There is more for this player to learn."

"Vadim, you don't need to do that . . ."

"Ah, but that is exactly what I need. Again, Bella."

"Again?"

"Yes," he said as his mouth sought hers and destroyed her brain with an all-in kiss. "Again."

And then he got started on *again* with that decadent Russian mouth trailing kisses down her stomach and beyond.

It was hard being Vadim Petrov's coach, but someone had to do it.

FOURTEEN

Vadim slipped out of bed, careful not to disturb Isobel. The clock on the nightstand said 2:15 a.m. Having lain awake for the past hour, he wanted to ensure that she was sleeping soundly before he took care of business.

Specifically, the business of his painful erection.

A night of firsts. The first time he had made Isobel come and the first time he had slept with a woman and not come himself. There was a cruel symmetry to this.

Not that the night's events had lacked for opportunity. But from the moment he'd slid her panties off her body, from the moment his fingertips had touched her soaking pussy, he had vowed to make the night about her. After the first time, there were three more times, each more intense than the last. He had much to make up for. His pleasure could wait.

With each new orgasm, she slipped further into a semiconscious dream state, her plaintive cries of, "Let me touch you, Vadim," fading until she finally fell asleep.

His cock had not followed suit.

He could wake her, but he'd rather take his punishment. The nearest of the two bathrooms in the suite was twenty feet away, but he passed it and headed to the one farther. Let his Girl with the Blazing Skates get her rest. She had earned it.

He would not be playing tonight and he understood that trade-offs needed to be made every day. Protecting Isobel from Shay's filth was more important than getting ice time. There would be other chances to play, just as there would be other chances to sink inside her.

A groan spilled from his mouth at the thought. Isobel's thighs falling open to finally embrace him, that shining invitation to line up his cock and push in, in, and home.

Facing the bathroom mirror, he wrapped his hand around this rampant beast that needed to be tamed. The first touch produced an instant leak at the broad head. This wouldn't take long, just a few strokes to get him there.

Thinking of Isobel, he might need only one.

"Vadim?" he heard outside the door. "Are you okay?"

Chyort voz'mi! He dropped his hand. "Da—yes. Give me a moment."

But he had left the door ajar, and she walked in, gloriously naked, her eyes wild. "What's going on, Vadim?"

Well . . . "I didn't want to wake you."

Her gaze fell to his cock, which turned harder at the sight of its mistress. It should have been impossible, given how close he was to blowing his stack, but apparently this was his life now.

"You were going to go solo with this?" Amusement tinged her voice. It was no laughing matter!

Irked at her teasing, he foisted the blame back on her. "I had given you all the pleasure you could handle tonight, *kroshka*."

She cocked an eyebrow. "I think we've determined that I can take anything you dole out, *baby*."

Perhaps, but he would not inflict his insatiable demands on her. "You fell asleep in my arms, Bella. It seemed rude to just take you while you were sleeping."

She stared at him in amazement, then stepped in and placed a hand on his chest.

"You spent hours giving me orgasm after orgasm after—"

"Orgasm?" he offered.

She pressed her body to his, and his cock jutted into her belly, a streak of liquid pleasure marking her warm skin. He inhaled sharply, desperately grasping at the tethers of his slipping control.

"So now you're here jerking off alone instead of taking what belongs to you?"

His nostrils flared, every masculine sense heightened. *Moya*. Mine. Yes, she belonged to him. Then. Now. "I was taking the edge off. I planned to fuck you properly when you had rested."

She brushed his lips with her own, then licked and

bit his lower lip. He moaned against her mouth and ground his cock into her stomach.

"Tonight you can have me anytime you want me, Vadim. Please don't jerk yourself off unless you invite me to watch."

An animalistic groan tore from his throat, and in a flash, he hitched her so she sat on the bathroom counter. His hands roved her body, not knowing where to start with this feast.

"What can I do, Vadim? Touch you? Suck you? Tell me what you need."

"You. I need you. I need . . . inside." He could barely form words. "Now."

She spread her thighs, her glistening pussy shining like a target, and he could no longer wait. He plunged into her and filled her to the hilt. She screamed her pleasure, clamping down with those strong, athletic muscles. Pure and perfect torture.

He withdrew, dipping his gaze to where their bodies had joined, and realized his error. No condom.

Frustration marred the ecstasy on her face. "Get one on. Now!"

Yes, my sweet. Fumbling with his toiletry bag, he found the packet and ripped it open. His cock was coated with her—she was wet, so wet—and the lubricant of her body ensured a quick roll-on of the rubber. He placed his hands under her ass and dragged her forward.

"Hold on, Bella. Do not let go."

But before he plunged deep again, he found her mouth with his and kissed her with all he had. She dug her nails into his ass and urged him forward. "Fill me up, Russian."

"*Koldunya!*" Witch.

He drove deep, a thick, hard thrust that would have smashed her through the vanity's mirror if he had not been holding her tightly. His rhythm was unsteady, ragged, every stroke an extension of the jumbled thoughts in his brain.

Harder. Faster. Make it better than before. Better for her.

Realizing that he needed to think of her pleasure, he slowed.

She moaned against his mouth. "Don't stop. Take what you need, baby. Make it fast. Brutal. Make it everything."

If only she knew what she asked. If he were to do that, he would consume her.

But his cock had heard her words and didn't care about the destruction it wanted to wreak. All restraint broke its bounds.

His hips flexed, pounding into her again and again. Taking what belonged to him. What had always belonged to him, though he had been too young to understand.

I will not last. I cannot last.

She heard his thoughts. Perhaps he had spoken them. Still holding on to his shoulder, she dipped the fingers of her free hand between their bodies and touched herself, freeing a lusty moan. He knew her body now. Knew she had to be on fire because that was her torch song.

"Yes, Vad, yes!" He felt the flood of her pleasure, a heat infusion even through the condom, and though he was ready, he stilled. Needing to feel her hold him caged through her orgasm.

Feel what it is like to have your woman come on your cock, you dumb fucking kid.

This time he had given pleasure that was her right. Two more thrusts and he let go, the peak reached, coming for what seemed like minutes. Hours. Forever.

Spent, he lay his forehead against hers, panting his way back to even. Their breaths found a steady tempo, a strange peace after an encounter that had felt like a battle.

Still buried in her, he kissed her softly. "That is why I left your arms."

"Because I don't deserve sex this good?"

He smiled at her take on it. "I knew I could not be gentle. It would be an invasion. A conquest."

"Good thing I have this need to be conquered." She stroked a line along his jaw. "You're the one who said we should be honest."

"Men will say anything to get what they want."

"So will women." She pressed her lips to his. "You know, I thought you woke me up. I could've sworn I heard you saying, '*Bella, I am here. Wake up.*' I must have dreamed it. I was so confused that you weren't there in bed with me."

"You have a common condition called orgasm brain."

"Let me guess. The cure is more orgasms?"

"How did you know?" Chuckling, he slipped from her and disposed of the condom. Then he scooped her up into his arms.

"Vadim! I'm too heavy. And you have to watch your knee."

"Yes, Coach." Ignoring her protests, he carried her back to bed. She was as light as air, and he felt invincible with her in the cradle of his body.

A satiated and showered Isobel found Dante in the hotel restaurant, fully suited up, perfectly put together, slicing into his eggs Benedict with a strange formality. Evidently the man was incapable of leaving his room without looking like David Gandy's runway understudy.

He'd had a short but successful career in the NHL until a bum knee—the same injury as Vadim's—prompted his retirement. Contrary to the image he presented now, he was known then as an enforcer at a time when there had been more violence in the league. She'd seen videos—this guy knew how to fight. Hockey brought out the darker, baser instincts of a person's personality.

She sat opposite him. His heavy sigh was a smidge over the top.

"If you wanted to eat alone, you should have ordered room service."

"The eggs are always better in the restaurant." He

placed his knife and fork down. "You're late to the begging party. I've already had St. James and DuPre knocking down my door this morning, not to mention the whole defensive line stopping by to give their opinion before I had my coffee."

"Then you won't mind one more. Not a peep on social media, so we're in the clear. You need to reinstate Vadim for tonight's game."

"The decision has already been made. We have a zero-tolerance policy for violence"—he acknowledged her brow lift with one of his own—"*off* the ice. It would be one thing if no one had witnessed it, but there were other players there. We can't be seen to favor one team member over another."

"If it hasn't made it online by now, then it won't at all. Reinstate them both. Put it down to bad judgment, crappy alcohol, cabin fever. This game is important, Dante. We have to win twelve of the next fifteen to be in with a chance of qualifying for the play-offs. Petrov needs to be on the ice tonight."

She'd left him in the early hours, sleeping off a night of use and abuse by hers truly. Hopefully he'd have enough energy left to play if Dante made the right call. And on the subject of use and abuse, she shifted in her seat, her body sensuously sore after the night's exertions. The Czar of Pleasure had *finally* lived up to his royal title.

"You know what I said when I came on board, Isobel. I'm not taking orders from the owners."

"I'm not asking as an owner, Dante. I'm asking as

a coach, a team player, and a Rebels fan. We've all got
something to prove, but let's not allow what I need to
prove to be at cross-purposes with what you need to
prove. The team is all that matters."

He smoldered in her general direction for several
seconds. Fortunately her time with Vadim had built up
in her a semidecent immunity to hot masculine glaring.

Finally, he muttered, "I'll take it under advisement."

"Dante—"

He held up a hand. "My eggs are getting cold, Isobel, and whining only makes them inedible."

Sensing victory, she hid her smile as she stood
before she and her whining left the restaurant, feeling
pretty damn optimistic.

FIFTEEN

Two months.

Two months since Vadim had skated onto the ice as part of a starting lineup. Tonight against the Spartans should not have been that night, but Coach Calhoun had approached him during morning skate and given him the news.

His temporary suspension was lifted.

Vadim sensed the hand of Isobel here. He had sent her a text of thanks. She had responded with: *Thank me with goals, Russian.*

There was no sign of her before the game. Usually she would show up in the locker room, or at the very least, rinkside, but no. Perhaps she was worried he'd be unable to hide what had happened last night.

And this morning.

And this morning, again.

Warmth flushed his veins, and it was not because the crowd had cheered his name. It was the memory of Bella's heavy-lidded gaze as she arched into his hand, her body seeking his magic fingers, her inner walls tightening around his cock.

Pride at the pleasure he had brought her puffed him up, fueled by the knowledge she had gone to bat for him to plead his case. Having Isobel in his corner invigorated him. Made him feel anything was possible. He hoped she didn't think there was an ulterior motive to his seduction of her. Although, looking back, he would say Isobel had seduced him.

Completely.

Once the game started, all thoughts of Isobel fled his brain. In the months since he had last played competitively, the pace appeared to have increased. More likely, it was Vadim's need to adjust. Blink and the game moved on. Hesitate and your mark left you behind.

By the end of the first period, he was sweating buckets and had barely touched the puck.

"Vad, you dill-hole, hit the damn puck!"

Vadim's sister, Mia, pounded the glass of the visitors' box at the Spartans' arena and let out a groan. For the last ten minutes of the first period, she had spent most of her time on her feet and all her speech haranguing her brother.

Harper and Isobel shared a smile.

"I think you're scaring Gordie Howe," Isobel said. She wasn't, because the pom, currently sitting in Harper's lap, looked right at home. Dogs were normally verboten in hockey arenas, but the pup was certified as a therapy dog because of Mia's prior illness.

Mia turned around and took the dog from Harper's arms. "Come on, Gordie Howe, time to see how your uncle is playing." She caught the eyes of the adults, including an amused Dante. "I'm sorry. I just get so excited when I see him play, and with him spending so much time on the bench last season, I freak out. He really should be playing better than this, shouldn't he?"

Yes, he should. Vadim looked slow out there, a step behind everyone else. Isobel could have watched from the sidelines but she didn't want him to feel awkward. Or perhaps she was more worried about how weird *she* would feel. How obvious her desire would play on her face. She may as well have *well-fucked* tattooed on her forehead and a *Vadim Petrov wuz 'ere* sign pinned over her jeans zipper.

You're his coach, Chase. Time to defend her player and her methods to the Rebels' management.

"He's a little rusty. Practice is all well and good, but nothing substitutes for actual game play. He just needs to get his ice legs under him."

Mia looked unconvinced, especially as Vadim was immediately dispossessed of the puck for the third time in the last five minutes. The end of the period couldn't come soon enough.

Had Isobel let her attraction for Vadim influence her decision to sign off on him? So far, he wasn't displaying the sharp skills and canny moves she'd come to expect. He looked awkward playing on the left wing, which was supposed to be his natural fit. She wouldn't be surprised if Coach Calhoun pulled him for good.

With the end of the period, Mia stood. "Time to go pee-pee!"

Dante raised an eyebrow at Isobel.

"She means the dog." And then to Mia, "Right?"

"Yeah, I do. He has a bladder the size of a pea."

Her phone rang, and her face crumpled. "Oh, I have to take this. Could you—do you mind—" She dropped Gordie Howe in Dante's lap, then left in a gust of wind.

Dante stared at the dog, then shifted so he was more settled in his lap. The pom gazed adoringly at all that Italian pretty and unmistakably preened.

"Vadim will improve," Isobel said defensively before Dante could light into her.

Their GM gave a rare smile. "I know. I just think we should have second- or third-lined him for this game. At least we're still scoreless."

"Yeah, Burnett's playing a barn burner," Harper said. "Some great blocks in that last five. Thank God he stayed."

"He wanted to leave?" Dante asked with surprising sharpness.

Harper nodded. "The possibility of a trade was floated a couple of weeks before the deadline, but I spoke to Cade and it seemed like it was coming from his agent more than him. He's so young that I think he's susceptible to suggestion."

Cade Burnett was only twenty-three and had been

with the Rebels for two years. Isobel saw that in hockey a lot—players looking for fast results, disappointed that it wasn't all happening immediately.

Dante was off in some weird headspace, his gaze focused on the empty ice, his hand rubbing through Gordie Howe's shiny coat.

"Don't worry, Dante," Isobel said. "Petrov will start playing better." He had to.

"From your lips to the hockey gods' ears."

Someone up there must have been listening, because when the second period started, so did the miraculous return of Vadim Petrov to pro hockey glory. The turning point looked inauspicious: the Russian in a one-on-one situation with a defenseman, which usually meant the goalie had the advantage. Really a one-on-two. Typically the defenseman's presence allowed the goaltender time to get to the top of the crease, and for most forwards, the opportunity was already dead because there was no opening. All you could see was the goalie crowding the net.

What did Vadim do? He changed the angle with a toe drag. Holding the puck at a distance outside his body, he then pulled it to his feet before taking the shot. Surprised by the release point, the goaltender had no time to react to the new angle and the Spartans' D-man had no chance to deflect.

First blood drawn by the Rebels, courtesy of the mighty Vadim Petrov.

Vadim sat heavily on the locker room bench, bent over while he unlaced his skates and caught his breath. His entire body was shaking, every cell burning with the aftereffects of a hard game. Adrenaline was still streaking through him. The Rebels had won, and nothing felt better.

Except perhaps being buried inside Isobel Chase.

"Good game, young Padawan."

He looked up to find the green-eyed witch herself standing over him. She wore a black turtleneck sweater that covered so much skin it should not have been sexy, yet it hugged her breasts in a way that was a capital crime. As for her dark-rinse jeans making love to every curve? Worth at least fifteen to life.

"*Spasibo*. Though the second goal was down to Bren. I was just there at the right time."

Bren shouted over to him. "As much as I love taking undue credit, Petrov, NHL rules dictate that whoever touches the puck last is assigned the goal. That first one you buried was a thing of fuckin' beauty, however. And it was all yours."

Vadim fought his smile. He was pleased, and especially pleased to get the kudos from a man he respected. Their captain was a straight shooter and didn't dole out compliments to just anyone.

He raised his eyes to Isobel. "This is down to you, Coach."

Two spots of color flagged her cheeks and her smile looked wobbly around the edges. "I'm glad if anything I did helped."

He held her gaze. *Oh, you helped, all right. You helped so well that I would really love if you helped again.*

She must have read his thoughts because she backed up a step and thumbed over her shoulder. "I should probably . . ."

"Yes, you probably should." Before he surrendered to temptation and pulled her down into his lap.

Violet had just come in with a loud shout of, "Ready for inspection, boys?" Dante followed, looking strangely pissed off. The GM said something to Cade, and Alamo's response only seemed to irk him more. Could the man not be happy that they had won after losing three in a row?

Vadim lowered his chin but watched while Isobel headed out. To keep up the illusion, she stopped and said something to Coach Calhoun and then to a couple of the other players. Wouldn't want to look like she was playing favorites. Ten minutes later, Vadim walked out of the locker room to a bank of microphones in his face.

"How's it feel to be back, Vadim?"

"The knee holding up okay?"

"We've heard you're receiving private lessons from team owner Isobel Chase. Care to comment?"

So it begins.

He needed to be extra careful about how he handled questions about Bella. Cade's warning came back to him: *You want to make that harder on Isobel or you want to calm the fuck down and figure out a plan?* Protecting her was key.

He gave clipped answers to their questions, careful not to dwell overlong on how Isobel had helped. He was also conscious that she was standing with Harper nearby, being interviewed by another reporter. When had his body become so aware of her presence, every cell thrumming to the beat of his need for her?

As his answers weren't interesting enough, the reporters moved on to other players, and Vadim headed down the tunnel on the lookout for his sister. The charter flight back to Chicago would be leaving soon, so there wasn't much time. That's when he noticed her.

She was not alone.

That woman. He had expressly forbidden her to come.

"Vadim!" Mia threw her arms around him, and the leash on her wrist pulled at the silly dog's collar. He tried to jump up on Vadim, wanting in on the affectionate exchange. "Bro, you played great. I was a little worried about you in the first period, but you *sooo* pulled it out in the second. I'm mighty proud of you."

He nodded, the rock of bile in his throat impeding any communication. He had told her not to bring Victoria. But his sister was barely sixteen, a child, who thought all problems were fixable. Leukemia, an injured knee, an irreparably broken relationship between a son and the mother who had discarded him like one would scrape shit from a shoe.

Sixteen months ago, he had seen the woman at the bedside of his sick sister for the first time since he was ten years old. The sister he had learned about one day prior. Fifteen years was a long time to go without seeing a once-beloved parent. Those years had added fine lines around her expressive blue eyes, yet left her beauty undiminished. Glossy onyx-black hair had framed her face in soft waves, different from the severely pulled back style she had worn when he was a boy. She was also shorter—or perhaps he was taller.

Tonight she glowed, and just as at that moment over a year ago when he had met her at the hospital, he wanted to stare at her all day.

"Hello, *pchyolka*," she said to him now.

His heart thrashed fiercely. That nickname—little bee—he would have happily gone the rest of his life without hearing it again.

Mia must have seen the look on his face. She leaned in close, still holding on to him. "I know you said not to bring her, but she wanted to see you so much. You can't ignore her forever."

He saw the desperate love rolling off the woman behind his sister, and it firmed his resolve.

Can't ignore her forever? Just watch me.

"I'll see you the next time I play in New York," he murmured to Mia, and kissed her on the forehead. She was a meddling menace, but he understood her desire to play at happy families. "Keep practicing."

"Vad," she said, her voice cracking slightly, its plaintiveness a fist around his heart.

"Thank you for coming, Mia." And then he walked by the woman who bore him without a second glance.

SIXTEEN

"Good game tonight, Russian."

Isobel plopped down in the seat next to Vadim, waiting for him to acknowledge her. If he didn't want company, he should have sat on the aisle.

He pulled his earbud from his right ear, his smile like the sun had gone supernova. He raised his head to check on the rest of the flight cabin. Most everyone was asleep, but they both knew they had to be careful.

Besides, that's not why she'd joined him. Or, not the only reason.

"Who was that woman with your sister?"

His smile faded. "No one."

"Well, we know that's not true. She's your mom, isn't she?"

He opened up his iPhone and started scrolling through the music. Isobel didn't know much about Vadim's relationship with his mother beyond the fact that she and Vadim's father divorced when Vadim was ten and she moved back to the United States. When

Isobel knew him as a nineteen-year-old, he didn't speak of her much. Meaning not at all.

"You guys on the outs?"

"We have never been on the ins."

"You and your sister are friendly. Close, even."

His expression was dark. "She is an innocent and had no choice in this. Victoria Wallace chose to walk away from her family because motherhood was too hard."

"Yet she raised your sister."

His eyes sharpened to slits. "You know nothing of it. She was pregnant when she left and never told my father about his daughter. Never told *me* until my father died and she needed something. Do not paint her as a saint, Isobel."

Oh. Well, that was just awful. She'd seen how he cut his mother dead at the arena, but only after that slow moment when the world seemed to stop for both of them. "I'm sorry. I don't know what happened, but she clearly wants to talk to you now."

"She can continue to want." Dismissing her, he returned to his iPhone. "You should get some sleep now before people wake up and start gossiping."

~

Five minutes later, Isobel stepped from the airplane bathroom to find a big, brooding Russian waiting outside. Two seconds after that, she found herself back in the bathroom.

The big, brooding Russian was still a big, brooding problem as he was now taking up all the space and using up all the oxygen.

"Can I help you?"

"This business with my mother, I will not answer questions about it."

"Okay."

"You will not use your powers of persuasion to get me to open up."

"Got it."

"It is in the past. My relationship with my sister is separate, and just because a child wants everyone to get along does not mean everyone should. Or can. We do not live in a fairy tale." He folded his arms, taking up more precious space, and stared so hard she felt she might combust. At this rate, the air supply didn't stand a chance.

Talking to someone about the thing you didn't want to talk about was a strange strategy, but then Vadim had clearly decided that more was less. Or something.

"I can see how difficult it is for you," she said in a neutral voice.

He gave a helpless shrug that cracked her heart a little. "It is difficult for everyone."

She rolled her lips in to hide a smile. Empathy was the first step. He might have been referring to his sister, but if Vadim recognized that his mother was suffering as well, then there was hope for them yet.

She placed a hand on his chest. "If you want to talk about anything, I'm here."

"As my coach."

"As your friend."

Heat flared in his eyes. "Last night, Bella . . ." He circled her waist and clamped a hand on her ass. "Was so fucking good."

Flames of lust licked along her skin. "It was, but . . ." She removed his hand from her ass, which was a damn shame because she'd never found a hand to fit said ass so perfectly.

"I think we need boundaries. Sex-free boundaries."

"If you wish me to discuss my many, many problems, it is better we do it after sex," he said gravely. "When I am at my most vulnerable."

She laughed. "My office door is always open for a chat with my players." Sliding toward the exit required she rub herself against him. So she might have lingered longer than necessary, but he had started this. "And my door will stay open when you visit so you don't get any ideas."

"I already have ideas, Bella. They are in my head and spreading to other, more interesting parts of my body."

Every time he called her Bella, her resistance reached for the white flag. *Stay strong.*

"Keep those ideas, and your body, to yourself, Russian." She opened the door, slipped outside before anyone saw her—and ran right into Dante coming from the galley. He appeared to be much more annoyed than a GM who'd just broken a three-game losing streak should be. Was it possible he'd seen Vadim coming in after her? That's all she needed.

She gently pulled the door shut behind her, praying that Dante didn't need to use the facilities. "Okay there, Dante?"

"What? Oh, yeah." He walked by her, back to his seat, his mind clearly elsewhere. *Phew*. It seemed everyone was in a mood tonight.

Swish, swish.

Vadim raced to the end of the rink, took the shot in the empty net, and raced back. Then he did it nine more times. He glanced over at Isobel, who lifted her eyes from her iPad.

"Two seconds faster than yesterday."

His knee was better. The urge to favor his other leg was gone, but the urge to win was as strong as ever. Other urges, too.

Three days since New York, and they were never alone. Even during these sessions, there was usually someone in the stands. Another trainer. Another coach. Yesterday, Dante sat through the entire hour, his thumbs working his phone feverishly. As soon as regular team practice started, he left, which meant he was taking a special interest in Vadim's progress.

In five minutes, the rest of the team would be on the ice. Removing his helmet, Vadim skated over to Isobel, who was making notations in his iPad chart like a doctor.

"I was worried game play might take it out of you," she said, not looking up, "but it's made you hungry.

There's no question about you being back on the ros-ter full-time."

As she continued to talk about gait speeds and skat-ing motions, he assessed whether there was tension between them because he had shut her down when pressed on the subject of his mother.

His relationship with that woman was not Isobel's concern. True, she had her own parental issues, but she'd had their support through her formative years. Vadim's father, on the other hand, had not been the warmest of individuals, and had become even frostier after his wife left him.

Left *them*.

Weeks would go by without Vadim seeing Sergei Petrov. Instead, he left Alexei as his proxy, ordering him to pick up a young Vadim from hockey practice, attend his first competitive games, even teach him chess. Alexei, the faithful retainer, had always been there.

Vadim'd had plenty of time to come to terms with Victoria's heartless decision, and he certainly did not need Isobel to play at therapist. Lost in a gloom, he realized that he'd missed much of what she was saying.

". . . these sessions should stop."

His neck snapped back. "Repeat, Isobel."

"If you're playing games and attending regular team practice, then we have to be careful about overdoing it. The gym conditioning has to continue, so something else has to give. It should be this."

Nyet. Something about Isobel's tutelage brought

out the best in him, and he wanted that to continue—in all the areas. Between the inability to touch her when others were around and the temptation of her beautiful ass at every turn, the last three days had been hell.

He weighed these competing needs.

"Fine."

Her green eyes widened. "Fine?"

"You will not be my coach anymore. That is fine."

A flicker of discomfort crossed her face. He hated to cause it, but his next words would dull any hurt. "If you're not my coach, then we can continue with what we have started. Properly."

"Oh, we can, can we?"

"Da, Bella. I have tasted you, drunk you down, yet my thirst has not been quenched. Any scruples you have about us will be wiped away now that this conflict of interest is a thing of the past." He looked at his watch. "As of three minutes ago, we should be in bed."

She laughed, and his balls took the hit. "One night only, Russian. That's what I said."

"Seven orgasms do not equal a one-shot deal. My throat is dry, and I think you're still thirsty, too."

Her breathing had picked up, her eyes flared with want.

He continued with his campaign to break her shallow resistance. No woman could withstand the Czar of Pleasure. "You're under my skin, Bella. I wake each morning, my cock hard and seeking your wet heat. The lessons will continue off the ice."

"I'm a team owner, Vad—"

His eyebrow reminded her of her sister's relationship with a player.

She countered by going in an unexpected direction. "Might be time to call Kelly off the bench."

"Yes, I'm sure he would love to hear he was your second choice."

She thumped him on the shoulder, a pointless exercise due to his pads. "You and I aren't about choices! It's just letting off steam because we rub each other the wrong way."

"Yes, Coach. Whatever you say, Coach."

She looked flustered and beautiful. Time to press home his advantage. "We'll start with nights in my bed and work to dinners. This is happening, Bella."

Not wanting to hear any further rebuttals, he skated away. Other team members were starting to come out on the ice, so it was a good time to cut the conversation short. He was confident he could steer her to his way of thinking. Her stubbornness was no match for that of a born-and-raised Russian.

Thirty minutes into morning skate and confidence was flowing through him like a torrent. Many reasons could be given: his goal-scoring performance in the last game, maybe, or the renewed strength in his body. But really, he attributed it to his mood. He had always been a player affected by the goings-on in his personal life. With sound mind came sound body and play. With Isobel came an improved Vadim—in every way.

In previous practices, he'd been aware of his knee,

and somehow that hesitation had spread like a contagion to the team. They were too careful around him, too conscious of his injury. This affected their own play, and while practice was not supposed to be overly rough, it was at least supposed to test a player's limits.

Since New York and his excellent turn on the ice, the crew had enveloped him in the fold. Coming into a new team injured was never a good way to start. There was no time to establish a rapport; you were always treated as "other" until you could contribute fully. Now he was one of them.

Yes, he was feeling invincible, his body close to its peak, his woman back in his bed. *His.* That was how he had felt about her then, and though he could deny it to her—or at least not scare her off so soon—he saw little point in lying to himself. Isobel had been his from the moment he had seen her on the ice eight years ago, her wild hair streaming from her helmet as she dispossessed a male player twice her size.

"Who is that?" he said in awe to the man beside him.

"My daughter," the man replied. "She's going to change the world."

Little did Vadim know that the world she would change was his.

An unexpected noise drew his attention, the sound a loud echo in the practice arena. Was that a bark? In the stands, Isobel had reappeared, now with a girl carrying a dog that looked just like his sister's yapping beast, the little dog with big shits. He skated closer, unsure that he should believe his eyes and ears.

"Mia, why are you here?"

Passing the dog off to Isobel in a leather bag, his sister stood when he reached rinkside and threw her arms around him. "I had a weekend off, so I thought I'd visit. See you play tomorrow." She clutched him tightly as if it had been months rather than mere days since he'd seen her.

He set her back and searched her face. Pale as ice, her lips dry and chapped. Outside in the March cold for too long, perhaps, but he remembered this cast to her pretty features when he had first met her at the hospital.

Isobel stood behind her with the stupid dog. "Vad, I don't think she's well. She lost her wallet and needed someone to pay the taxi. I think she might have the flu."

Mia waved that off with typical Petrovian drama. "It's just a little cold . . ."

At which point his sister—dramatically—fainted.

SEVENTEEN

"I'm fine," Mia said around a phlegmy cough. "It's just a cold."

Vadim stood at the end of the bed in the ER, glaring alternately at his sister and the doctor, who looked no older than twelve. Isobel felt a little intrusive staying in the room, but Dante had insisted she mark their left-winger the moment he heard Vadim's sister was sick.

If he catches anything and can't play, I'm holding you personally responsible, Chase.

As separating Vadim from his sister was impossible, her only choice was to hover close and ensure that he didn't get within contamination distance.

"She should see an oncologist," Vadim said to the ER doc. "She had a bone marrow transplant fifteen months ago. Perhaps she is having a relapse."

"The blood work came back fine, Mr. Petrov, and I've spoken to her doctor at NYU." Doogie Howser pushed his glasses back up his nose. "This is a virulent case of the flu. We're seeing a lot of it."

"See, bro?" Mia sat up, though she swayed like a windblown reed. "I just need to lie down for a bit." She shivered, looking around with something like dread in her eyes. "But not here, Vad. I can't stay here."

Never taking his eyes off her, Vadim spoke words clearly intended for the doctor. "She can leave?"

"Sure. Bed rest for a few days. Plenty of fluids. Tender loving care." He looked at his buzzing phone. "Our usual prescription for the flu." He left to attend to the truly sick.

"Vad, I'll see you outside in a minute." Mia steadied herself with a splayed palm on the bed. "I just need to get my stuff together."

Vadim didn't move an eyelash.

"Bro! Leave!"

"I will turn my back while you dress. Isobel will tell me if you have fainted again."

"Vadim Petrov, stop being a dill-hole! I should have drained all your freakin' marrow when I had the chance." Mia looked to Isobel for help.

Isobel pushed at Vadim, which was roughly equivalent to negotiating with a giant statue. "I'll stay to make sure she doesn't fall over. Go take care of her paperwork."

With one last mutinous look at his sister, Vadim stalked out. Isobel picked up Mia's clothes and handed them to her.

"Where's Gordie Howe?" the girl asked.

"Igor—I mean, Alexei has him."

She looked relieved. "Good. Alexei loves Gordie

Howe. That man is such a softie. Could you—?" She turned her back and gestured at the bow of her johnny. Isobel stepped in and undid it, then helped her with her underwear and clothes.

Something Mia had said thrummed through her. "Vadim was your bone marrow donor?"

"Uh, yeah." A furtive glance to the door, and she went on. "I'm not supposed to tell anyone. We're trying to keep our connection on the down low so I won't feel the pressure of being Vadim's sister. People will have a lot of questions, especially . . ." Her voice petered out.

"Especially as that's how you and Vadim first connected? Because you needed the transplant?"

She nodded, tears welling. "Mom was worried my father would try to get custody of me, so she kept me a secret from him. About a month after he died, we found out about the leukemia, so she had to fess up. I mean, she would have gotten in touch with Vadim anyway, but it moved up the timetable." A tear finally fell, and she wiped it away with a watery smile. "Vadim was amazing. He didn't even hesitate, but he won't talk to her. He can't forgive her."

Who'd blame him? His mother had left him as a child and only reached out when she needed his genetic material for the child she kept. That had to have hurt him deeply. Neither could this situation be easy on this poor girl torn between two people she loved.

"The Vadim I know is a pretty forgiving person." After all, he hadn't held on to a grudge about how

Clifford had treated him in the wake of their doomed teenage hookup. Or, he hadn't held on to it for long. She patted Mia on the shoulder. "Now let's get going before he Hulks out on the discharge nurse."

"Nyet."

Isobel moved a foot over the threshold, though she didn't hold out much hope of it making a difference. Alexei had braced his body so it filled the space between the doorjamb and the open door he refused to let her through.

"Listen, Alexei." She considered smiling, then decided it would be wasted on this guy. He'd hated her eight years ago, his face always in a permanent scowl at her for leading Vadim astray. Nothing had changed. "I'm here to see the patient."

"Flu," Alexei grunted. "In bed." He pushed the door toward her.

She splayed a hand against it. *Try me, Igor.* "I brought soup."

"We have soup." He looked like a bulldog who had eaten a lemon and enjoyed it. So maybe he was a borscht-producing master and soup was his stock in trade, but she had an ace in her back pocket.

"It's in a bread bowl, Alexei. They put the soup"— she held up the bag containing the majestic offering— "in a bowl made of bread. *Comprendez?*"

He didn't look like he *comprendez*'ed.

She tried again, slower this time. "The bowl is made of bread."

From a distance, Vadim said something in Russian, and Alexei answered with a string of guttural hacks that put her in mind of cats being murdered.

"Vadim, I have soup!" Isobel called out, just in case it wasn't clear who was at the door or that soup was in the mix.

A resigned Alexei held the door back. As she stepped inside, her eyes were immediately drawn up.

So much light, like it had somehow been bottled and was being pumped into the foyer. Set back off the main road in Winnetka, from the front, this rented lakeside mansion looked like a typical playground for the rich and famous, about as palatial as you could get in the Midwest. Moving farther in, she realized that the front was a model of deception, as the foyer led to a great room styled like a Mediterranean villa. Floor-to-ceiling windows overlooked the wave-torn lake, which lashed against the ice-fringed edges of the property. In the summer, it would be epic. In March, it merely looked spectacular.

Adding to the spectacular, at the center of the tableau was the man himself, looking like a louche Regency duke. He lay sprawled on a massive L-shaped sofa, his legs covered by an afghan, his chest exposed and gleaming. Gordie Howe lay curled up beside him, auditioning for the part of "villain's pet" in the latest James Bond.

"You brought me soup?" Vadim asked.

"Hell no. That was just my toll." She turned to a looming Alexei and placed the package in his hands. "This is for Mia. I'm guessing it's about time for her to eat."

Isobel had offered to let Mia stay with her until she was healthy enough to travel back to New York. No way in hell did they want one or more of their players coming down with something that kept them from making money for the franchise. But Vadim wouldn't hear of it. So here she was, ostensibly on Dante's orders, ensuring that their star left-winger wouldn't catch the flu.

"Where is she?"

"In one of the guest rooms," Vadim said. "I will wake her."

Isobel raised a hand. "Nope. You are not getting sick, Russian. I'll do it, if necessary, but we have to keep you out of harm's way."

Alexei cast a glance at Vadim, who muttered something in Russian. It was enough to send him off to another part of the estate. She couldn't imagine the impenetrable Alexei ever getting sick, so this worked out nicely.

Isobel slipped off her parka, sat down several feet from tattooed temptation, and crossed one booted foot over her thigh.

Vadim's brow furrowed. "The soup is in a bread bowl?"

"Sure is. They scoop out the bread and fill it with soup."

"What about the bread that's scooped out?"

"They wrap it and put it on the side for dipping."

Vadim didn't want to look impressed, she could tell, but no one in his right mind could fail to acknowledge the genius of the bread bowl. His wistful look toward wherever Alexei had retreated was confirmation enough.

"Any sign of fever?" Moving closer—purely in the guise of visiting nurse, mind you—she placed a palm on his forehead. He felt fine, but looked H-O-T.

Taking her hand, he rubbed it along his chest, then his abs, heading south. "Just down here."

"That's not why I'm visiting. I'm on a mercy mission."

He curled a hand around her neck and drew her close. "Then have mercy, Bella." His kiss was as hot as he looked, and she was weak. So weak. Probably coming down with the flu.

Drawing back, she kept her eyes at chest level. "You really ought to cover up. This can't be helping."

"Can't be helping whom?" He had her bang to rights there.

"You're pretty funny for a Russian, Vad. You weren't like this before."

"I am half American. It took a while for my sense of humor to develop." Seeming to realize what he'd said, he frowned and tugged on the edge of the afghan. He looked a little lost, and Isobel's heart softened.

Sensing an opening, she took her shot. "Does your mother know about Mia?"

His expression hardened. "Alexei called her, so I expect she will show up soon. She may have even planned it. Sent her sick daughter here."

"Paging paranoia."

He regarded her with half-lidded eyes. "It is a Trojan horse gambit."

"I'm sure your sister would love to be compared to a Greek classic. Or a wooden horse." Or a battle in the war between her brother and mother.

"This is how she plays the game. My father is dead, I am rich, she is back. And look, I have a sister!"

Waiting until Vadim's father died definitely put an odd spin on it, but Isobel refused to judge. Her own mother had left her father for good reasons: lesbianism and adultery were pretty much top two, she'd say. Walk a mile and all that.

"Mia told me you were her bone marrow donor. I don't remember you being off the ice for long over a year ago."

He smirked. "Keeping tabs on my career, Bella?"

"Keeping tabs on my team's assets, Russian. It wasn't in your file."

"I only needed a week to recover and I convinced the Quebec team doctors to keep it secret. My life is very public, and she has enough pressure as it is, being the next great thing in female hockey."

Isobel could relate. "So if you didn't meet your sister until recently, how come she plays hockey?" Not many girls "fell" into hockey by accident.

"Mia says she was encouraged to play all sports: soccer, tennis, swimming, lacrosse, hockey. But the ice is in her blood."

"The genes are strong with this one, huh?"

Vadim allowed himself a moment to look proud. "Have you seen her play?"

"Only online. It's amazing how strong she is, considering she's not fully grown. But she's not a muscle factory, either. Her speed reminds me of yours."

"She will be an all-time great. I have no doubt."

Isobel blinked away threatening tears. How petty of her to think of her own ruined potential while admiring another player. Even Isobel could see that Mia was more talented than she'd been at that age.

"Well, my work here is done, so I should go."

He grasped her wrist. "Have you had a flu shot?"

"Uh-huh."

"Then you will stay."

"Shouldn't you be napping?" Hockey players were big on naps, and this would be about the right time for one.

His lips curved. "Get under the blanket."

"Vad . . ."

He pulled back the blanket to reveal wafer-thin sweatpants, ridiculously low on his hips. Her Kryptonite! Those V indents were something else, absolutely lickable. His arm stretched along the back of the sofa, inviting her into paradise.

"There are people here." She looked around as if the people were actually present in this room. Gordie Howe, proxy for society's judgment, eyed her with ambivalence. "This is crazy."

Sex she could handle. Insane, lights-out monkey sex, maybe against that floor-to-ceiling window overlooking the lake. But the comfort of his body was another thing entirely. Becoming accustomed to it would not be good for her mental well-being.

"Mia will sleep after her soup. Alexei has an errand to run that will take all afternoon. Lay your head on my chest and take a nap with me, Bella."

She *was* pretty wrecked, and a few minutes wouldn't hurt, she supposed. Feeling completely overwhelmed by his sheer Russian-ness, she threw an arm around his hard body, snuggled in the crook of his arm, and closed her eyes.

EIGHTEEN

Vadim woke up to indescribable pleasure. Isobel's hand was stroking his cock.

He turned his head, noting her dark lashes fanned over her cheekbones, her breathing steady and even. Still asleep, yet she pleasured him in her dreams?

This girl—this woman—had completely bewitched him. Had she any idea how sexy she was or how much he wanted her? Likely she credited this attraction between them to proximity. Coaching had thrown them together in a relationship that was pressurized and adversarial. Sex was a natural way to relieve the intensity.

So strange, when it appeared that he was barely a blip on her radar all those years ago. His trade to Chicago was not his choice, but he had embraced it, his curiosity about her almost overwhelming. Now he was here, and he was determined to see this through.

Isobel would be his.

Because there was no doubt he was hers.

She owned him with every stroke of his cock inside

his sweatpants, not hard enough to be deliberate, but tantalizing enough to drive him wild. He wanted to wake her, to make her aware of her actions so she would take it to the next level. Hard, fast strokes that would hurl him over the edge. But he also wanted to stay in this twilight where Isobel didn't realize he was about to tilt her world off its axis as she had done to his.

So he watched her, half in agony, as she continued to give him the comfort he refused to admit he needed.

A moment later, her eyes fluttered open. She flushed bright red. Her hand stopped moving.

"Hi," she said, a shyness in her voice that warmed his chest.

"Hello."

"Did you put my hand down your pants?"

"Do not be ashamed of your dreams, Isobel."

She looked confused. "I thought I heard you say something when I was asleep. Telling me you were here, the same as in New York." Shaking herself awake, she sat up, dragging her hand away from his cock, which twitched in misery. "It was just supposed to be a nap."

"If it's any consolation, my cock usually undergoes a vigorous workout during my naps. It's nice to get an assist."

"You should see how your sister is doing."

"Ah, the perfect way to make my boner go away." He stared at it. "Usually."

She held up her palms. "Magic hands. Extra long-lasting boners even when sisters are mentioned." She smiled. It destroyed him. "How about I go see if she's okay? Keep your germ exposure at a minimum."

A minute later, she returned. "She's still asleep. Gordie Howe's curled up on the end of her bed, watching over her."

He hoped Alexei remembered to pick up food for the dumb dog. "Come here, Bella."

"Think I'll stay over here." She moved to the window. "View's much better."

Yes, it was; Isobel framed against the white lunar landscape like an ice princess.

"You look cold," he said.

"Then warm me up, Russian." She didn't even turn, so sure of her power over him. But hadn't it always been this way?

Switching the afghan to his shoulders, he stalked toward her and covered her body with his, chin on her shoulder, the blanket shrouding them both.

"This place is going to look amazing in the summer," she murmured. "All that impossible blue, but then you probably like the white. Reminds you of home."

"I couldn't wait to get out when I was a kid. Come to America, the whole cliché."

She stiffened, and he wrapped his arms around her waist. "I was bitter at first, Isobel, but no more. And my father was as much to blame. We are where we are supposed to be."

"I had no idea Cliff would do that. Mess with your

visa. Blackball you in the league. I only found out later. He was always so worried I'd meet a boy and let him lead me astray. He didn't have enough faith that I'd put my career first. As if I'd—" She broke off.

"As if you would've put hockey second to go moon-eyed over a boy? I knew that. I knew you."

She relaxed. "But my father didn't. It's the model for how relationships in pro sports work. Everything revolves around the male player, not the other way around. He was used to women putting him first. His wives gave up everything, and to be honest, he didn't give them a whole lot back. But I wanted to succeed in hockey more than anything and I wouldn't have let a guy stand in my way."

"So even if I'd stayed, visited you at Harvard, tried to make something of us, we were doomed?" He said it lightly, though his heart mourned the conclusion.

"Hockey was all I cared about. Sure, I liked you—I had a giant crush on you—but given the choice, you would have lost."

"Of course I would. I couldn't even satisfy you in bed."

She laughed, her body rocking against his. "You've made up for it, Russian. But it wasn't the right time."

No. Clifford Chase, who didn't trust his daughter to choose her first love—the holy trinity of a stick, a puck, and an ice oval—had decided to remove the temptation to the other side of the world. But the old man was dead, and his daughter was in Vadim's arms where she belonged. Was it the right time now?

To stop himself from saying something stupid, he kissed her neck, held her tight.

"I'm sorry about how he treated you," she said. "I'm sorry I didn't stand up for you and that your chance to play here was delayed."

"I made it back." *To you*, his tricky heart finished. Was this what he'd been striving for all along? An open path back to Isobel Chase?

He wished she didn't make him crazy and tie him up in knots. He wished he didn't want to take care of her and snuggle with her on the sofa. He wished this feeling were merely lust.

But with Isobel, it had always been so much more.

Eager to unite his mental and physical needs, he crept a hand to the waistband of her tracksuit bottoms and broke the border. Down, down he inched, to paradise.

"Vad," she moaned, and he heard encouragement that sent his hand deeper, his fingers parting and entering. All this wetness, all for him.

His mouth moved along her jaw, the shell of her ear, the delicate feathered wisps at her dark hairline. Beneath his lips, he felt the pinched skin of her healed scar. That night in Buffalo, he had thought he had lost her when an opponent's skate sliced through her skull.

Never again.

Stroking through her slick heat, he caught her clit with his callused finger on each return. He knew what she liked now, a steady rhythm, a slow build, barely-there glances against her pleasure center so she wouldn't go off too quickly.

He shoved her pants and underwear down, encouraging her to part her thighs and give him better access. It also gave his rock-hard cock, still confined in sweatpants, a home to nuzzle against. The cleft of her bare ass invited him to settle in and grind hard. He could come like this. So easy. So good.

But it would always be his Bella first. Her moans increased in volume, and she wrapped a palm around his neck to anchor herself. Her other hand shot out toward the window, and he reached for it and locked his fingers with hers. Needing to connect at every extremity. They were twined together, moving as one mass of heat and sex and pleasure. Who would have thought he would find so much satisfaction with his raging cock positioned outside his woman's body?

Beyond the glass, the shadows of late afternoon stretched over the lake. Lace-frilled waves pounded the shore of his private beach, the wildness on the other side matching the passion on this one.

"Vad—yes, yes."

As he couldn't bury his cock inside her—condoms were in the bedroom—he used the next best thing: two fingers slipped inside just in time to feel the clamp of her muscles as she exploded in release. His cock continued to thrust, his hips flexing, his body demanding. Feeding his fingers into her mouth, he bit down on the sweet juncture where her neck met her shoulder, and she returned the favor with a clamp over his hand to muffle her cries.

Her pussy jerked around his fingers again. She still had more to give him!

"Moya!" Mine. A lusty suck on her neck soothed the sting. His Bella, so insatiable.

She was not the only one.

Her liquid pleasure flooded his hand and triggered a response that hadn't occurred since Vadim was a schoolboy.

With a stifled roar, he came inside his pants.

NINETEEN

"I should leave."

It was at least the tenth time she'd said that, yet she found it impossible to move. Apparently, she'd checked her spine at the door and now her post-orgasmic lethargy kept her pinned to the sofa. The perfect weight of Vadim's arms around her wasn't helping her bid to go, either.

Every time she brought up her departure, he kissed her. On her eyelids, her nose, the corners of her mouth. Outside, waves crashed and night descended. Oddly, she felt as if she'd made some peace with Vadim over how they'd parted all those years ago. Not that it changed anything going forward. He was still a hockey player, and she knew all too well that pro athletes always put themselves first. Two cheating college boy-friends and a father who couldn't keep it in his hockey shorts had skewed her frame of reference.

Her mind returned to the one and only time her father had taken her to an away game, long after he'd given up playing and just after he'd bought the majority share in the Rebels. Barely twelve years old, she'd been excited to have her own room with its pillow chocolates and a minibar fridge—fun-size Pringles!—and especially pleased that it adjoined her dad's. So cosmopolitan, she'd thought. Big mistake, as she found out later.

A nightmare had jerked her from sleep, and she'd sought out her dad for comfort. But as she approached the door leading to his room, she heard it: the giggle of a woman not her mother. A hockey groupie. Isobel didn't need to go in or listen further to learn more— her heart knew the score, and in that moment, her all-encompassing love for him cracked. Violet wasn't on her radar yet, but Isobel understood then what he had done to Harper. What he had done to both his wives. How he took what he wanted because he was a man of reckless appetites and minimal compassion.

He never asked her to lie. At the time, she had thought it was because his infidelity was so accepted by her mother that there was no secret to keep. She saw it differently now, how complicit she was because she knew he would never treat her with such contempt. He might break his marriage vows, but he would never betray Isobel. Only later did she realize that he hadn't seen her as a daughter. Not really. He had put her in a box that fit his ambition: the son he never had. The son he would mold into greatness.

She sat up, determination in her bones, tugging her sweatpants higher on her waist and pulling her hoodie's zipper as high as it would go. *No more funny business*, that zipper pull said. "Really, this time."

Arrogant Vadim Petrov, a man who had women at every game proposing marriage and more on huge signs held against the Plexi, watched her beneath hooded eyes, so sure of his control over her body. He'd changed into jeans, which, along with his shirtlessness, was an unreasonably unfair check in his favor.

"Yet you continue to stay."

She opened her mouth to protest—*no, really, this time, I must*—but was cut off when Alexei walked in with a rolling suitcase, a small figure trailing him.

Vadim snorted. "What did I tell you?"

The dark-haired woman Vadim had snubbed at the Spartans arena in New York stood apart from Alexei, clearly frantic with worry. "Where's Mia? How is she?"

"She's asleep and she's fine," Vadim said. "Or she will be. There was no need for you to make the trip."

The woman, with fiery blue eyes like her son's, shot momma-wolf daggers in his direction. "Excuse me if I don't take your word for it. Now, I'd like to see my daughter."

With a disgusted glare, Vadim jerked a hand at Alexei. "Show her."

Once they'd left, Isobel turned to Vadim. "She's worried. She doesn't need your attitude making it worse."

"I told you before to stay out of it. That hasn't changed."

She debated this, but decided that there was nothing she could do. At least, not now. She turned to leave, only to find that Vadim's mom had returned, her face crumpled with worry.

"Her temperature is 103. I'd hoped to take her to the hotel with me."

Vadim stood and crossed his arms over his bare chest. "She will stay here until she is better. Alexei can inform you when she's awake."

"Vadim!" Isobel couldn't believe his bullheaded insensitivity. "Your mother can't stay at a hotel."

The petite woman thrust her hand out. "I'm sorry. I didn't introduce myself. I'm Victoria Wallace."

Isobel shook it, enjoying the strong grip. "Isobel Chase."

She brightened. "I know. My daughter adores you. Your picture is on her bedroom wall along with Vadim's."

"That's scary." And wasn't that an image, the two of them paired together on a teenager's bedroom wall? Isobel cut a look to Vadim, who evidently wasn't as impressed with this news as Isobel.

Victoria addressed her son, her expression chilly. "I'd like to be here when she wakes up, so I'm going to sit in her room."

"Alexei can call you—"

"Of course it's all right," Isobel cut in. "And there's no need to stay in her sickroom. You might catch the flu. I'm sure Vadim can put you up elsewhere in the house." She led Victoria gently to the sofa. "Now have a seat while he and I go into the kitchen and talk about you behind your back." Then to Vadim: "Petrov. Kitchen. Now."

She steered him into the kitchen, but only because he let her.

"She should be staying at a hotel," he grated.

"While her daughter is sick?"

"I can take care of my sister. That woman should not even be here!"

Isobel placed her hands on his chest. His hard, broad, perfect—*focus*. "Vad, it'll just be for a couple of days. Let's eat, and if after that you still can't bear it, then Victoria can stay with me. It's a ten-minute drive from here to my place, and she can visit her sick daughter while you're at practice."

"Unacceptable."

"Then you can move into a hotel and leave this place to the two of them."

Color flagged his aristocratic cheekbones while his decadent mouth twitched in annoyance. He wanted to shout at her, but he didn't want his mother to hear. Perfect.

She smiled sweetly. "Now, what've you got here that could be turned into a meal?"

"Alexei cooks. He will make dinner." He squinted at her. "I do not enjoy when you interfere in my life, Isobel."

"I know," she said with a pat on his arm. "Now, go put on a shirt. You're blinding us all with those pecs."

⌐

Dinner was a strained affair, a lot of "Could I have some bread, please?" and "Oh, this carbonara is lovely." (It was. Alexei had it going on in the kitchen and looked almost human in an apron with cartoon cats and the slogan OCP: Obsessive Cat Person.) Isobel did her best to keep the conversation rolling and learned that Victoria was an office manager for a real estate company and that the bakeries in Park Slope, Brooklyn, were out of this world.

"So, Isobel," Victoria said after Vadim's grunts became unbearable. "I understand your father isn't around anymore. What about your mother?"

"She lives in Scottsdale with her partner. After she divorced my dad, she came out and lived happily ever after chasing the rainbow."

Vadim's head snapped to attention. "Gerry is gay?"

"You remember my mom?"

"She was always flirting with the players."

"Overcompensating." Isobel smiled at Victoria. "Speaking of overcompensating . . . There was a time not so long ago when Vadim wished *I* was a lesbian. It was the only explanation that fit the facts as he saw them."

Back to grunting from the Russian man-child to her right.

Victoria smiled. "He was always like that as a boy. No gray areas with Vadim."

"Yes, please discuss me as if I am not here."

"You can always contribute," Isobel said, but by some mutual silent agreement she and Victoria stopped talking about Vadim's childhood foibles. It was still too raw for them to be in the same room together.

"So, do you like being a coach?" Victoria asked after a few more bites. "I understand there aren't many women coaches at this level."

"She's an excellent coach when she's not being a pain," Vadim offered, which Isobel took as progress, because the statement could only be directed at his mother. Or Alexei.

"Some would say the two things go hand in hand," Isobel said, then to Vadim's mom, "I like it. I like working with people who want to learn."

"Pro players are pretty set in their ways, I imagine."

"Damn straight. Younger players, especially ones younger than Mia, are more receptive. Definitely more rewarding."

"I am unrewarding?" Vadim asked.

She heard unexpected cheekiness in his voice, so she gave it right back. "Not . . . completely. A vast improvement from your misguided youth."

His smile lit up the room and her world with it.

"I've been doing some work with a youth hockey charity here in Chicago," she said to Victoria, eager to mute the charge coming off Vadim. "Giving kids, especially ones that don't have a lot of economic resources, opportunities to play sports can have a real impact on their lives."

Vadim frowned. "I did not know about this."

"Well, our interactions usually focus on you, Russian. Center of the universe and all that."

Alexei's cough sounded like agreement, and even Victoria had trouble hiding her smile.

"It is not always about me, is it, Bella?"

She'd give him that. He'd certainly demonstrated his generosity as a lover. She wished he'd stop flirting with her in front of his mom, though. As if this situation wasn't awkward enough.

"If you're feeling like spreading some of that love around, there's a charity fund-raiser next week."

"I would be honored to attend."

Alexei and Victoria watched this exchange with interest—or at least, Isobel assumed that was the meaning behind Alexei's squint. And she hadn't missed how Alexei snuck furtive glances at Vadim's mother every time she sucked on a noodle. That wasn't merely a casual interest in whether people were enjoying his food.

Victoria continued. "Mia never stops talking about your performance in Sochi, Isobel. She watches it over and over. Even more than Vadim's games."

Vadim rolled his eyes, refusing to be drawn in.

"Yeah, well, Vadim only got a bronze."

He raised his chin. "I will get gold next time."

She couldn't resist. "So will I."

He looked taken aback, bafflement darkening his expression. After a long pause, he asked, "What does that mean?"

Deep breath. "I was invited to Plymouth next week for tryouts."

"Isobel, that's wonderful," Victoria said.

"Thanks."

Vadim stayed silent and merely continued with the moody stare.

"Well, say something," Isobel muttered.

"Say something? How about, 'You cannot do this'?"

Not that. Her heart squeezed. "This might be my last chance."

He slammed his fork down, its loud clatter making everyone at the table jump. "Have you forgotten what you went through two years ago? When you almost died? You are not fit to play."

"Players take risks all the time. Guys play with blood clots, concussions, injuries, but they'd rather leave it out there on the ice. They'll probably just make me sign a waiver, exempting them from liability."

He threw up a hand, all Vadimesque drama. "How wonderful, Isobel. There will be no one to sue when you are dead."

"What would you do? If someone said you should never play again but you still had the strength in your legs and the torque in your body and the fight in your heart? If they said your next skate might be taken at the same time as your last breath, would you retire gracefully?"

His mouth curled in a sneer. "I would not risk my life to play hockey."

"Then I guess it doesn't mean as much to you as it does to me."

Victoria looked at Alexei, then back to the bickering couple. "Perhaps we should let you discuss this alone."

No, thanks. She'd had quite enough of Mr. Know-It-All Petrov. Isobel stood, her heart sputtering. "No need. Thank you for dinner, Alexei. It was very nice to meet you, Victoria. I hope Mia gets better soon."

She took her plate to the sink, rinsed it, and placed

it in the dishwasher, then left with the heat of Vadim's condemning stare burning into her back.

Tvoyu mat'! How could Isobel think this was acceptable? Vadim had only recently acknowledged his feelings for her, and now she wanted to put herself in harm's way?

Two minutes after she left, he checked to see if she was still outside, perhaps sitting in her clown car, psyching herself up to admit her error. But she was gone, her exit fueled by her stubbornness. No matter. Soon she would recognize the foolishness of this plan.

He returned to the kitchen, relieved to see no sign of his unwanted guest.

Alexei was filling the dishwasher. On Vadim's entry, he spoke in Russian. "She is with Mia."

"You should have talked her out of coming."

"It is time you acted like a man and faced up to your problems."

Vadim pointed. "I do not employ you for your opinions."

"And yet I have given them to you all these years."

This was true. Alexei was never afraid to comment on Vadim's choices and mistakes. Vadim put up with it because he needed the occasional sounding board, but that didn't mean he had to listen to the man's opinion on every topic.

"You were loyal to my father. How can you take her

side in this? She left him." She left *them*. "Ever since she wedged her way back into my life, you have acted as though you work for her, not me. I am your employer."

"Your father was not perfect."

"He did not abandon his son!" Though that wasn't strictly true. He provided a roof over Vadim's head, yes, but he was a hardworking man with myriad business interests, not all of them legal. If he couldn't attend every—or any—of Vadim's hockey games, it was because he was earning money to provide for his family.

But apparently that wasn't good enough for his mother. She hadn't wanted to be a parent anymore. But fate had the last laugh, leaving her pregnant with the child of the husband she hated.

He placed his hands on the kitchen counter, holding in his agitation by a thread. "Did he abuse her? Hit her?"

"No." A crystal clear voice rang behind him. "Your father never raised a hand to me."

He turned to Victoria—he could not call her anything else, even in his own mind. She had abdicated all rights to the title of mother seventeen years ago.

"Alexei, could you give us a moment?" she asked in rusty but serviceable Russian.

With Alexei gone, Vadim searched for the most restrained thing he could think of. He refused to let her feed off his pain. "I know he was a difficult man, but you can't reenter my life after so many years and expect open arms."

"I understand. And I understand if you're not ready

to talk about any of it. But please know that not a day went by when I didn't think of you, Vadim. The boy I loved—*love*—more than my own flesh."

Evidently not, or she would have put up with whatever inconvenience his father had inflicted. A little distance from a rich and powerful man? Surely a small price to pay to be with the boy you claimed to love more than your own flesh.

Isobel would know what to say. How to handle this. But he couldn't even trust her to stick around. She would rather foolishly put her life on the line instead of be here for him when he needed her.

Annoyed at his weakness, he cleared his throat and sought neutral ground. "How is Mia?"

"Sleeping. Her temperature's still high but not as bad as before. She'll be furious to miss your game, but perhaps she'll be well enough to stay up and watch it on TV."

"There is a media room on the other side of the house, but she might be more comfortable in the living room. I will move the TV in there." He threw a glance that way, as if he needed to choose a place for the television right now. Looking directly at her was too painful. "Shouldn't she be in school?"

"Yes, she should. But she stayed home with a sore throat this morning while I went to work. I didn't even know she had left New York until Alexei called." She crushed her hands together. "It's hard to keep track of her sometimes."

He was tempted to say she had chosen this life of

single motherhood for herself, but he was tired and no longer in the jabbing mood.

"She is willful, that is for sure. This is good for a hockey player, not always so good in a daughter or sister."

"I wouldn't have her any other way. Her spirit, especially in light of all that's happened to her, is awe-inspiring."

They were silent for a moment, thinking on the illness that had brought Victoria back into his life and the girl they both loved who was trying to bridge the chasm between them. Existing fissures widened, and Vadim's mind worked hard to plug every single one. He would not allow her in. And he especially would not allow their common denominator—Mia—to be used as a pawn, even if Mia had set this chess match in motion.

"I should go to sleep," he said, though he doubted he would get much rest tonight.

She looked crushed, and he hated her for making him feel guilty.

"I just wanted to thank you for letting me stay to take care of Mia. As soon as she's well, we'll leave."

Yes, you will.

TWENTY

"You started without me?" Harper came click-clacking into the den at Chase Manor and threw herself onto the sofa. Heels off, hand grab for the wine, and— "No spare glass?"

Violet pressed pause on *Dirty Dancing*—the original, of course. Baby and the fam had just arrived at Kellerman's Resort in the Catskills. Sexy shenanigans were on everyone's dance card. "We thought you couldn't make it."

"Have I missed a single Awkward Sister Bonding Night yet?"

Isobel smiled. She had to admire how Harper had stepped up to the sister thing since they'd been thrown together six months ago. Not inheriting the team to run solo had been tough for her, but she handled it like a boss, making a real effort to broker their fractured sibling relationship. Now big sis hopped up and grabbed a wineglass from the sideboard.

"We'd understand if you wanted to spend more time with Remy," Isobel said.

"Plenty of time for that." Her swallow was audible. "I'm, uh, thinking of moving in with him."

Violet and Isobel exchanged *oh really* glances. "That's serious."

"Too soon?" She poured the wine, and as she often did, answered her own question. "Maybe it is. But he wants to start trying for a baby and—"

"A baby?" Violet grabbed the bottle from Harper before she'd made it to half a glass. "You don't need alcohol. It sounds like you're already mentally impaired."

"Vi . . ." Isobel warned.

"Come on. She knows him less than six months and they're already trying to get preggers. That's crazy!"

Harper looked amused at Violet's overreaction. "Take it you're not a fan of kids."

"In exceedingly small doses, and I wouldn't have thought you would be, either. When we get to the play-offs, we'll have fulfilled the terms of the will. We—" She stopped. Self-corrected. "*You* don't have to sell off, which means you are still running a professional hockey team, Harper. How are you going to be the bitch in the boardroom if you also have to be the babe in the bedroom and now the baby mama with a spare diaper in her Kate Spade purse?"

"Well, here's my secret." She leaned in, those green eyes they all shared sparkling. "Remy plans to retire at the end of the season and he'll be staying home to change the diapers. It's all he's ever wanted since he was a little girl."

Isobel felt a pang in her heart. How wonderful to have found someone so willing to step up to the plate like that. "That's pretty hot."

Violet clearly didn't want to agree, but how could she not? "Remy with the BabyBjörn? Yeah, hotness at ovary-exploding levels."

"So we have to start looking for another center," Isobel mused.

Vi thumbed in her direction. "Always the team with this one."

"We have to make the play-offs first," Isobel said. "Twelve games to go, and with the way the standings are now, we need at least eight points to be assured of the wild card."

Harper set her chin. "Ten points would be better, so we can straight up qualify and don't even have to consider wild card. You think Petrov has it in him?"

"Physically, yes. Mentally? This business with his mom is distracting him." Isobel had filled them both in on the latest Petrov drama. The news of how Mia and Vadim were related was also prompting questions, and Rebels' PR was currently whipping up a statement for the media.

"What about this business with his coach?" Harper asked after taking a sip of her wine. "Is *that* distracting him?"

Isobel stiffened. After Vadim's overreaction to her tryout news, there would be no returning to that well. Could the bastard be even a little bit pleased for her? Oh no. Heaven forbid anyone else draw focus from the mighty Vadim Petrov.

"We're not—I mean, we did but—" She held up her hands. "We had some unfinished business from years ago and now it's all tied up. The itch has been scratched."

"Multiple times, I hope?" Violet asked, and when Isobel laughed her agreement, her younger sister nodded. "That's my girl. So proud."

"Hmm."

Isobel hated when Harper did that. "Don't, okay?"

"What? Remind you that itches have an annoying habit of staying, y'know, itchy? That's what I said about Remy, and we all know how that turned out."

As if there were any comparison. "Remy's not like other hockey players. He's not hanging at clubs. He's not signing bare tits at the Empty Net. Not once have I seen him look at a puck bunny since he was traded in. The man has only ever had eyes for you."

"Yeah, the minute he laid those Cajun peepers on you," Violet chimed in, "he was all, 'Me Remy, you Remy's baby mama. Take my seed. Take it all!'"

Harper's smugness wasn't annoying at all. "You've got to be kidding. I'm *so* not what he had in mind for his future, but once I figured out what I needed, I realized that Remy was the one. You know how you wake up, and you can't remember what you were dreaming about? It's there, just out of reach, so close but so far. I think I was dreaming about Remy all along. Then one day I woke up, the dream sharpened, and it all fell into place."

That was strangely poetic from the usually plain-speaking Harper. Even Violet looked affected.

On the subject of dreams, a curious memory returned to gnaw at Isobel. *Wake up, Bella. I am here—* the words she'd thought she heard while she napped in Vadim's arms and gave him a sleepy hand job. It was like something in a reverie, just like those brief moments when she and Vadim appeared to be on the same page.

Harper sipped her wine. "You're right, though. Remy's about as far from Cliff as any man could be."

The weight of that statement loomed over Isobel's head like a heavy object waiting to fall.

"Well, you won't catch me falling for a hockey player," she said defensively. "I'm not going to be that woman, waiting around, knowing he's—just knowing."

She caught Harper's eye, expecting judgment, but saw only compassion. They had both experienced their father's failures as a parent in different ways. Clifford thought Harper too weak to run the team and Isobel too strong to be wasting her time on coaching. *Hockey's not for pussies, Izzy.* Only this year had the sisters found common ground, and ironically, it was Clifford Chase's last will and testament that had forced them into a new understanding of what the other had suffered.

Violet, who had never met him, was definitely more circumspect on the subject of Clifford. And by circumspect, Isobel meant completely silent.

The youngest Chase poured more wine. "Things seem to be looking up, for sure. The team's on a winning streak. Harper's managed to snag a guy who actually wants to be a stay-at-home hottie. And now that Isobel's hit it and quit it with Petrov, it means you won't have to worry about conflicts of interest when you become a full-time coach."

Right, when she became a full-time coach, the great compromise. As much as she enjoyed it, it didn't fill her heart to overflowing like actual professional play and competition.

Don't be a pussy, Izzy.

Should she tell them about the tryout? After Vadim's overreaction—ooh, the man was impossible—sharing didn't seem like such a good idea. They'd only fret.

She picked up the remote. "Enough chitchat. Let's get lost in the glories of Swayze and the merengue."

"You won!" Mia's congratulations devolved into raspy coughs that sounded like a seal with a three-pack-a-day smoking habit. Lifting her head off her mother's lap, she tried to sit up on the sofa in his living room.

"Do not get up." Vadim knelt beside her and felt her forehead with his palm. "She is still hot."

"Her temp went down one degree," Victoria said. "I've been trying to get her to go to bed, but she insisted on waiting up for you."

"Vad, you rocked it on the ice," his sister sputtered. "Though you could have gone all the way with that second goal instead of laying it up for DuPre." She coughed again. "Too generous."

"There are plenty of goals to spread around. And these decisions made in the moment should not be second-guessed by armchair forwards, especially when they result in wins."

She made a face, and in that moment she looked just like their father. Anger barreled through his veins at the woman who had denied the man the chance to meet his daughter.

Mia was too ill to notice his change of mood, but Victoria's mouth thinned in discomfort. "Do you think Isobel might come to visit?" Mia asked.

"We shall see. For now, you must get your rest. Off to bed, pchyolka."

"What does that mean?"

"Bee," Victoria said, her eyes flashing. Always with the searching looks. "Little bee."

Standing, he curved his arms under Mia's body and lifted her close. "Because you are always buzzing around. On the ice, especially." She was fast, possibly faster than Isobel had been in her prime. Not quite as strong yet, but she would get there.

Her forehead fell to his shoulder. "I'm glad people know."

He carried her toward the guest room where she was staying, and though he suspected what she meant, he asked anyway. "Know what?"

"That we're related. As soon as I found out, I wanted to tell the world. I was so proud to be your sister. But then when we met first, I was sick and I didn't make a good impression."

His heart ached in memory of her weakened state that first time he'd met her in the hospital in New York sixteen months ago. He had fought so many emotions that day: anger, regret, hate, all at Victoria. But as soon as he saw how ill Mia was, this beautiful girl who couldn't help the decisions of her parents, he vowed to do everything in his power to cure her.

"You made a terrible first impression, *sestrichka*. But it's understandably difficult to shine with the great Vadim Petrov in the room."

Her soft giggle fluttered against his neck. At the door to her room, Victoria went ahead to turn down the bedcovers. He laid his sister down, and she curled up on her side while he placed the comforter over her.

"You saved my life, bro."

"The flu is making you delirious."

"I haven't thanked you enough."

He remained grave. "You have come to visit and brought your germs. This is gift enough."

She groaned and he laughed, then dropped a kiss on her forehead to let her know he was teasing. "Go to sleep, and we'll dissect my game choices tomorrow."

"Night, Vad."

"Good night, Mia."

He left the room, his body itchy in a way it often was after a game. Adrenaline still rippled through him, but he'd left the arena quickly so he could tend to Mia—and avoid Isobel. Now that he'd seen his sister and ensured that she was safe, he wanted to blow off some steam. Fuck or fight.

As sinking his tension inside Isobel would not be possible until she came to her senses, he would have to satisfy his need with a fight.

Victoria emerged from the room, followed by the dog, and closed the door behind her. In silence they walked to the living room with the pup trotting quickly on his tiny legs to keep up.

"She's getting better," he said.

"Yes," she said, her relief evident. "As soon as she can travel, I'll take her home."

"You would not leave her behind?"

Her face reddened, the jab having the desired effect. Pettiness pinched his chest. Why should *he* feel this way, caught in this no-man's-land of suffering? All wrong. He refused to pander to her need to explain herself, because as soon as he asked, it would be a slippery road to accepting she'd had a good reason.

Bad mothers always have good reasons.

She sat on the sofa while he sat in the armchair farthest away. "How's your knee?"

Neutral ground. This he could discuss. "Better."

"Isobel seems to be good for you."

"She is an excellent coach."

"Only a coach?"

He scowled. "I am not discussing this with you."

"Too old to take my advice?"

"Too old to take your bullshit."

She smiled, and it sliced deeper than when she had looked wounded by his earlier jibe. "That's fair," she said. "I'm not exactly the best qualified when it comes to love."

"No one said anything about love." How typical. All women, even terrible mothers, apparently couldn't help making assumptions. He had smiled at Isobel and showed concern that she was trying to kill herself; it must be love!

The silence expanded between them, and just when it felt like something would snap he felt a nudge at his leg. Gordie Howe. The silly dog likely sensed the tension and was seeking comfort. Needing something to occupy his hands and thoughts, Vadim picked up the ridiculous creature and settled it in his lap.

"He likes you," Victoria said.

"He knows where his next meal is coming from." Absently, he stroked the dog's shiny coat and was strangely gratified to feel him relax. If only his own comfort could be bought so easily.

"You were always good with animals," Victoria said softly. "Cats, dogs, even hamsters. Remember when you lost that horrible ball of vermin, and we had to turn the house upside down looking for it?"

"That horrible ball of vermin was Boris, my closest friend. He liked to sleep in warm, dark places."

"Yes, and he liked to leave turd-shaped gifts. I threw out so many shoes."

Good old Boris. Vadim found himself smiling against his will. He reached for the hardness inside him, but it was becoming more difficult to find.

Apparently encouraged, she spoke again, her voice now more animated. "What was the name of your dog again? The big, black mutt?"

"Fyodor." He hadn't thought of him in years. He might have been a mongrel, but he'd held himself like a king.

"Fyodor! He followed you everywhere."

She was laughing now, confident she had found a way to break him down. He could feel himself slipping as memories inundated him from all sides in colorful, jagged pieces. One soared above the others: the swings in Maritime Victory Park in St. Petersburg.

Push higher, Mama.

That's as high as it goes, pchyolka.

More, Mama. Don't stop.

"Whatever happened to Fyodor?"

"Papa ran him over, backing up out of the garage." Fyodor had liked to sleep under the car, though it made no sense, as it was warmer in the house. Poor mutt, another dumb animal who had sought comfort and paid the price.

"Oh," she said quietly, the wind ripped from her sails. And yet again, that guilty pang checked his heart. She had liked Fyodor, always ready with a treat for him under the dinner table.

He could feel the storm rising again, the war dueling in his chest. She had no right to dredge up these memories or make him sorry for her. She had no rights at all.

"Let's get something straight," he said. "You're here because of Mia, no other reason. So you can quit with the journeys down memory lane. We won't be reminiscing about the good old days, so stop trying so hard. Just stop."

He got up, placing Gordie Howe on the floor. The dog looked up at him expectantly, then switched his attention to the other person in the room, assessing his options. So fickle.

"Understood," Victoria said, and instead of the hurt he expected to hear in her tone, something else rang clear. Something that sounded a little like victory.

Chyort! This woman thought she had gained some advantage over him, and while the power shift was subtle, he felt it as he left the room. He felt it in the gaze she transferred to her phone instead of to his departing back.

Gordie Howe, the traitor, remained with Victoria. Apparently the dumb pup knew who had eked out a win in this round.

TWENTY-ONE

"Gather around, guys. Time to meet our special guests."

Isobel watched as the faces of her juniors lit up when their guests came onto the ice. Seeing Ford Callaghan, Cade Burnett, and the mighty Vadim Petrov himself up close was a thrill for them. Normally, seeing the Russian would be a thrill for her, too. But they had left things in an odd place. At least it hadn't affected his play. In the week since, they'd won two games at home and were about to head out to Vancouver tomorrow.

"Hey, Coach," Burnett said to Isobel, and then to the group. "Got ourselves any future pros here?"

Half of the kids shot their hands up, and the rest looked like they wished they'd thought of it.

Isobel smiled. "Guys, you probably recognize these troublemakers, but I'll introduce them all the same. The one with the funny accent is Cade 'Alamo' Burnett, the bulwark on the Rebels' defense line."

"Aw, you're makin' me blush." He winked at Natasha, causing her to color furiously.

"And you've met this guy before," Isobel said, gesturing to Ford. "The guy who looks like a marauding Viking is Coach Callaghan's brother, Ford 'Killer' Callaghan. Currently the leading goal scorer in the Western Conference."

Ford saluted them with the butt of his stick. "Team."

"And last but not least, meet Rebels' left-winger Vadim Petrov, no nickname necessary."

"Except Czar of Pleas—"

"Ladies," Isobel cut off Gabby, who was pumping out enough teenage hormones to knock Vadim over. Unfortunately the Russian was looking particularly hot today, not a wrinkle or pimple in sight. "Let's remember these are our guests."

The girls giggled like girls their age are wont to do. Vadim raised an eyebrow at Isobel, then held her gaze unerringly. She had no idea what to do with it, so she merely reddened to the point that she and Natasha were a matching set.

Moving on. "I thought maybe we'd play a couple of periods. How about we start with Captain Callaghan and Captain Petrov?" She looked at the Rebels players. "Okay?"

"Hell—I mean, heck yeah," Ford said. "Might be my one shot at wearing a captain's band."

Vadim graced them with speech at last. "Perhaps we shall start with girls versus boys."

The girls perked up, and Gabby spoke for the group. "But there's only three of us girls."

"There's also your coach. Last time I checked, she is a girl." Vadim assessed them. "What positions do you play?"

"Forward, center, and defender."

"Marcus, you good with being goaltender for Captain Petrov's team?" Isobel asked.

"Yes, Marcus, I need you on Team Petrov."

Marcus gazed in wonder at Vadim, like he'd been chosen first by the most popular kid in school. All he could do was nod dumbly.

"Hey now, Ruski," Callaghan said. "Pretty sure you're trying to bamboozle me by picking the quickest players. Not to worry, we boys will take care of business. I need four good men and a goalie."

With the teams set, the remaining players sat rinkside, where Cade would officiate. "But no swearing, Alamo, 'kay?" Isobel cautioned.

"Rebels' honor, Coach Chase," he drawled with a dirty grin.

They set the period to five minutes so the other kids would get a chance to play. As well as officiating, Cade kept up a running commentary throughout that had the kids on the bench in stitches.

"The Czar with the puck now and he passes to— what's her name—Gabby?—I'm never gonna remember that. Let's just call her Skittles. So Skittles rushes the zone, only to run into trouble with a dispossession by Tall Dude. Not bad on the stick-handling, TD. And now they're on the break with Killer comin' up the side for support. Quick pass and . . . and back to TD and . . .

foiled by Team Petrov's tender! The Crease Monster rules!"

Vadim and Ford were obviously operating at about 30 percent, given the youth of their teammates. Not once did they try to score themselves, always making sure to pass back to one of the younger players. After five minutes, the teams switched out with their classmates, Cade went in for Petrov, and Jackson Callaghan offered to referee the next period.

Which is how Isobel found herself sitting on the bench with Vadim.

"Hi," she said softly.

"Hello."

"How's Mia?"

"Improving."

Another pause. "Thanks for doing this. I thought maybe you weren't talking to me."

He kept his eyes on the rink, where Cade was still announcing the game, even while playing.

"Freckles with the puck . . . and now he sees an opening . . . but Alamo slaps it away . . ."

"I thought maybe I wasn't talking to you, either." Vadim turned slightly, eyes blazing. "I have not come around, Isobel. But then you don't need me to, do you? You are your father's daughter. The game will always come first."

He had a point, but she also knew this: if she wanted to succeed, she couldn't live in anyone's shadow. Not her father's. Not Harper's. And certainly not Vadim Petrov's.

"When is your tryout?" Each word sounded like it practically choked him.

"Saturday." She nudged his shoulder. "Wish me luck."

"The Girl with the Blazing Skates doesn't need luck." He stood and twisted to face her. "She needs her head examined." And then he stormed out onto the ice.

On Saturday morning, Vadim walked into the kitchen, found Victoria cutting up fruit at the counter, and turned to walk out again.

"Vadim."

He stopped, every muscle in his body straining with tension. Stay? Go? Punch the fridge door?

"I was about to take Mia some breakfast, then the kitchen is all yours. I have to walk Gordie Howe."

On hearing his name, the stupid ball of fluff rubbed against Vadim's legs and gave a little yip.

"I can walk him."

She waved off his offer. "You played well last night. Mia was so excited to see you score that winning goal."

Throwing all his emotion into the game in Vancouver seemed to be the best—the only—thing to do. His home no longer belonged to him. He felt oddly unmoored from his own life. And then there was Isobel, who wished to risk it all to get back this part of herself she claimed was missing. No helmet could protect her from the one bad check that could end her life. Infuriating woman!

Her tryout was today in Massachusetts, and guilt pinged him that he had not wished her well. But doing so would condone her choice. He refused to be a party to such madness.

He should call the coach and insist she be sent home. *To him.*

This was where she belonged, wrapped in his arms, taking naps on his sofa. Not wanting to be solo with his miserable thoughts, he edged back into the kitchen and approached the coffeemaker, only to have another scent invade his nostrils. Previously hidden from view by Victoria's slim frame, a teapot sat on the counter, a canister of Russian Caravan beside it.

"You are making tea?"

His surprise teased her smile. "Of course. I drink it all the time. Your sister can't start the day without it."

Mesmerized, he watched as she went through the time-honored ritual. She poured a splash of the *zavarka*, or tea concentrate, into a cup from a small teapot that looked vaguely familiar, then added hot water and a spoonful of jam.

His heart thrummed violently. It was how he used to take it as a child, following the lead of his mother.

"You don't drink tea anymore?" she asked. "Alexei had to dig this teapot out of storage for me."

"When I moved to Canada, I got into the habit of drinking coffee." He couldn't avert his eyes from the spoon as she stirred the jam into it. "I am surprised you would take this piece of Russian culture back with you to America."

"I wanted to . . . stay connected to that part of my life in some way." She coughed slightly. "You used to like your tea with raspberry jam. I asked Alexei to buy a jar just in case."

Irked at her transparent efforts to curry favor, he snapped, "Why are you making Mia breakfast anyway? She's well enough to get up." Well enough to travel, too, yet he was in no hurry to shove them out the door. He liked having Mia around, even if she came with the baggage of Victoria.

His mother smiled serenely, and the remembrance of how she used to grace him with that sunshine was a sharp, stabbing ray of light.

"I like to spoil her," she said. "Soon she'll be at college, and I won't have a chance."

Already close to college age and he had just found her. Would his sister still want to know him once she had made a life for herself elsewhere? That made him think of Isobel again, who was in such a hurry to leave him for the next world. These women.

"Where is Alexei?"

"He went to the store." She opened her mouth to say something, then closed it again.

"What? Speak."

"I'm surprised you haven't parted company with him."

Vadim leaned against the counter, his arms crossed. "He has always been loyal to my father."

"Yes, but your father isn't around anymore, and you are perfectly capable of looking after yourself."

He eyed her speculatively. "It is good to have an assistant, one who will not gossip to the tabloids about my personal life. The last one I had simpered and made googly eyes at me all the time. And I do pay him well."

Her blue eyes watched, searing him once more. "You seem upset."

A stupid statement. His arched eyebrow let her know this.

"More so than just your usual annoyance with my presence," she teased. How wonderful that she could joke about it. What progress they had made!

He shrugged. "Isobel has set out on her mission of self-destruction today."

She mouthed *ah*. Back to stirring the tea. "Perhaps you should support her. Not everything has to be so black and white, does it?"

People in the wrong always said that. Vadim knew exactly who was right here.

Before he could argue his point, Victoria coughed hard, her hand reaching for the counter in support.

In a flash, he cupped her arms. "You are ill?"

"Just a sore throat. It's nothing."

"It's not nothing. You have the flu."

She shook her head. "I'm fine. Another day or two, and Mia will be well enough to travel."

At which time Victoria would be worse. This was his life now, the family reunion that refused to end.

"Off to bed with your tea. I'll take our invalid her breakfast."

"Vadim, there's no need. I have to walk Gordie Howe and—"

"I will walk the little dog with big shits. Do not argue with me. Why must all the women in my life argue with me?"

She smiled, a wobbly curve of her lips that appeared to come apart around the edges. The image she projected as he peered down at her was so frail, so vulnerable, almost deserving of his pity. Of his affection.

Only then did he realize that he was touching her for the first time in seventeen years. He dropped his hands.

Her expression clouded over. "I don't want you to get sick."

As if that was the reason he had recoiled.

"Go to bed. I will take care of everything."

TWENTY-TWO

Isobel had spent a good chunk of her life in locker rooms, but she'd never been so grateful to sniff the stink of this one at the Team USA training compound in Plymouth, Massachusetts.

This is it. My last shot.

Only Vadim knew she was here. She didn't want to tickle anyone's hopes, or in Harper's case, judgment. Better to focus on her dream without worrying others would take a dump on it. Even so, when she checked her phone one more time, her heart plummeted at the blank screen. No good-luck messages.

Fine. Let him pout.

"Chase!" Stefan Lindhoff, head coach for Team USA, crashed into the locker room and pulled Isobel into his arms for a bear hug. "Thought you might chicken out."

Isobel pulled back and punched him in the shoulder. White haired at the age of forty-three, he'd enjoyed an on-again, off-again career in the NHL before he'd found his true calling: yelling at people to haul ass down the rink.

"Screw you, Coach, I'm here to skate. And, uh, screw you."

He laughed his head off. "You always had a cheeky mouth on ya. Ready to get out there?" He was already walking toward the rink, expecting her to follow him. "So you'll probably recognize a few of the players from Sochi, and there's no shortage of talent from the college ranks," he threw out over his shoulder. "This year the pool is pretty deep."

"Yeah, yeah, I've been warned. Look, Coach . . ." She stopped, and he faced her. "I appreciate that you've given me a chance here. I know I haven't played competitively for a while, but I haven't stopped training. I haven't stopped believing I could get back here."

He nodded. "We have your medical records, and the team doctor's already looked at them. I didn't know it was so bad, Iz."

Damn, she was going to lose this chance before she'd even made it to the face-off circle. "It's just medical opinion. I know what I can do. I know what my body is capable of. Put that waiver in front of me and I'll sign. This won't come back to you."

He gusted out a weary breath. "Let's see if you can still skate, Chase. Then we'll figure out how to tie up the legalities in a big red bow."

Out on the rink, about ten women, all suited up, were skating figure eights on the ice. One of them broke away and raced toward her.

"Chase!" Jen tackled her and held her tight. At this rate, she was more likely to die from overhugging than from a hard check against the boards. "Girl, it's awesome to see you. How's the noggin?" She knocked gently on Isobel's forehead.

"Still attached, Grady. Thanks for the push."

"Yeah, well, you might not be saying that after I put you through your paces." She winked. "Coach's orders, of course. No mercy."

"All right, ladies, let's get this show on the road," Coach said. A couple of assistants skated over, along with a few of the players. Isobel nodded in recognition at each of them, having played with some and kept tabs on the rest as they made their mark in the NCAA and beyond.

"Three full periods." Consulting a clipboard, Coach started divvying them up into two teams. "I'll call the shift changes for both. First line is Grady on left, Chase in center, and Jensen on right."

First line, back in the mix.

This was worth any risk.

Vadim answered the door, gloriously shirtless, as usual. Late in March, but the man cared nothing for the Chicago winter. The world was a better place for it.

His surprise at seeing her was obvious. "Isobel?"

"I got your text."

"I didn't—" He shook his head ruefully. "Mia must have sent it."

His message to her an hour ago had made her smile and given her hope that he might be willing to make peace. On reflection, she now realized that the text wasn't really Vadim-speak.

Flupocalypse is upon us. Send supplies.

His gaze fell to the shopping bags. "What have you brought?"

"Soup," Isobel said with a grin to hide her disappointment that the text hadn't come from him.

His eyes lit up. "In the bread bowl?"

"Of course."

"You may enter." Smiling, he took the bags from her.

Mia lay sprawled on the sofa in the big room, gazing out the window at the waves crashing against the icy beach. Gordie Howe was curled up beside her and the large TV showed the *Friends* crew splashing about in their nineties glory.

"Isobel!" The effort of greeting sent Mia into another coughing fit. "I'm getting better."

"Sure sounds like it. Where's your mom?"

"In bed sick. Alexei, too." She giggled, which turned into more coughing. "Not together, of course."

As if. Alexei had always struck her as sexless, humorless, and with little to redeem him beyond his loyalty to Vadim and his spaghetti carbonara. But apparently even hard-ass bulldogs could be felled by the flu. *Faith in the universe? Restored.*

"Back in a sec," Isobel said, and headed into the kitchen.

Vadim was removing the soup from the bags. He

looked so earnest, his big hands wrapped around the small take-out containers as he placed them carefully on the kitchen counter.

He raised his chin. "How did it go?"

She'd flown in late last night, caught a few Zs, and headed over when she got not-Vadim's text. She knew he didn't agree with her choice, but she assumed that the fact he was talking to her meant conciliation was on the table.

"Good. I won't hear back until next week, but Lindhoff said he liked what he saw."

As had Isobel. Her body had come alive on the ice, her competitive juices flowing with every defenseman rushing to take her down. This was what she should be doing. Not coaching reluctant male players who resented every piece of advice she gave them.

Vadim continued unpacking the soup, though he kept his steel-eyed gaze on her.

"And they're okay with your medical history?"

"Lindhoff thinks it'll be fine." She moved in and rubbed his hard bicep. "I don't want to fight."

"Then we will not fight," he said cryptically.

That was surprisingly easy. "Three of the players are down with the flu." They had a game tonight, so Dante and Calhoun were understandably concerned about the other players' health. "Coach might want to play you on the right to take Callaghan's place and start with Shay on the left. You okay with that?"

He folded his thick-as-oak-branches, gloriously inked arms over that blockbuster chest.

"I've played much of my career on the right wing and I am more versatile than Shay. This will not be a problem."

"I was referring more to the beef you have with him."

His handsome face scowled. "As long as he passes when I'm open, we will work fine together."

"Isobel!" Mia called out. "I'm bored, and Vadim doesn't know how to entertain me."

"I gave you bone marrow, you ungrateful brat," he shot back. "Entertainment was not part of the deal. Neither was little dog with big shits."

"Don't call Gordie Howe that. He's very sensitive."

Isobel laughed. "She sounds better."

"She's on the mend. Go sit with her and talk about hockey, but stay several feet away from her germs." He kissed her forehead, and predictably, she melted into him. "I wish you to stay strong so I can fuck you without conscience after I win tonight."

"Your. Ego."

"It is large, yes." He pulled her flush, giving her a preview of his ego. "I will need a moment to calm it down to less epic proportions. This time shall be spent preparing lunch." He turned her and pushed her back toward the living room. Sounded like she was forgiven, or Vadim had decided his sexual needs were more important than his disapproval.

Fair enough. They were more important to her as well.

Isobel plopped down on the sofa beside Gordie

Howe. "How's it going, sickie? Bet you're anxious to get back to New York and on the ice."

"Ice, yes. New York, meh." She lowered her voice to a whisper. "Don't tell him, but I like hanging with Vad. He's an absolute hoot, and half the time he doesn't even realize it! He promised he'd let me play a few minutes of practice with the Rebels when I'm better. Oh, and he also told me you used to practice together years ago. That's how you met."

Isobel smiled at how quickly Mia jumped from topic to topic. "Yeah, seems like forever. Another lifetime."

"*My eyes!*" Phoebe screamed from the TV.

"Oh, I like this one." It was the episode where everybody finds out about Monica and Chandler.

"I'm usually too busy for TV, so I've never seen this show," Mia said. "I didn't expect to like it, but it's hitting the spot." She rubbed her dog's head indulgently. "Gordie Howe likes it, too. He makes happy yelpy sounds whenever Joey opens his mouth."

Too busy for TV—didn't that sound familiar. That's how Isobel's life had gone, on instructions from her father. No time for anything that wasn't about getting to the top of her game. Only when she was injured was she able to relax. She hoped Mia wasn't overdoing it.

The girl's phone rang and, frowning, she declined the call.

Curiosity piqued, Isobel asked, "Who's that? A boy?"

"No way." She bit her lip. "Boys just get in the way, don't they?"

That's what she'd thought. But there was no doubt that she'd missed out on . . . fun. "Mia, if you want to have a boyfriend, you should go for that. Especially if he's hot."

The girl glanced at her phone. "That was an agent."

"Wow, already?" Isobel had signed on with her dad's agent, not that she was ever talented enough to get any significant endorsements, just that one Wheaties commercial after winning silver at the Games. The world had changed in the last few years.

"Yeah, he wants to sign me now. Says he has lots of ideas to take me to the big time."

"What does your mom say?"

"I'm not telling her. She'd freak out."

"Then you should talk to Vadim. To be honest, I think there's going to be plenty of time for that— agents, sponsorships, deals. Right now you should be focused on getting better, getting good grades, and getting into the college of your choice. It's going to be hard enough once you're NCAA. You need to make time for yourself, and if you're worried about endorsements and making money now, it'll be a distraction."

Mia considered this. "Do you ever wish you did it differently?"

"What?"

"Any of it."

Isobel inhaled deeply. "I would have watched more episodes of *Friends*."

Another buzz sounded, and they both looked at

Mia's phone again, but it was the other one on the ottoman. Vadim's, Isobel guessed.

Mia picked it up. "Whoa! Sexting alert."

Isobel couldn't help leaning in for a closer look. A text message from someone called Marceline said: *Bonjour, Vadim, I am in town next week. Call me.* Then, in case the verbal encouragement wasn't enough, a photo of two very perky breasts with a red heart tattoo on the left one sweetened the offer.

"The Czar of Pleasure strikes again," Mia whispered with a giggle.

Isobel snatched the phone from her, bile-tinged jealousy climbing her throat. "That's private. You shouldn't look."

Rein it in, dummy. Isobel had no claim on Vadim. If anything, it was better to know that she was just one of several options for him.

"We have soup," a deep voice intoned behind her.

She dropped the phone like it was a hot coal, then peeked up to find Vadim coming toward them with a tray carrying three soup bread bowls. Like everything else, domestication looked superhot on him.

"Oh, that's not supposed to be for me," Isobel murmured. "It's for your mom and Alexei."

Vadim put the tray down on the ottoman/coffee table. "There is enough. You will have lunch with us, then Mia will take a nap." He winked at Isobel. "I must nap, too, to prepare for tonight's game."

Heat flushed Isobel's cheeks. She was fully aware of what a nap with Vadim invariably led to and, with that text message still doing a number on her sanity, she realized that her feelings for the Russian were skirting the edges of falling into a deep pile of shit.

While Vadim made sure Mia had numerous cushions supporting her, Isobel grabbed a bread bowl filled with potato and leek soup, her favorite. The bready container quickly got soggy, so it was best to eat it fast. *Pig at the trough* was not her most attractive look, but what did she care? Vadim had a French-speaking, buxom playmate—with a heart tattoo on her boob, no less!—coming for a visit.

Once Vadim had Mia settled in with her soup, he picked up his own.

"This is excellent," he said after the first mouthful. "Better than Alexei's borscht."

"Ugh, borscht. The worst," Mia said with great passion.

"It is the soup of your people," Vadim said. "You must be respectful."

Isobel tried to say with a straight face, "Yes, Mia, respect the soup of your people," which set Mia off laughing, and then Isobel couldn't help joining in.

Vadim shook his head at their silliness, but Isobel could tell he enjoyed being teased.

"I've been meaning to ask, Vadikins," Isobel said. "What's with the shirtless thing? Not a fan of the above-waist articles of clothing?" *Or just keeping it simple for the quick sext and pic you might need to shoot off to that French-speaking hussy?*

Mia giggled. "It's freezing out, and he insists on walking around like he's on a modeling shoot." She touched a finger to his shoulder. "What's this tattoo for?"

"It is a jaguar, signifying strength and grace. It also eats schoolgirls who do not finish their soup."

"What about this one?"

"*Matryoshka.*" At Mia's querying frown, he explained. "A babushka. Russian nesting doll. Your cultural education has greatly suffered, I see."

Isobel added, "It signifies many layers."

"Not for me," Vadim said. "What you see is what you get."

So not true. Mia continued asking for the meaning of the tattoos, and Vadim explained when he had gotten each one and why. Isobel enjoyed how easy he was with his sister, their undeniable love for each other making them glow.

"What about this?" Mia asked around a yawn. Isobel tilted her head, wondering which one she meant. Ah, one of her favorites: the skates bursting into flames.

"It represents speed on the ice. *Devushka s goryshimi konkami.*"

Mia squinted. "What does that mean?"

"You, young lady, should learn your mother tongue." He took the remains of her bread bowl from her and placed it on the tray. "Now you must sleep. And I must check on the others."

"I can do that," Isobel said. Dante was still being an annoying pain in her ass about Vadim's proximity to the plague, or the "Petrov contagion" as he'd dubbed it, especially since he'd caught it himself.

"You will wait here, Isobel. We must discuss strategy." He lifted Mia into his arms.

"I can walk, you know, bro."

"I know, pchyolka."

Isobel cleared up the tray and put the plates into the dishwasher. When she returned, Vadim was back in the living room, sitting on the sofa.

"They are all asleep. I'll wake Alexei and Victoria in a while to feed them." He patted the seat cushion. "You will stay and nap with me."

Oh, God, what was she doing here? It seemed she was incapable of resisting that blue-eyed stare, those chiseled cheekbones, and that to-die-for tatted body.

She was addicted to Vadim Petrov.

That one night in New York should have been enough to sate her hunger, and if not that, the orgasm against the window a few days later. Napping together was a dreadful idea.

Yet, like a sex-starved zombie, she went to him and settled in while he covered them with a faux fur blanket. There was no missing the part of his anatomy that was opposed to the idea of a power snooze.

"Napping," she said firmly. "That's all we're doing."

"Yes. Napping." He kissed her softly, a prelude to so much more than a nap. She sank into him, but he didn't take it any further and neither would she, not when there were flu survivors likely to wander in at any moment. Kissing was okay, though. Pretty harmless, she insisted to the parts of her that were flirting with self-control.

"Mia's already getting interest from agents. I think she needs advice."

"Then give it to her."

"Her brother's advice."

He blew out a breath that ruffled the hair at her temple, close to her scar. "She is too young to be tying herself to all of that. And it's not as if she will ever want for a thing. Half of our father's wealth belongs to her."

"You're just going to give it to her? Millions of rubles?"

"A million rubles is only twenty thousand dollars. We are talking billions. It is her inheritance, and her father would have wanted her to have it."

Sure it was Vadim's to do with as he pleased, but she suspected Victoria would have an opinion here.

"That doesn't really answer Mia's problem about an agent. She's going to be under a lot of pressure and . . ."

"And, what?"

"Promise me you won't push her too hard. Let her be a teenager. Let her enjoy college and hang with friends and fall in love. Go dancing and watch *Friends* episodes."

"This is why I've been trying to protect her. Now that everyone knows we are related, she is getting more attention."

"It was going to come out eventually. I just worry about her. About girls like her."

Vadim cupped her cheek and stroked his thumb along it. "You missed out on so much, Bella."

"I suppose."

"And now you are making up for it, greedy witch."
His hand cupped her ass and pulled her over his body.

She swatted his hand away. "Maybe we should talk."

"I thought this was a booty call."

He pronounced it "beauty," which was sweet, especially as Vadim's English was excellent and she suspected his mispronunciation was deliberate.

"I came to feed the ill, but now I'd like payment with the deep stuff. I'd like to know more about you and your life in Russia."

"This is not a good time. I have more urgent needs, and then you can delve into my sordid history when I am weak and depleted. I need to be inside you, Bella."

She laughed, loving how honest he was. She wasn't sure she could ever be that honest with him, yet he had become the only person she wanted to talk to. The only person who could understand a tenth of what she was going through. So he didn't approve of her choice to try out for Team USA, but she knew he would cheer her on if she made the grade.

"You need to sing for the right to give me an orgasm, Vadim."

"I cannot sing."

"Then answer a few questions."

———— ⌐ ————

Vadim sighed. Isobel was relentless, and while he admired this attitude on the ice, he was not so enamored of it on unfrozen terrain.

"You may ask questions. I can't guarantee I will answer."

"Do you miss your father?"

He wasn't expecting that. "Yes. He was a difficult man, but he had my best interests at heart."

"How was he difficult?" She leaned up on her elbow.

"Like yours, he had high expectations. He wanted me to go into the family business. He thought that hockey was just a phase. But when he realized I intended to make it my life, he relented. Or, rather, he ignored it."

"What kind of business was he in?"

"Telecommunications, tech, energy. A lot of fingers in a lot of tarts."

She firmed her lips, clearly holding in a smile.

"Did I not say it right?"

"Pies, Vadim. A lot of fingers in a lot of pies."

He moved his fingers between her legs. "Pies, tarts, it is all warm and welcoming and tasty."

Grabbing his hand, she placed it outside the blanket, then wagged a finger. "Nuh-uh."

"I know what you are doing," he murmured.

"What *I'm* doing?"

"Yes, you are trying to force me to admit my father had faults so I will be sympathetic toward Victoria."

"There are two sides to every story."

Not to this one. "Perhaps she did not like Russian winters or she missed McDonald's french fries—they are different in St. Petersburg, you know. Perhaps she had a hard time making friends with the wives of my father's business associates or she did not want to put in the effort. Perhaps my father had an affair or she found someone else she loved more. Yes, there are two sides, but only one of them left me without a mother at the age of ten."

She laid her head on his shoulder and made circles with her finger on his chest. "When she gets better," she said, "they'll go back to New York."

In her words he heard her judgment: this was his chance to get all the answers he sought, if only he would not be so stubborn. He sighed, knowing the ice was starting to crack under him, yet he wasn't ready to greet the inevitable cold rush of water.

"Mia is my future. Victoria is my past."

"Tell me about the first time you met Mia."

He smiled, though the memory was a mix of pleasure and pain. "It was in a hospital room in New York a couple of months after my father died. Victoria had called the day before." No preamble, no buildup from the woman who had borne and abandoned him, and he supposed it was better that way. Her reasons for contacting him were blunt. He'd hoped his father's death would prompt her to get in touch, now that this last barrier to her contacting him was gone. But no, not even that was enough to bring her back into his life.

"Mia looked so weak, lying there. She had only learned who I was that morning. Victoria did not want to get her hopes up until I agreed to come out and be tested as a donor."

"You didn't hesitate?"

"No. The blood of my ancestors runs in her veins. There was no choice for me. I was a match, and we went from there." Angry again, he drew back from her. "My father should have met her."

"What do you think would have happened if he'd known about her?"

He shifted to face her. "He would have welcomed her into the family. Made sure she wanted for nothing."

"Maybe fought for custody?"

So transparent. "It would have been his right."

"And what about your mother's rights? Maybe she was afraid because your father could buy his way into Mia's life."

"He would not have needed to do that. Every girl wants to know her father."

He could see her clever mind working overtime, seeking another access point to his compassion. She wouldn't find it. He was all tapped out as far as Victoria Wallace was concerned.

"You said your father might have had an affair, like that was normal. Like your mother should have put up with that."

"*Your* mother put up with your father. Though the fact that she is gay may excuse his behavior."

She sat up. "He cheated on Harper's mother with mine. He cheated on mine with Violet's. And I know there were more. But of course, hockey players always defend their own. The ice brotherhood, right?"

"All I am saying is that an uninterested woman in your bed changes the situation."

"Of course, the woman is always to blame."

"Your mother is a lesbian! There is fault on both sides there, Isobel."

She pointed a finger in his shoulder. "Exactly. But my mother's sexuality didn't give my father an excuse to bang everything that's not nailed down. Harper's mother can't give him a son, he moves on. My mother can't satisfy him, he moves on. He knocks Violet's mom up and abandons her."

"Yet you loved him."

Her eyes reflected her hurt. "Yet I did."

"As I loved my father. For all his flaws."

She leaned in, her breath soft against his lips. "We can acknowledge they had faults, that they were not perfect, but they were still the men who shaped us. You can forgive him his faults, but not your mother hers?"

Back to this. "People make sacrifices all the time for their children. For the people they love. My father was not perfect, but surely she could tolerate his faults for a few years. Until I was old enough to not care if they were no longer together."

"He might have cheated on her, and she should put up with that? Is that what you think marriage is, Vadim? One person calls the shots because he has the power? Or because there are children who would probably be better off with their parents apart? Never mind that he's unfaithful. That he screws around. That he's unable to resist the women throwing themselves at him because he's powerful and rich."

He sensed she was accusing him of crimes he had yet to commit.

"I am not my father, Isobel." *Nor yours.*

"That's not what I meant." She looked rattled. "Not everything is so clear cut, Vadim. You've heard your father's side of the story. Get your mother's now while you can."

TWENTY-THREE

"Chica, you look hot!"

Isobel handed off her coat to the cloakroom attendant at the Drake Hotel, site of the Hockey for Everyone fund-raiser, and faced Violet, who was shrugging off her jacket.

"I do a lot with this foundation, so I don't want to look like I just crawled out of a sweaty gym bag."

Violet passed off her coat and ran a hand through her hair, to which she had recently added purple streaks. With her gleaming skin, emerald eyes, and floral tattoos on her upper arms, she looked so sexy in a red shift dress and thigh-high boots. Dominatrix chic. Isobel didn't look sexy in the slightest, let alone hot, but she was mildly pleased at how this green dress matched her eyes and draped over her body, giving her curves that were previously nonexistent. With the kitten heels, she wasn't too tall—though Vadim would always be taller no matter how high her heels.

"The Russian's going to think you're totally bangin'."

Isobel grimaced. "I'm trying to cool that off." *And*

doing a fantastic job by nagging the guy to talk about his deep, dark problems. Go, me!

"Ladies, lookin' fine."

They turned to see Cade, Erik, and Bren walking in, rocking smart suits with ties. Even though the guys wore suits on game days, there was still something about seeing a big hunk of brawn all dressed up that got a girl's senses a-tingling.

Cade, complimenter in chief, kissed Vi on the cheek and then pulled Isobel in for a hug. "Off the clock, Coach, so just accept my affection."

Isobel laughed. "If I must. You ready to flash those pearly whites for the children, Alamo?" One of the fun parts of the evening was a bachelor auction with the single players. According to Felicia in Rebels' PR, anticipation was at a fever pitch, especially as the team had six games left in the regular season and was on the cusp of making the play-offs. Charity events always raised the profile for the team, and getting the Rebels behind this one was great for their image.

Cade grinned big. "As long as some cougar doesn't expect me to put out on the first date, we should be good."

Violet was eyeing Bren, who was doing his utmost to ignore her. "Should we expect to see you on the block, Highlander?"

He scowled. "Doubt anyone would be interested."

"Oh, I don't know about that," Violet said, all mischief. "I think I'll set conditions for my bid. I'd like to see you in a kilt on our date."

Bren raised his scruffily bearded chin—almost a play-offs beard, which was definitely tempting fate—and held Violet's gaze. His eyes ran a disapproving arc over her hair, then a not-so-disapproving arc over her body. "Not bloody likely, Ms. Vasquez."

Her smile was slow, all flirtation. "I bet I could get you to wear one by the time the season is over."

"How much is this foolish bet worth to you?" His Scottish brogue sounded like he'd just dropped in from a Sean Connery sound-alike convention.

"Hundred bucks," Violet said.

Bren spoke low, husky. "I don't need the money, but I'll think of something in kind."

That made Violet blush. The tension prickling between the two could have charged every iPhone present. Playing with fire, this girl.

Oblivious to the mating ritual, Erik said, "Let's go in. I bet they have good canapés." Their goalie was obsessed with finding his next meal.

Cade held an elbow out for Violet and his other for Isobel. "Yes, I can handle you both, ladies."

Giggling like schoolgirls, they took the offered arms and walked into the ballroom, which was already jam-packed. No immediate sign of Vadim, however. While Isobel had mentioned it to him a couple of weeks ago, she hadn't brought it up since. But she wanted to see him, especially as she felt foolish for inserting her Clifford issues into her heart-to-heart with him about his father.

Everyone drifted toward the bar, but Isobel broke

away, needing to check her phone. Coach Lindhoff was due to call any day now with news of whether she'd made the team. The restrooms were as good a place as any for privacy, but her phone screen remained frustratingly blank.

On her way out, she stopped short at a surprising sight at the end of the corridor: Cade and Dante, engaged in what looked like a heated conversation.

Well, *engaged* wasn't quite right. Cade's usually easygoing expression was a mask of intensity as he leaned intimately close to Dante. The Rebels' GM was listening closely, not saying a word. Until something Cade uttered had him responding with a palm flat on Cade's chest.

The Texan jerked back clumsily, his back crashing against the wall. It shocked her. Isobel would never have thought him homophobic, but it was as if Dante's touch repulsed him.

Dante stood back, giving Cade space to leave, which he took like a bat out of hell. Alone, Dante did the oddest thing—he touched the wall where Cade's back had leaned, then curled his hand into a fist. On a deep breath, he raised his gaze and locked it with Isobel's. The flash of pain on his face faded, but not quickly enough. Didn't she feel quite the voyeur.

"Isobel."

"Oh, hey there." *Let's just pretend I didn't witness whatever the hell that was.* "Surprised to see you here," she said, moving forward.

"I'm up for anything that makes the organization

look good," he said with a smile. He really had the most gorgeous smile, even when forced. "And I hear you're being honored with an award."

The foundation wanted to give her a token for her efforts. All nonsense, really. "Oh, that."

"No need to underplay it. I know you work hard with those kids, just as I know you did a great job with Petrov. And I understand your skills are already in demand. I'll have to talk to Coach Calhoun and the rest of the staff, but I think it's safe to say you'll have a full-time position next season."

Isobel nodded, her throat tightening. Two of the Rebels' defensemen—Cade and Kazinksy—had asked her if she would work with them on their skating skills now that her methods had proven successful. A full-time coaching position; plan B achieved.

But plan A was still a possibility.

"Not worried we're bucking the status quo too much, Dante?"

"I think the Rebels are just living up to their name. Nothing succeeds like success. In the end, that's all anyone cares about." He frowned. "I thought you'd be happier."

"Still adjusting to the new world order."

Evidently distracted, he merely nodded. His phone went off in his hand. "Excuse me." He moved farther down the corridor to answer it.

She left him there, pondering how we always want what we cannot have. Dante appeared to have a crush—or something—on Cade, who as far as Isobel knew was about as het as they came. Nothing but heartbreak down that road.

Back in the ballroom, she did the rounds like a politician. Harper, wearing a strapless black and silver sheath, was doing the same on the other side, and they met in the middle.

"Ever get sick of pretending Dad was awesome?" Harper asked with a fake grin.

"Hey, if the name gets us butts in seats and extra green for the kids."

"Yeah, I know." Harper smiled, for real this time, and grasped Isobel's arms. "You look gorgeous, Iz. Absolutely stunning."

Isobel tamped down on the part of her psyche that had always craved her sister's approval. "Just doing my part for the Chase name."

"What do you think the old coot would say if he could see us now?"

Isobel had no idea. He had been a great player, a good coach, a bad husband, and a demanding father, but she would never claim to have understood him.

She hazarded a guess. "He'd say he knew we could do it all along."

Harper laughed. "He would! God, he was such a know-it-all asshole."

"*Minou*, you talkin' about me behind my back again?" Remy's lips grazed Harper's shoulder. Apparently he had a thing for her shoulders; odes had been composed, according to Harper.

"Well, I see Mac Farnum trying to catch my eye,"

Isobel said, and smiled her excuses as she went to meet the foundation head. Five minutes later, she had extracted herself from Mac's orbit—he'd been trying to persuade her to give his grandson personal coaching lessons—and was skirting the edge of the stage when she felt a tug on her arm. Foxy-fast, she was shanghaied and dragged behind a curtain.

Six feet five inches of built-for-pleasure Russian held her immobile.

"Vadim!"

He pressed two fingers to her lips. "Shush, Bella. Do you want to alert the world?"

She rolled her eyes. "You could have just walked up and said hello out in the open."

"Then I wouldn't have been able to do this." His mouth sought hers, all sweet hunger and sensual rawness. Her lips parted to give him access. The sweep of his tongue, a luxury she couldn't afford, was divine. She took it anyway because she'd missed him.

Lust. Not a good foundation. But it certainly filled the horny cracks.

"You look like an angel, Bella. A beautiful green angel."

She clamped her lips shut. Vadim's usually excellent command of the English language sometimes clashed with his absolute sincerity.

"What's so funny?"

"A beautiful green angel sounds like an environmental activist."

He winked. Winked! "We have done good things for the environment, you and I. Sharing showers."

She gave a solemn nod. "I accept this important role."

Smiling, he coasted his hands over her hips and molded them to her ass. "I wish you to do something for me. As I will be unable to spend any time with you this evening because when I'm next to you, my cock has a mind of its own, you will have to give me your panties."

She swallowed. "My panties?"

"Yes, your panties."

"You can't be close to me because of your raging erection, so I'm to give you my panties. Not seeing the logic here, Vad."

"This is why the USA is a failing superpower. You do not make the necessary connections."

Never get involved with a Russian. "Enlighten me."

"If your panties are in my pocket, I will know that you are suffering as much as I. Without that slip of fabric between your thighs, your senses will be heightened." Each word was a seductive thrust of temptation. "That sensitive little pussy of yours will feel naked. It will get wet. It will think about why and will know that I carry your panties around in my pocket."

Her head fell against his shoulder, her breathing quick and shallow. Oh, God, what was he thinking, saying all these wicked, delicious things?

He wasn't finished. "Perhaps I will finger them. Perhaps I will slip away to a quiet corner so I can bury my nose in them and smell you."

Jesus. "Okay, I get the connections."

His tongue traced the shell of her ear. "I'm not sure you do. Perhaps I will take myself in hand and wrap your panties around my cock while I jerk off. I will have to put my fist in my mouth to muffle the sound of your name on my lips."

Stop don't stop. "You'd better dry-clean those puppies before you give 'em back."

He laughed, a rasp of appreciation against her ear, then he gave the sensitive lobe a gentle nip. "Panties. Now, Bella."

Feeling heavy with sensation, she looked over her shoulder. All clear. "I need to hold your arm."

"Better you hold my shoulders." He fell to his knees, his hands on the backs of her calves. "I like to see you in dresses, Bella. You have beautiful legs." His hands trailed to the backs of her thighs, and she ransacked her mind, trying to remember what she was wearing.

Something old and gray?

Something new and sexy?

All would be revealed! He hooked a finger in the elastic and pulled. As the panties cleared her thighs, she glanced down. Thank the lingerie gods. A black silk bikini from Addison's collection.

They pooled at her ankles. She lifted a kitten-heeled foot, but he held it down. "Wait."

With his palms roving inside her thighs, he moved back up, up, up, until—oh, God—both thumbs stroked her.

She swooned.

"You are wet, Bella." He lifted his gaze to meet hers,

and everything she adored about him reflected back at her in those crystalline blues.

With eyes never leaving hers, he lifted her skirt. One inch. Two. *Total, wicked exposure.* His tongue gave one solitary swipe of pleasure over her dripping center. He knelt back on his haunches, his face in ecstasy.

Then he picked up the panties, stood, and put them in his pocket. One lascivious lick along his lower lip completed the torture.

"Are you okay?" he asked, as if what had happened had not just happened.

"No," she managed to croak out.

"Good."

He drew back the curtain and sent her out into the crowd.

For five thousand dollars a table, one would expect the food to be better. But then that was probably the point—spend as little on the food as possible so that all the funds could go to charity.

Before the meal, Vadim had mingled with the crowd, signing autographs and fending off women who said he would be their first choice during the bachelor auction later. He didn't care about the auction, but he would do it for Isobel. During this time, whenever their eyes met, he patted his coat pocket and watched her blush.

Damn, she was beautiful with that color infusing her creamy skin. The taste of her still coated his mouth, and it had taken a Herculean effort on his part to stop after one lick. Tonight they would find a hotel, because when you had relatives in town, it put an unbearable crimp in your sex life.

"Not gonna eat the chicken, Vaddy?" Erik, who had the appetite of a woolly mammoth, eyed Vadim's barely touched meal. Their goaltender had already eaten Cade's, not that the usually amiable Texan noticed or cared. He was in a strangely foul mood tonight, barely grunting when spoken to.

Vadim pushed his plate toward Erik. "It's all yours."

"Awesome!"

Bren was on his other side, a finger tracing the rim of his water glass, his expression contemplative.

"Okay, there, Captain?"

"Yeah. Just not a big fan of these kinds of events. Reminds me of my ex. She was big on parties and glitz."

"How are your girls?" Bren had two beautiful daughters who visited once a month from Atlanta for a few days. It was hard on him to be separated from them.

Bren's face brightened. "Amazing. Though my youngest doesn't really like her mom's new boyfriend. Says he's a Philistine."

"That's a big word. How old is your youngest?"

"Almost nine," he said proudly. "Smart as a whip, and she doesn't suffer fools gladly. My ex is shacking up with Drew Cassidy. You heard of him?"

The wide receiver for the Atlanta NFL team. "Your wife has a type, then."

"Ex-wife. And yeah, she does. But she likes a once-a-week athlete versus the NHL schedule. The girls want to live with me, but I'd have to find a nanny, and how is that any better than what they've got now?"

Some women were not cut out to be mothers. "A nanny might be an improvement."

Bren smiled knowingly. "Heard your mom's in town, along with your sister."

Vadim sought out Isobel, two tables over. "Yes, it's not the most ideal situation."

"It never is. So, you and Isobel, huh?"

"What?" His protective instincts surged. "She is my—" *Mine.* "—my coach."

The Scot rubbed his beard. "Sure she is."

Denial was on the tip of his tongue, but he was saved from having to do so when someone tapped the microphone. A white-haired man on the stage thanked them for their attendance and launched into a spiel about the charity.

"We've raised over $420,000 for Hockey for Everyone tonight, including one single donation of $100,000 from the Rebels' Vadim Petrov." The crowd erupted in appreciation while Erik elbowed him in the ribs.

"Good work, Vaddy!"

The rest of the table congratulated him, but when Vadim caught Bren's eye, he saw sly humor.

"Yeah, good work, Vaddy," the Scotsman said softly.

Unable to resist, Vadim looked over to Isobel, who

had an eyebrow raised and a smile on her face. This charity meant a lot to her, so of course he would help, especially as he had wealth beyond what he earned on the ice. One hundred thousand dollars was a drop in the bucket of his millions, but he didn't want to overdo it in case people would gossip. Which is why he had asked that his name not be mentioned.

In for a ruble . . . He stood to accept the applause and shouted out, "The rest of my teammates will match my donation." The players might be here to mingle and lend some star power, but there was no reason why they shouldn't also put their hands in their pockets. They could well afford it.

The room broke into louder applause, even his teammates, who shook their heads at his audaciousness in volunteering their hard-earned cash.

"I will pay out for any of you who are cheapskates," he said as he retook his seat.

"Before we start the fun with the bachelor auction," the man on the stage said, prompting several women near the bar to scream their appreciation, "we'd like to take a moment to honor one of Hockey for Everyone's founding members and an unstinting advocate for the cause of bringing hockey and sports to anyone who wants to play. First, let's give you a brief recap of her great career."

A video started up, beginning with footage of Isobel playing as a five-year-old, fearless even then while her father passed pucks to her. Her childhood and teen exploits on the ice were well documented, and the rest

Vadim knew because once he had met her, he'd followed every step of her professional life: the glory in NCAA, the silver medal in the Games, the one and only night fulfilling her dream as a hockey pro.

While everyone watched the screen, he watched her as the lights flickered over her face with each milestone. The winning goal against Russia in the semifinals in Sochi (the one time he had actually cheered *against* his country) right up until the first few minutes of the game in Buffalo.

He had stood in the stands that night, covered with a winter cap, seeking and embracing anonymity. It was her night, and he didn't want to take away from that.

Lightning fast, she feints left and whips by the Montreal defender, her skates on fire, the puck hers to command. She's already scored two goals and her team, the Buffalo Betties, is ahead by one. With four minutes left to the second period, another goal would place them in a commanding position. The first win in the new National Women's Hockey League will likely be hers.

The goaltender spreads, filling the crease, leaving no gaps, except Isobel sees a chink of light. Her hockey IQ is nothing short of phenomenal. She passes left to her winger, moves into position, and when the puck is back on her blade, snipers to the top shelf. A drive of beauty, it will win the game, though she won't be on the ice when the final buzzer sounds.

This was where the highlight reel ended, but Vadim's brain picked up the next frames of that fateful night two years ago. Each move, stride, and hit was stamped into his memory.

A minute after that beautiful goal, she's checked hard by a defender and falls to the unforgiving ice. Her helmet slips off— she's always liked to wear it loose—and an opposing player is unable to brake in time.

A skate slices through Isobel's skull like it's the softest butter.

Blood pools on the ice, and I know. I know this is not a typical rink injury. I know this will end her career.

Possibly her life.

The crowd shoots to its collective feet, everyone in a horrified hush as her teammates and game officials huddle around her.

Too long. She's been down too long.

I start out of my seat, pushing past the rubbernecking crowd, my mind racing as fast as my heart. If it's a minor injury, they will bring her through the tunnel, back to the locker rooms, but if it's as bad as I suspect, she will be in an ambulance before I can make it to the arena's back area . . .

"You all right, Petrov?"

Vadim took a moment to haul himself back to the present. Bren was eyeing him as if he'd been speaking in his sleep.

"*Ya ne znayu.*" I do not know.

Thankfully, this video recap ended before the worst moment of her life. But just like him, she was thinking about it. Stark paleness blanked her face as she headed up to the stage. He knew it was the one moment uppermost in her mind.

The moment she lost it all.

TWENTY-FOUR

Vadim shook hands with Lenny, the Rebels' HQ head of security.

"Sorry 'bout this, Mr. Petrov. I could have called Ms. Chase or Mr. Moretti, but I figured you might be the best person to handle it, seeing as how you're no stranger to night skates yourself."

"You did the right thing."

Lenny shuffled alongside Vadim as he headed toward the practice rink.

"I thought about shutting the lights out, force the issue, so to speak, but I didn't want her to have an accident. She wouldn't listen to me when I told her she should take it easy and come off the ice."

That sounded like Isobel. "How long?"

"Going on ninety minutes now."

Vadim mentally kicked himself. After the fundraiser, she had disappeared, not even telling Violet where she had gone. No answers to his texts, either.

That video.

He should have known when he couldn't find her

that she would come here. The rink was her cathedral, the ice her touchstone. It was where she would always return.

But ninety minutes? That was more than any set of legs, even those of a powerhouse like Isobel Chase, could endure.

"I will take care of it, Lenny. Thank you."

"All right, Mr. Petrov." Lenny turned and walked back to his post near the entrance.

Should Vadim go back and grab skates from the equipment room? Deciding against it, he continued to rinkside, the sound of ice being crisscrossed and shredded getting louder with each step.

His heart stuttered, stalled, and crashed at the sight before him.

Bella on the ice, the green fabric of that sexy dress flapping behind her. Her dark hair flew like the wind, her silhouette that of a Valkyrie as she corralled the puck and shot it into the net.

But even a Valkyrie needed armor. On her body, no pads. On her head, no helmet.

Fury reared up in his blood, chasing away his admiration. If she fell and struck her skull—that would not happen.

"Isobel!"

She spun on her blades to face him, a glare already daggered his way. Then she pivoted and skated back to the center, where she had lined up several pucks.

Fine. He would play her game.

Two minutes later, he was out on the ice. He'd left his

jacket and tie behind and rolled up his shirtsleeves. Skating in suit pants and a dress shirt felt odd, but maybe the moment deserved oddness. He would give her this.

And then he would put her over his knee and give her the spanking she deserved.

"Ready?" he asked, thrusting a helmet toward her. A foolish question. This woman was born ready. She was the daughter of greatness, the child of Clifford Chase's destiny.

"I don't need that."

"Then I will be forced to take it easy on you. No checks. Hockey for toddlers."

Growling, she grabbed the helmet and forced it over her head. He grasped the chin straps, absorbing her ire while he took care of securing her safety. As soon as it was tight, she shoved him in the chest.

"Don't spare me."

"Never."

It took him a few minutes to catch up, to warm to the rhythm of the ice. The rhythm of her. His clothes restricted his movement and he would not be surprised if his pants split right down the center on his first lunge. Perhaps that's why she was able to whip the puck away from him twice in a row.

"Come on, Russian, you're going easy on me." The words were a tease, the tone was disgust.

She floated the puck in front of him, inviting him to slap at it. Instead he circled so he hovered behind her, a predatory move.

"It is colder than I expected," he said against her ear.

"You've gotten soft since you moved to the NHL. What would your countrymen think of poor little Vadim who can't handle a little chill?"

"They would think I should find a woman to warm me."

She turned and passed the puck to him. "Try to score."

He moved until he was close enough to kiss her. The temptation was almost unbearable, but he resisted. "Try to stop me." Then he struck the puck so it hit the board behind the net and ricocheted back.

The next ten minutes were spent in a game of wits and hits. He was careful not to check too hard. She didn't give him the same consideration.

At the third slam of his body into the Plexi—and der'mo, he did not enjoy playing without padding—he dropped his stick and flipped their positions. Covering her body with his, he held her securely against the plastic.

Skating with her turned him on. Isobel had always excited him, but watching her talent as she danced rings around him, the balletic ice moves of a master—this made him feel alive. And with that life, that zest spiking his blood, he knew he was back to where he had started.

In love with Isobel Chase.

Had he ever not been in love with her? He could barely remember a time he did not want her. Did not need her. Did not adore her with every part of his body and soul.

"Why are you here, Bella?"

"On this earth?"

"Tell me."

Her eyes flamed behind her mask and he released the strap, pulling it off her head. He needed to see her properly. See her pain. He lifted her chin to look her in the eye.

"Lindhoff called. I didn't make Team USA."

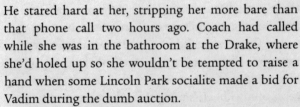

He stared hard at her, stripping her more bare than that phone call two hours ago. Coach had called while she was in the bathroom at the Drake, where she'd holed up so she wouldn't be tempted to raise a hand when some Lincoln Park socialite made a bid for Vadim during the dumb auction.

She shouldn't have answered the phone. She should have let it go to voice mail, so she would have one more night of hope.

"What did he say?" Vadim's tone was careful. Of course it was; he was dealing with a time bomb.

"What you said. What everyone has been saying. He was clear this wasn't an indictment of my talent." The words were choked out, dripping with bitter understanding of the position Lindhoff was in. "But he ran it by the lawyers, and they can't risk the liability. One minute winning gold, the next their center bleeding out on the ice. Think of the optics."

She dropped her stick, the clatter of it against the ice loud and final. It was over. She was done.

"Bella," he whispered, his voice soft with pity she neither needed nor wanted.

She pushed him away, but he crowded her back, all brute Russian strength. His power mocked her weakness. His health scorned her failure. Nothing was stopping him from reaching the pinnacle of his sport. Their sport.

She shouldn't begrudge him, but she did. Oh, how she did.

"And now you are here, unleashing your fury on these poor defenseless pucks." He gave a half grin at that, but she couldn't see the humor in it. Not yet.

His fingers tunneled into her hair, and he traced his warm lips along her jaw, her cheek, her hairline. Giving him permission, she turned her head slightly, anxious to get it over with. He smudged his thumb over the raised ridge of flesh, his eyes riveted to the path his thumb took.

"You have your trophy, Bella."

This scar? She made a noise between horror and sadness. "Thirty-seven minutes. That's what I got."

"Most men never accomplish in a lifetime what you did in those precious minutes." He cupped her jaw and held her in place while his lips moved over the physically healed wound. "You fought well, my angel."

"Did—did you see it? The game?" She shouldn't ask, but she had to know.

Sadness dimmed his eyes. "I saw it. Your goals were beautiful, your skating sublime. There was nothing you could not do on the ice."

Her chest constricted on hearing his compliments.

Was this what she wanted, fishing for praise just as she had with her father all those years ago? Yet Vadim's words chilled her—they were all past tense. She would never achieve those heights again.

She must have drawn back, for he pulled her close to him, his eyes ripping her heart open until it was butterflied and bleeding.

"I know that you are trying to find your place again, Bella. That since your injury, you're not sure where you fit in."

"Hockey was my life for so long, and I can't imagine it not being my—my everything. That's why this shot at the Games meant so much. Otherwise, all I've got is coaching and—it's hard, Vadim. It's hard trying to get respect, and I'm really not helping my case by fooling around with you."

"Fooling around? Is that what this is?"

"What would you call it?"

"It is what we are meant to do. We are who we are meant to be, and I want this with you."

It sounded like Russian doublespeak. She didn't understand it, but she knew it scared her. Was she trying to sabotage her coaching career by messing around with Vadim? But if she didn't have that, who was she?

Not a hockey player. Not a coach. With Vadim—if that's what he wanted, if she could stop being a jealous shrew about his star-bright career and the sexting hordes—she'd be a WAG. A player wife or girlfriend.

"I don't know who I am without hockey, Vadim."

And a WAG is not enough.

He circled her neck with his hand, his chest flush with hers, his heart beating hard against hers. "You are Bella. The girl who can do anything. The woman who drives me crazy. There is plenty for you to be." He kissed her, and after a soft press, she kissed harder, then pushed him away, scooping up her stick as she went. But not her helmet.

She didn't want to be the woman who drove him crazy. She didn't want to be defined in relation to a superstar, because as soon as that happened, she would slip away into the shadows as Vadim Petrov's woman. Surely she was more than that.

"Bella," he said, resignation in his voice. Tired of her drama, no doubt.

She raced to the end of the rink, sliding a loose puck into the empty net with ease, but her skate caught on the goal frame and she fell to the ice.

He was on her instantly, down on his knees.

"Isobel!"

"I'm okay," she whispered, but her tears contradicted her desperate assurance. That womanly weakness her father despised.

"This stops now. You have been on the ice for long enough." He stood and held out his hand.

She hesitated, but then she allowed herself to be pulled up. To be supported.

The notion made her ill.

Back in the locker room, he placed her on the bench and knelt before her to unlace her skates.

"We were like figure skaters out there," he murmured, evidently trying to make light of what had come before. "In our sparkling costumes."

She inhaled a deep breath, though her lungs seemed incapable of filling. "What would you do if you couldn't play hockey, Vad?"

He stopped unlacing and considered her question.

"I would take more naps and drink more tea."

He grinned at her, and she grinned back, suspecting she looked like a funhouse mirror version of herself. But *his* smile? It was like this rare outbreak of spring sun after a long, hard winter, and unfortunately it wasn't only her hormones that skipped in delight.

Bella, I am here. Wake up.

Yes, my love, you are.

She inhaled a sharp, cutting breath, barely able to cope with the shocking recognition.

She was in love with Vadim.

Oblivious to her distress, he kept on smiling, that devastating, soul-destroying grin. It was either cry her eyes out or punch his perfect jaw or—she bent down to taste him. To absorb his life force and beauty into her blood. His hands fell away from her skates and crawled up her legs, plotting his way to the heart of her.

Bastard.

His mouth on hers was the only thing keeping her grounded in this world, but she didn't want the security his strength would give her. She didn't want the love. She wanted the danger.

She couldn't have hockey, but tonight she could have him.

With a shaking finger, she traced his perfect cheek-bones, ran her thumb over the seam of his lips. She'd fallen for him in a way that was a million times worse than all those years ago. Then, her future was mapped out, and no man—not even the destined-for-greatness Vadim Petrov—would stand in her way. Now her future was uncertain, and this man on his knees before her was either her port in the storm or the rocks she would happily dash herself against.

She loved him.

She hated herself for it.

And in this sublime moment of realization, something else struck her. "My ass is cold."

He blinked. "Your ass?"

"You took my panties, remember?"

"You were skating for over an hour with no panties?"

She pushed him back and slipped from the bench to straddle him.

"Either you give them back or you figure out another way to warm my ass."

"I refuse to return what belongs to me. I have many dirty fantasies designed around them." He pushed his hands up her thighs to cup her chilly rear. "I shall take care of this problem of yours if you take care of this problem of mine." He slid her flush over his problem.

She moaned softly on coming into contact with his erection, pushing against her slick softness through his pants. "Have you ever fucked with skates on, Russian?"

"It has never seemed wise."

"Let's live dangerously, shall we?"

Never removing her eyes from him, she unzipped him slowly—a tough job given how much resistance his dick was putting up. With determined hands and his help, she pulled his boxers down to free him.

She tilted her head, left, then right, taking him in like a centerfold. "You're so beautiful, Vadim. So perfect."

"Only when I am inside you. Don't leave me waiting, Bella. I am cold, too." He lifted her, spreading her ass cheeks and parting her with his thumbs. She shivered wonderfully as he stroked through her wetness.

"Condom," she murmured. Her hand patted his pocket and he obliged with his wallet and the rubber.

"Before the next time, we will discuss this," he said. "Skin on skin. I want that."

It might happen, if she could survive this moment with her sanity intact.

"Next time," she said as she slipped her body over his like a glove.

In keeping with the location, her mood, the proximity to dangerous weapons on their feet, it should have been frenzied and urgent. So why did it feel like a dream? Possibly because she was trying to hold on to the essence of herself.

She closed her eyes against the intensity waving off him, but he was having none of that. Beneath her, he shifted his body up and closer. His hand palmed her neck.

"Do not hide from me, Bella," he whispered, his breath a warm wisp of entreaty.

Her eyes fluttered open to find him smiling at her. That damn smile. The hand at her nape shifted, and his thumb swiped at her cheek, coming away damp.

Oh, God, she was crying. During sex!

She jerked back from him, intending to separate altogether. He already had her heart. Anything more was far too selfish of him.

Still, the tears fell. He sopped them up with his thumb and put that thumb in his mouth, just like that night in New York when he had tasted her pleasure. Now he got to taste her pain.

"Yes, my beautiful girl. I see all of you now."

He pushed her dress—this stupid dress she'd worn because she wanted to look pretty for him—up above her waist.

"Take everything you need from me, Bella."

Dreams abandoned, she thudded to the reality of now. The pain, the pleasure, Vadim. Only and always. This she could control, and so she moved up and down, sliding along that hard length, marveling at his power to hold himself and fuck up into her with long, liquid pulls. They found a rhythm that rhymed, a tempo that teased, a pleasure that knew no beginning or end.

They found each other—but a part of her knew she was forever lost.

TWENTY-FIVE

Vadim let himself in quietly, not wishing to do anything that would wake Victoria. Mia had returned to New York two days ago, where an aunt Vadim had never met would stay with her. She'd already missed too much school, and with Alexei on the mend, Vadim would not have to worry about spending more time than necessary with her mother.

But Alexei couldn't be here twenty-four hours a day, so Vadim had stopped in to ensure that Victoria didn't need anything. Merely the actions of a good host. Then he would go see his woman.

On the ice, Vadim's life was perfect. The Rebels were close to the play-offs, needing only one win out of their next three to guarantee a wild card spot. Two wins would place them in the top three in the division. Tonight it had been four-two against Nashville at home, and two of those goals belonged to Vadim.

Off the ice, his life was not so rosy. In the week since Isobel had heard the news of her decimated dreams, she was not rebounding with the resilience he had expected. Her smiles were beautiful, but sad. Her eyes deep pools, but dull with her pain. Tonight he would see her, comfort her with his body. Tonight he would tell her he loved her.

Knowing the landscape of his rented house well, he didn't bother to turn on the lights, so he was surprised to encounter an obstacle in his path. *What the—?*

He switched on a lamp. The obstacle in question was a leg.

And it belonged to Alexei, who sat at one end of the sofa, his face fire engine red, his shirt unbuttoned halfway down his chest and revealing a thick pelt. At the far end of the sofa sat Victoria, looking equally flushed, but thankfully still dressed.

Why had he not seen this coming—and how could he go about unseeing it?

"I thought you were sick," Vadim murmured to both of them.

"I'm feeling much better," Victoria said, her embarrassed tone pronouncing her outrageous guilt. With Alexei! "Actually, I've booked a flight for tomorrow."

"Good."

She winced, and he rejoiced in hurting her. But she was brazen now that she had slid another knife between his ribs and cracked him open again. "You played so well tonight. Congratulations."

"I'm surprised you had time to watch!"

"Do not speak to her like that."

Vadim stared at Alexei. His employee. His friend. His . . . he did not know anymore.

"She is your mother and deserves your respect."

His mother placed a hand of restraint on Alexei's arm. "Let him be angry."

He did not need her permission. The anger inside him was his right, and it was time she realized this.

"He doesn't know how hard it was for you, Vika," Alexei said.

Vika? Since when did Alexei call his mother by such an affectionate nickname? All his pent-up emotion found release now that Mia wasn't here to curb it.

"How hard it was? My father wasn't an easy man, but what woman abandons her child?" He rounded on his mother. "I imagine the only reason you took Mia is because she was physically tethered to your body!"

Her eyes grew wet, but he refused to buy it. Where were the tears when this thief of his childhood left in the dead of night?

"I—I'll be back in a moment."

When she left, Alexei stood, closed the gap between them, and punched Vadim square in the jaw.

Chyort voz'mi! The old man still had fire in his fist.

He switched to Russian. "You are acting like a brat. You need to hear her out."

"Hear her lies. Hear how she left me alone."

"You weren't alone. I was there."

Vadim froze. "You were there because my father ordered it. Because your family owed me service."

Alexei sneered. "Really? That may be how it started out, but I've had opportunities to move on. You think I want to stay here and clean up after a sniveling child?"

"I pay you enough, don't I? Why stay if you hate it?"

"You are so like your mother." Something like a smile hooked his mouth. "Such drama. That is your American side. She was always so—" He stopped talking, his memories taking him somewhere—or some *when*—else.

Vadim's heart pounded. This could not be happening. The old fool had been bewitched. "You were in love with her."

"Yes."

"And now?"

His lips curved. "I'm too old to be in love."

Not too old to indulge your lusts, though. With my mother.

"You watched over me." Recognition dawned, the knowledge filling him with horror and shame. "For her."

"I was loyal to your father."

"That's not an answer."

Alexei skewered him with a look. "It is the only answer I will give you."

He needed more. Anything. The whole sorry tale. "If you know so much about it, why don't you explain why she left me behind?"

"Because I was a coward." Vadim turned to his mother, who had just spoken those words. In English, too, because Vadim had made his plea in the language she would understand best. Baited the trap.

This was what he wanted to hear. Victoria admitting her weakness. Victoria down on her knees. Victoria failing.

But even as those thoughts swirled, seeking vindication, he couldn't grasp at them. They slipped away like waking dreams, impossible to grab hold of in the face of her obvious distress.

"Alexei, I need to speak to my mother alone."

Alexei looked at his mother, his expression filled with love. Victoria nodded, her power over him undeniable. His so-called right-hand man shot one last look of warning at Vadim and left the room.

"Seems he's no longer my man, not while you're here. Perhaps he never has been."

"He's always been protective. Of us both."

"The times he goes away, weekends here and there—is he seeing you?"

Victoria sat, her hands in her lap. "Would you think of that as a betrayal?"

"His life is his own." Though he never acted like it. Vadim felt foolish for knowing so little about Alexei, and not a little jealous that the man knew how to love Victoria with such generosity.

What else didn't Vadim know? What else had he chosen to block out?

He sat on the same sofa, a few feet away from her. There was conciliation in it, and the look on her face said she understood. It was the best he could do at the moment.

"I remember the night you left," he said. He knew this was her tale to tell, but it was his story as well. He needed to expunge it. Confront the pain as that terrified boy remembered it. "There was a suitcase at the bottom of the stairs, and you were running around, frantic about something. You looked so worried, and that made me worried."

"I was searching for your passport. Your father was on an overnight trip to Moscow, and I knew it was my best chance. I had the tickets for both of us—me and my little ice warrior. I'd put your passport in a drawer under some papers, but it wasn't there. I'd been planning for three months and now this!" She threw her hands up in the air, as if this horror was happening now.

"Papa came home." It filtered back to him in fragments. Doors slamming. Adults shouting. Soul-wrecking tears.

"He had found out. He had spies everywhere and somehow he found out. He walked in the door and held up your passport and said, 'Looking for this?' and I knew I was done. I'd already asked for a divorce, and he'd said if I wanted it, I would never see you again."

"So you left anyway?" Gave up just like that.

"No. Your father had one of the staff take you to another room. I told him I'd stay, that we could forget about what had happened, but he refused. He couldn't trust I wouldn't try to take you away again. I'd shown my hand, you see. He picked up my suitcase and gave it to one of his goons. Then he ordered me into the car.

"I tried to stand my ground. Dig in my heels, literally. I wouldn't leave, but he dragged me into the car and drove me to the airport. I didn't even get to say good-bye to you, my—my—" She pressed a hand to her breastbone. "But I vowed to get back to you. Once in New York, I hired a lawyer, who said I had a good case for visitation. But your father had a lot of power and influence. The fight would be a long slog, but it would be worth it if I could get to see you sometimes."

Recognition clobbered him. "Then you found out you were pregnant."

She nodded, every hurt she'd ever endured playing on her face. "There was no way I could fight him, and even if he had given me visitation, he would never have let you out of the country. Not after I'd tried to take you. I would have put up with that if I could have seen you even twice a year—"

"But he would have taken Mia. You—" He couldn't finish it. She chose her unborn child over the son she left behind.

"Vadim, I'm so sorry. If I thought your father would be reasonable I would have come to some arrangement. But if I had visited you, I would have lost you both. I could never be a mother to either of you. Not properly."

"But you would be the best mother you could be for Mia." The sharp lance of her initial confession twisted slightly, as if to let the blood around the wound flow more easily. He needed to shore it up. Choke it off.

He buried his head in his hands. Was knowing better or worse?

A soft hand on the back of his neck soothed. Mothered.

"A part of me died the day I left, Vadim. The rest

of me the day I realized I couldn't see you again. Not until he was gone for good or Mia was eighteen.

"He never hit me. He never raised a hand. But he was a cold man, Vadim. A cruel man. My parents warned me not to be taken in, but I fell in love. I thought I could soften him after marriage, but it was a mistake to think he could change. Men don't change."

Even now, she insulted her son, but he couldn't blame her. Inside he was an immutable block of ice, incapable of seeing beyond the worldview crafted by his father. *It is right or wrong. It is black or white. It is love or despair.*

"I cannot do this now," he said. Not without Isobel. She would tell him how to act. She would coach him to the correct response.

Isobel would know what to do.

TWENTY-SIX

Isobel couldn't sleep.

Too much plagued her: the play-offs, the tryouts, her future.

Vadim. He was worried about her since the news of her failure to make Team USA. He wanted her to snap out of it, but it would take time to wrangle her self-confidence and make it her bitch again. And with this slip in her assurance, all those niggling doubts about her worth returned.

Like Vadim, confidence in one arena of her life had a direct impact on the rest. Injured and not playing, she'd lost what little mojo she had around men. But these past six weeks with him had boosted her up: coaching him back to his winning ways, feeling useful for the first time since her injury, Vadim's attraction to her—all combined to create a heady cocktail of "Yes, you can!"

Now her confidence was at dirt-low levels, and relying on Vadim to buoy her up would be a mistake. He would tire of her soon. Of that she had no doubt.

Her phone buzzed with a call from someone she'd

been avoiding. She hadn't spoken to Jen since Plymouth, and the last thing she wanted to hear was her friend's pity.

But things were looking up, weren't they? She tried to force cheer into her body, so it would be heard in her voice. A coaching gig with the Rebels, a spanking-new career in the pros! Plan B was better than no plan at all.

Answering, she pressed the phone to her ear. "Hey, Jenny-Benny!"

"Congrats, Iz! Great game tonight. Your boy was on fire."

She covered her mouth to hide her smile. *You're heading for a crash.* "He's not my boy."

"Well, *he* seems to think he is."

She could feel the stupid smile slip from her face. "What does that mean?"

Jen coughed slightly. "Maybe I shouldn't tell you this."

"Tell me what?"

Another throat clearing. This was getting ridiculous. "Jen?"

Finally, her friend spoke, and Isobel listened with a sinking heart while the last shreds of her strength shattered into dust.

She opened the front door of Chase Manor and let him envelop her. But her body refused to respond, her arms dead weight at her sides.

"What is it?" he whispered against her temple, and

when she didn't speak—when she couldn't because her anger choked off her words—he drew back, his beautiful sonofabitch face crumpled in confusion. "Bella, are you all right?"

"No, I'm not."

He moved forward. She stepped back.

Hurt came over him briefly.

"You killed it," she whispered, each word torn and raw. "You killed my dream."

He inhaled a breath, and in it she heard his relief. He was glad to have it out in the open. Maybe it had been eating him up inside.

He expected her anger, then he expected her forgiveness.

According to Jen, Vadim had called Coach Lindhoff and threatened to go to the media if Isobel was chosen. He would tell everyone that Team USA didn't take concussions and player injuries seriously. That they'd do anything to win, even risk killing a player in their desperation to win gold.

He had known all along. That night at the practice rink a week ago when she had gone to mourn, he had come onto the ice with her. Skated with her. Made love to her.

All this time the reason she would never play for her country again—for *herself* again—was because of him.

"Yes, I called him," Vadim said, his mouth hard with self-righteousness. "Lindhoff is using you for his own glory. He does not care if you live or die. He cares only for the gold."

"*I* care only for the gold!" she spat out. "You had no right to do that. This is my career—"

"This is your life, Bella," he boomed. "There's a reason you retired from play after your injury. The doctors told you of the dangers, and you were willing to heed them at the time. But then your father died. You were lost, unmoored, not yourself. I know how this feels and I know you think you have failed him by not getting back to competitive ice, but that is no reason to risk everything. You are incapable of seeing this, so it must be shown to you. For your own good."

For her own good. Where had she heard that before? Oh right, the mantra of the late, great Clifford Chase.

"You condescending prick! I'm a grown woman, Vadim. I make my own decisions, and that was my decision."

He held her face with both hands, all drama because everything he did had to be drenched in it. "I have waited my entire life to love you and I refuse to let your stubbornness take you away from me."

Her heart beat faster—or faster than before—at his mention of love. But love didn't sneak around crushing dreams because it knew best. Love didn't get to sugarcoat this turd.

She jerked away. "That's not good enough. You can't throw out the love card and use it to excuse this."

"I can and I will. That night in Buffalo, you nearly died. So don't tell me that my love for you isn't big enough to excuse my behavior. My will to protect you will always be bigger than anything you can throw at me."

A tiny kernel in her brain saw his viewpoint, even if he couldn't see hers. He wouldn't back down, because Vadim Petrov always knew best. How to recover his skills. How to handle his mother. How to deal with the woman he supposedly loved.

"Isobel, tomorrow is not promised, but there are things we can do to make it more likely. For you to go onto the ice, play hard, risk the life that means so much to me . . . these are not on the list of those things."

Always back to him. "So you're not sorry?"

He set his chin, all Slavic imperiousness. "Nyet."

Having reached this impasse, they stood staring at each other in a frigid face-off. Pound for pound, she had always been a better player than him, but the time for games was over. This was her life, her future, and he had damned it with one phone call.

"Then what comes next, Vadim? You've made this decision for me. What's next for Isobel Chase?"

She sounded so forlorn—she was referring to herself in the third person, for fuck's sake—and she hated it. She hated *him*. Yet she wanted this man she hated to soothe her and tell her it would be okay. Then one night while he was sleeping, she would lodge a puck in a very uncomfortable place.

Vadim, the man with all the answers, now outlined his plan for Isobel's life. "You will be a coach. You have done well with me and other players want to work with you. Moretti will hire you. He will do this when I tell him how good you are."

Maybe he was behind Moretti's offer. "So you're going to fix it. Again. I skate by the grace of Vadim Petrov's favor."

His brow lined in recognition of that little dose of sarcasm. "You will have me stand back and let you put yourself—put *us*—in jeopardy?" He stalked her until she was back against the banister in the marble-walled foyer, making his intent clear. "It has been a circuitous route, but we are here now. Together, the way it's supposed to be."

"You've got it all worked out, don't you? I'm exactly where you want me. Fawning over the great Petrov, second fiddle to his career. Working to ensure *you're* the center of the hockey universe."

He placed hands on either side of her, gripping the handrail. "I know you are angry, Isobel. In recognition of this, I will not rise to your bait. In time, you will realize that this is for the best."

The best? Her skates yanked from under her by the man who has everything? The god who can have anyone? Was she supposed to feel blessed that he had chosen her to love above all others? Because it didn't feel like a blessing. It felt like a leash, on which she was forced to stay two steps behind. Vadim was the sun, and she was a pale moon, whipped by forces beyond her control.

"I want to live my life on my terms, not yours."

"There are always checks on our lives. Years ago, I

had mine, but I made it out. I made it here. You will adjust in time."

"And meanwhile I hang around with the other WAGs following the career of my man?"

He smirked in victory at how she had referred to him. *My man.* Apparently the dumbass Russian's sarcasm meter was broken.

"Good, this is what we will talk about. Real things, our future." He cupped her jaw, his touch so tender after he'd bruised her beyond belief. "So you want to be a W or a G?"

She jerked out of his grasp. "Remember how my dad pushed me, how he blackballed you in the NHL because he was worried I'd throw my career over for a boy?"

"And he was wrong. You would never have done that." He stared, recognition arriving a second later. "I'm not asking you to do that."

"Yes, you are. You're asking me to hang tight at home while you hit the road and get hit on in return."

"You do not trust me? There is no one else. There has been no one else since I returned to Chicago."

"Not even Marceline with her tittie tat? Yeah, I saw that text, Vadim."

He didn't have the decency to look cornered or guilty. "That is history, and sometimes women from my past will contact me. You know there is only you." He said it so simply that she never doubted it for a second.

She trusted he wouldn't stray—at least not immediately—but there were other ways trust could be frayed.

Broken. And by going behind her back, he had shown what loving Vadim would be like. His way or none at all.

Isobel a WAG? It was ridiculous.

Yet she was tired. So tired. Staying still wasn't in her nature, but maybe taking a break . . . No. Once she did that, it would be over. Once she submitted to Vadim's dominance and his definition of love, she would be finished. Subsumed.

He held her by the shoulders. "Have I ever treated you as second best? Have I ever told you that your career was secondary to mine? I know what hockey means to you, but you cannot use this need to prove yourself worthy to throw away our chance together, Isobel. We're not kids anymore. Your father wanted you to be independent, not to rely on anyone, to be second to no man. And perhaps he meant that you should grab life by the balls, but no father would want his daughter to put her life in danger. No father would want his daughter to slap love in the face."

Then he didn't know Cliff.

"I can't do this. I see you on the ice, and my body rages with envy. I want your career, your skills, your resilience after injury. Even if I can get past what you've done—and that's a big if—I'm going to end up resenting you because you have everything I don't have."

His look was all pity. "Isobel, that's crazy."

Yes, it was. Since her injury, she had been grieving for her lost career like she'd miscarried a child. Seeing Vadim on the ice—this man she loved—was like watching him nurse the child that should have belonged to her. Deep down, she knew this made no sense. It wasn't as if he had stolen it from her or only one of them could have it. But why did it feel like it? And her bitterness at losing this thing that had defined her for so long would end up destroying them both.

"You took away my last chance, Vadim. I know you think it was for my own good, but all my life I've had people telling me that." *Train harder. Study more. No boys. Skate, skate, skate.* There had to be something to show for it. There had to be.

Dumb tears were falling now. "This was my decision to make, and you ripped it away from me."

"Bella." Two sad little syllables.

She pushed at his chest, absorbing the beat of his big heart, loving and hating the owner. "Go. Please."

He looked torn, but she checked him again, using the last vestiges of strength in her failure of a body until he stood outside the threshold.

Anger glittered in his shockingly blue eyes. "I will not watch you die on the ice."

"Instead you'd watch me shrivel to nothing off it."

Then she shut the door, knowing her heart lay on the other side.

And as she sank to the floor, one thought fought its way out of the tangle of all the others: eventually she'd rise above these setbacks, both her crushed ambitions and her ambitious crush.

It's what her father would have expected.

TWENTY-SEVEN

Stevie Nicks's "Gold Dust Woman" increased in volume as Isobel approached the cottage on the Chase Manor estate where Violet had lain her Fedora for the last seven months. Vi's love of the Fleetwood Mac front woman was a tad obsessive, and knowing that she probably couldn't hear the knock, Isobel walked right in.

On Dante Moretti, lounging against the kitchen counter and looking very much at home.

"Oh, hi," Isobel said.

"Morning, Isobel." Unfazed by her arrival, Dante sipped his coffee from a mug bearing Lionel Richie's face and the slogan "Hello. Is it tea you're looking for?"

At a loss for how to proceed, Isobel was immensely grateful when the music stopped and Violet walked in, wearing overalls and a purple T-shirt that matched the streaks in her hair.

"Hey." Violet looked at Isobel.

Isobel looked at Dante.

Dante looked . . . bored.

So, they were all caught up.

Dante placed the mug down in the sink. "Any idea where Petrov is, Isobel?"

"What do you mean 'where Petrov is'?"

"He took a personal day. After last night's loss, we are now in the unenviable position of needing to win the day after tomorrow. Against Philly, the Eastern Conference leader. The last game of the season, and perhaps of all our fucking careers, and your charge decides he needs to go find himself and practice is optional."

That was not good. Vadim played better when he was happy, and last night he had not played well. In the week since their big fight, the Rebels had blown two chances to earn a top three in the division, leaving it all to ride on the final game. Breaking up with the player you're banging *before* you make the play-offs should probably not go in the coach's manual.

But she wasn't his keeper. He was a grown man, and if he felt it was perfectly legitimate to make decisions about her career, then he could sure as hell make decisions about his own.

She folded her arms, recalcitrant. "He's going through some stuff. Family stuff."

This earned her Moretti's squint. "Why do I get the impression there's something you're not telling me?"

"It's none of your business, Dante."

"None of my business? This team is my business! Let me guess. Just another episode in the Chase Family Telenovela."

"And pray tell, Dante, why are *you* here?" Isobel snapped. "Getting acquisitions advice from Violet?"

Violet coughed out a laugh, but then assumed a guilty expression when she saw Isobel glaring in her direction.

"Violet, thanks for the coffee," Dante said, and then he left the building with his three-piece suit and his hot-assed scowl.

"What the hell was he doing here at eight in the morning?" Isobel asked.

"He's helping me with Italian character work. For my improv class." Violet headed to the counter. "Is this a wine conversation?"

Isobel took a seat at the scratched farmhouse table, marred by splotches of blue and red paint that looked recent. Painting, improv classes, wine for breakfast—Violet definitely led a more fulfilling life than the rest of them. "It's a two-bottle conversation, but I have to drive to Rebels HQ to work with Burnett, so I'll stick with coffee."

While Violet poured, she asked, "So, where is Petrov, exactly?"

"I've no idea. If he's not answering his phone, then he doesn't want to talk to anyone."

"And . . ."

Wasn't this why she'd trekked two hundred feet from the big house? "We broke up. Parted ways. Whatever you want to call it. I found out something, something he did."

"Freakin' hockey players. He cheated on you?"

"No. Not that I know of. It's worse."

Violet placed two mugs of coffee on the table and took a seat. "You're on the air, caller."

She blew out a breath. "So, I tried out for Team USA and I would have made it except Vadim sabotaged it."

"*What?*"

She didn't have far to reach for the indignation still simmering below the surface, so she let it fuel her explanation of what Vadim had done. Once unburdened, she felt supremely vindicated in her decision to kick the manipulative bastard to the curb.

Except Violet had this weird look on her face. Also weird? She had remained uncharacteristically quiet.

Feeling edgy, Isobel plowed onward. "And then he had the nerve to tell me that he did it because he loved me. I mean, who does that? Total dick move, right?" *Right?*

Violet pursed her lips. Twitched her nose. She opened her mouth to say something. Closed it again.

After two more false starts, she finally spoke in a low voice, like she was summoning it from a deep, dark place. "Are you *seriously* telling me that you were going to play hockey again—*real hockey* with checks and knocks and all that shit—even after the doctors told you one bad hit or fall and it might be kaput, *bye-bye, Isobel?*"

Isobel squirmed in her seat. "Doctors always err on the side of caution. That's their job. But my job is to skate. I know what I'm capable of, what my body can handle."

Athletes are consummate liars.

Women in love often are, too.

"Oh really?" Exasperated, Violet waved at an empty

chair at the table. "What does Harper think? How does she feel about you lacing up your skates so you can go off and—and—and—" She pointed to some far-off point. An imaginary ice rink of doom, Isobel supposed. "And *die*?"

There was a reason Isobel hadn't told anyone but Vadim, and it wasn't only because she didn't want to jinx it.

"Stop being so dramatic. I haven't told her and I'm not going to because it's not happening now anyway. I'm done, no more pro hockey for me!"

Flustered, Isobel shot up, then sank to her chair again. She needed to explain it better. Violet had gone through her own rotten year with her breast cancer and had embraced her second chance with more zest than a bowl of lemons. Surely she would understand.

"You don't know what it's like to lose the thing that defines you, Vi. This has been everything to me since I was yea high. Dad would take me out and practically fling me across the rink. On the ice I danced. I was free. This is what I was supposed to do. It's what Dad wanted, and now . . ." She knuckled her eyes. Some of her happiest memories were of Clifford teaching her to skate. "I've let him down. I've let the old bastard down."

Her heart shriveled into a tiny lump, coal-like and blackened, incapable of sustaining life and love and happiness.

Violet was still scowling. She didn't get it, because she had never cared for hockey. The only person who understood was the same person who snatched it away from her—for her own good. Turdweasel!

"First, Harper almost fucks her life up trying to impress a dead man, and now you're doing the same," Violet said. "Jesus H. Christ on a bike, Clifford was an asshole. He screwed around, left his baby mamas high and dry, and then thought he could twist you all up in knots from the grave with his legal shenanigans. And I bought into it. I said I'd hang with you for the season and not take the cut I had coming in the will until later, so your Rebels dreams wouldn't die. But I didn't sign on for this crap."

Isobel opened her mouth to protest but shut it when Violet made a *zip-it* gesture with her hand. "And now you're using this thing the Russian did for you because he loves you as an excuse to push him away. It's like you desperately want to please old Cliffie-boy, yet you're terrified that any guy you meet will be like him."

That made no sense, except she guessed it did. "Well, you have to admit the Russian is out of my league."

"Yes, he is! He has a brain and you don't. The man doesn't want you to die playing a stupid game with sticks and a ball—and yes, I know it's called a puck but I'm making a point. He doesn't want you to end your days getting your head bashed in. I can't believe your selfishness. Sounds like Vadim is better off without you."

This was outrageous. Isobel was the one suffering through a breakup and mourning the death of her career, and Violet was acting like this was a crime against *her*. Why the hell did she care how Isobel lived her life? If she ended up on a stretcher or in a coffin, it'd be no skin off Violet's nose. They hardly knew each other.

Oh.

Shit.

"Violet, I—"

"Look, I've got stuff to do." Violet jerked upright and put her mug of coffee in the sink beside Dante's. She hadn't even taken a sip. In profile, it looked like she was—oh, hell, she was crying.

Isobel stood again, even more discombobulated than she had been ten minutes ago when she walked in and saw Dante in her sister's kitchen.

"I'm sorry," Isobel whispered. "I didn't mean to upset you." *I didn't think I could.*

"Doesn't matter. After we lose this dumb game the day after tomorrow, it'll all be over anyway. You can go skate yourself to death, and I won't be around to see it."

She stomped out of the room, leaving Isobel floundering.

Vadim stepped off the elevator in the high-rise building in Park Slope, Brooklyn, and looked left, then right. His mother stood at the doorway to the apartment where she lived with Mia, a crimp at the center of her forehead so deep it was visible from twenty feet out. He headed down the corridor to meet her.

"Mia's not here," she said quickly. "She's at practice."

He could fib and say that he had not known this, but the time for lies was over. Isobel had said he needed to see this from his mother's point of view. His woman might despise him, but her advice about his family had always been sound.

"I knew Mia was out. I am here for you."

Her blue eyes flew wide. Vadim had always assumed he had his father's eyes, but he saw the ring of fire in hers now. Just like Vadim's, a signifier of deep emotion. His father had never been an emotional man.

"Come in." She wore a blue silk blouse and a well-cut black skirt. Not expensive, but smart and professional.

"You are just home from work?" he asked as he stepped into the foyer, though *foyer* was too generous. Mia had told him it was a small two-bedroom that, like all New York real estate, cost a fortune. He placed his overnight bag near the coat closet while Gordie Howe sniffed it, and then him. Ridiculous creature.

"About an hour ago. I was just about to open a bottle of wine. Would you like a glass?"

"I am not drinking alcohol this week. We have one more game, and I don't want to jinx it." They had lost their game in Denver, the one that would have been their cushion. Now there was only one shot left in Chicago against the Eastern Conference leaders, Philadelphia.

He should not be here. He should be home getting ready. But he could not be where *she* was, not without falling to his knees before her and apologizing. He refused to say he was sorry for saving her life!

"Tea?"

He nodded. She left the room, and he found his gaze avidly drinking in everything before she returned and made more of his curiosity than was warranted. Clearly this was a lived-in place, a weathered and well-loved home. Interesting art graced the walls, and photos covered every flat surface. Most of them were of Mia, or of mother and daughter.

His breath hitched.

Not all of them.

He picked up a gilt-edged frame with hands that would lose the Rebels the last game of the season if he let them tremble like this. Taken when he was nine years old, it showed him wearing hockey gear and carrying a trophy that was almost as big as he. His first big win.

Had she hidden it away all these years while she kept his identity a secret from Mia? Did she occasionally remove it from its storage place, unwrap its protective wrapper, and pore over it with a desperate longing?

He suspected she had. He suspected this separation had been as hard on her as it had been on him.

"Do you remember when you wanted to give up hockey?" He heard her voice behind him.

A stress laugh spilled from his mouth. "I was too small. And Papa said it would never work out for me. I was always getting checked and pounded. I loved hockey but I hated competitions."

She smiled. "And I told you that if you couldn't be the biggest, you would be the quickest. Buzz around the ice like a pchyolka."

Little bee. That is what she called him. But after she left, he had an unexpected growth spurt, his muscles came in, and he no longer needed his quickness. His power came from brute strength. His speed never left, but he did not rely on it.

He forgot what had made him so suited for hockey in the first place. He forgot a lot of things.

"I've made a mistake. Screwed up with Isobel. I thought what I did was for the best, but she doesn't see it that way." He noticed his mother's wry arch of her eyebrow. "Yes, tell me, Mama, how we men know nothing about our women."

"Oh!" Tears welled in her eyes. What had he done now?

Ah. *Mama*. He had called her Mama.

She sniffed and knuckled the corners of her eyes.

He cupped her shoulder. "Don't cry. I won't call you Mama again."

That only made it worse, though it was hard to tell if she was laughing or crying.

She swiped at her cheeks. "I'm such a blubberer. Let me see to the tea, and then you can tell me about Isobel and how you messed up."

An hour later, the front door opened and Mia called out, "Whose bag is this?" She stopped, mouth agape, on seeing Vadim on the sofa.

"Don't be so surprised, sestrichka. I said I would visit."

"But . . ." She looked at her mother, then back at Vadim, who was sitting with shoes off, legs stretched out on a footstool, and Gordie Howe in his lap. Yes, he had made himself quite at home while he explained what had happened with Isobel. His mother had listened, not judging. Isobel would need time to come around, she advised. He had threatened her independence, and now she was figuring out how to align this with her feelings for him. Vika had no doubt that Isobel was crazy about him—she knew it from the moment she saw their dinner table teasing of each other in Chicago.

Only a mother could be so sure that her son was loved despite all evidence to the contrary.

He stood and enveloped his sister in his arms, while Gordie Howe yapped around excitedly. "How was practice?"

"Uh, good. What are you doing here?"

"I cannot come to see my family?"

"Sure you can, bro." She thumped him on the shoulder, her eyes soft and wet. "I just didn't expect you. Are you staying the night? You can have my room!"

"That would not be very brotherly of me. I have made a reservation at a hotel nearby. I will come back for breakfast." He turned to his mother. "If that is okay."

"Of course it is." Vika looked as teary-eyed as Mia—well, that would increase tenfold with his next move. He had forgotten all about it until now.

"I have something for you. Wait one moment." He went to his overnight bag and pulled out a package.

"For me?" Mia said.

"No. This is for our mother."

With shaking fingers, Victoria opened the boxed gift and flipped the cardboard lid. Peeling back the tissue paper, she yelped in surprise.

"Vadim, it's beautiful!" She lifted it out of the box: a samovar used to make tea in the Russian tradition. Made of polished brass, this one was less ornamental than many, more functional. Watching her face transform with emotion was still too painful, so instead he fixed on her blurred reflection in the burnished metal.

He cleared his throat. "Do you already have one?"

"I do, but it isn't as beautiful as this. It's on its last legs, actually." She stood and threw her arms around him, sinking into him, and he found himself holding on to her, as if that could replace every hug he'd missed for the last seventeen years.

It couldn't, but hugs were contagious, were they not? He was happy to become infected.

"What time should I come over for breakfast?" It was Saturday, so he didn't want to force them to rise too early, but his flight back to Chicago was at two.

"Eight. It'll give me time to get to the bakery."

"I'll bring the baked goods. You provide the tea."

Swiping at her eyes with one hand, Mia gripped his forearm with the other. "You could just stay here tonight. On the sofa."

"Ah, but is that not where Alexei will be staying?"

His mother blushed. "Alexei? I—I don't know what you're talking about."

"Oh, don't you?" He called out loudly in Russian, "You can come out now, you old fool!"

The durák put his head around a corner, his expression sheepish. "The walls are thin. You will wake the neighbors."

Mia laughed, all amazement. "You mean he was here the entire time? Hiding?"

Vadim shook his head in pity. "I saw his shoes over by the armchair. Fools in love are not known for their common sense or the ability to cover their tracks." To Alexei, he commanded, "Do me the service of treating my mother with respect and court her with pride in the open."

The old bulldog scowled. "I do not need your permission."

"No, you don't, *priyatel'*." Friend. He kissed his sister, then his mother, on the forehead. "Until breakfast. And, Alexei?"

He placed a hand on his old friend's shoulder, the man who had attended every hockey game, given unsolicited opinions, and stepped into his father's shoes for very little reward. "Please take this with the kindness it is intended. You are fired."

And then he left his family awestruck.

TWENTY-EIGHT

Vadim sat on the bench, tying his skates. He put a double knot in one, then looped the end through and triple knotted it. It was unnecessary, but he had been doing it since his KHL days. Hockey players were a superstitious lot.

Dante appeared in the locker room and moved through quietly, speaking a few words to each player. Sometimes he gave a short speech, but before an important game—against a tough opponent, a long-time rival—he preferred to float, aware of the tensions and not wishing to add to them. Tonight was their last shot, the final game in the regular season. Lose now and be ready with the refrain of failed seasons every-where: *there's always next year*.

The big speech was left to Remy, whose gift for rousing the troops was incomparable.

"Well, *mes amis*, I could say it's just like any other game but it's not, n'est-ce pas?"

"Hell, no," Burnett said, shaking his head.

"I know it's been tough the last few years. This year

has looked a whole lot better. But anyone who thinks we gave it a good shot and better luck next time had better rethink that position. Because this could still happen. *We* could still happen."

Murmurs of assent greeted this statement.

Remy looked around, his gaze touching every player in the room. "Now, not to pile on the pressure, but this is my last season in the NHL."

"No way, Jinx!"

"Fuck me, you're kidding!"

"Lazy fuckin' bastard."

This last observation was from Bren St. James, who, by the looks of that crooked half smile, was not surprised at his friend's announcement.

Remy let loose a big grin. "Win or lose, I'm retiring to cook, get fat, and make babies."

Huge guffaws all around tempered the tension. It was no secret that the Cajun craved a family life on retirement and that his jambalaya was a thing of beauty.

"You've probably heard this rumor that I'm considered the unluckiest guy in the NHL. When I was traded to this piece-of-shit team, I thought it was just another sign I was cursed. But then a few things happened. We won a few games. We gathered some confidence under our skates. We started to play better. I—" He shook his head, a small smile on his lips. "Well, my life sure changed a whole lot."

Remy was a man in love, with everything to play for. *This*, Vadim could appreciate, even if the object of his particular affections was unable to see his point of view. Fine. His anger would power his performance tonight, though this is what he had said for the last two games. Games they had lost.

Remy was still talking. "You all know I had a chance to leave a few months ago. I stayed. I'm here. And now we're here on the cusp of something we haven't seen for over fifteen years. A play-off spot. We can do it. We will do it. *Bon chance, mes amis. Laissez-nous patiner.*" Let's skate.

They moved out, heading for the tunnel. Just outside the door, Vadim's heart hammered triple time at the sight of a dark ponytail belonging to a stubborn head bent toward one of the trainers.

Close together, Isobel and Kelly discussed something on her iPad. Always with her charts and assessments. She raised her eyes just as he walked by. He saw something soft in there, something he could work with. She did not hate him completely, and this knowledge was like a bird soaring in his chest.

"Whore," he heard in a loud mutter behind him.

Vadim closed his eyes briefly. *Shay, you have chosen the wrong night to test me.*

He turned and fisted the asshole's jersey, yielding a satisfying yelp of pain. Leon Shay was dressed, but he had not been playing well and would likely not make a shift tonight. Less ice time fueled doubts and dimmed confidence—a vicious cycle. But these doubts did not change the man's personality, which was as ugly as it had been on the first day Vadim met him seven weeks ago.

"What did I tell you about speaking, Shay?"

"Screw you, Petrov! Everyone knows you've got your spot because of your history with one of the team's owners."

All the players had stopped now. Isobel watched, her color rising, her eyes alive with concern.

Cade stepped in. "Shay, you'd best apologize."

"Fuck that! I'm not saying anything that isn't true. She might not be banging him now, but she sure as hell banged him all those years ago." Shay glared at Vadim's woman, and then dared to speak to her. "Should we take a number, *Coach* Chase? Make sure you rate us on all aspects of our performance?"

"Shut up, Shay," Cade spat out with a guilty look at Isobel.

Coach Calhoun moved in, pretty quickly for a man of his lumbering bulk. "Get out on the ice. Now!"

When no one moved, Isobel took a step forward, only to be checked with a hand on her arm by Kelly. Vadim knew it was harmless—he knew his Bella would not have moved on so quickly—but he still saw only a red blur in front of his face.

His fist clenched. He raised it, but in half a heartbeat, found it covered by Isobel's hand.

"Don't, Vadim. Tonight's too important."

"Do not protect him. He has wanted this for a long time."

But before they could come to blows, both Dante and Bren stepped in, ensuring that Vadim would have to go through several hundred pounds of pure muscle before his fist connected with its ultimate destination: Shay's jaw.

Luck was on this dúrak's side today.

Dante divided a look between the two men. "Anyone care to explain?"

No one was inclined to answer.

Coach Calhoun spoke up. "Petrov, Shay, if either of you would like to continue this conversation, then consider yourselves on an indefinite suspension that *will* extend into next season. That's not to say it won't already be happening, of course. We are in an all-or-nothing game situation, and you shitheads want to put all that in jeopardy over what?" He flicked a glance to the *what* in the room: Isobel herself. Returning his disgusted attention to the entire team, he yelled, "Get out for warm-up now!"

"A word, if you don't mind, Coach Chase," Dante said to Isobel.

The team headed out, except for Vadim. He couldn't leave Isobel, not after what Shay had said.

"Bella." He grasped her arm and pulled her aside, making it clear that they had a deeper relationship than player-coach. He no longer cared.

"Does everyone know about what happened between us years ago?" She lowered her voice, though this was pointless. "And now?"

"The before . . . yes, they know. The now, they may have guessed." The perceptive stares of Dante and Kelly affirmed this.

She balled her fists and held them to her temples.

"How did they know about before?" She waved a hand at him. "Because the only other person who knew was Violet. And you."

"I was not the one who overheard your conversation with your sister. It was Shay. That is the source of our enmity, among other things."

"So he told you and—"

"Cade, Erik, and Ford."

She shook her head in resignation. "Well, it doesn't matter, I suppose. It's just one more shit brick in this giant, steaming wall of shit."

"I'll fix this with Moretti. You won't lose your job—"

Her expression was all pity for him. "Vadim, stop trying to protect me. Stop trying to fix my life. In fact, just quit while you're behind."

And then she left him, with him feeling lower than a dog.

What a dumbass she'd been. She had assumed that when Vad and Shay had clashed previously, it was all innuendo and trash talking, but apparently it was her own big mouth that had set this in motion. Now her inability to keep her greedy mitts off a player she was coaching had washed her up, once and for all.

Dante stood at the door to the locker room. On catching her eye, he pushed it open and jerked his chin. "Let's talk."

Kelly placed a hand on her arm. "Isobel, are you okay?"

She smiled at him, this kind man who had always been far too nice for her. "I'm fine, Kelly. Thanks, and—I'm sorry."

He didn't pretend to misunderstand, his nod speaking his thoughts. They weren't a couple, but she had intimated that they might be one day, which was less than classy of her.

She walked into the locker room, her heart in her stomach. She respected Dante and she didn't want to disappoint him.

"If it's any consolation," she started, "we're not together anymore." It was certainly no consolation to her.

"You want a full-time coaching position, Isobel," he said as he paced the locker room with hands on hips. "You want the men to respect you. But how the hell can you get that if you're playing favorites? It's bad enough Harper's with DuPre."

"Oh really?" Harper walked in, twitching her nose at the aroma unique to locker rooms. "We really don't need your judgmental commentary, Dante. I think you'll agree that my relationship with Remy has brought a lot of positive media attention to the team."

Dante rubbed his chin. "This isn't a soap opera, Harper. This is a professional sports franchise that's in danger of collapsing under the weight of its owners' egos."

Harper caught Isobel's eye. "Did he just call us fat?"

Isobel battled a smile. She had never loved Harper more than she did right this minute, but she couldn't let big sis fight her battles.

"Dante," Isobel said. "Believe me when I say I didn't want this to happen. I made a mistake and I'm fully prepared to accept the consequences. Effective immediately, I'm resigning my consultant position and I won't be throwing my hat into the ring for a coaching job."

"Isobel, take a moment to think about this," Harper said.

"I have. Dante's right. I'll never get the players' respect after this. And once it gets out, which it will, I'll have a hard time getting respect from any organization at the pro level."

Dante looked uncomfortable, as if his wish had been granted, but the genie had a rotten case of BO.

"Dante, you don't want to do this," Harper said, unexpected steel in her voice. They stared at each other for a good five seconds, an entire conversation conducted under Isobel's nose. And then the oddest thing occurred.

Dante blinked first.

"We don't need to make the decision now," he said quietly, but there was no missing the strain of anger in it.

Mind made up, Isobel held out her hand. "Thanks for giving me a chance."

He stared at it for a second, then shook it. "You did great work with Petrov, Isobel. You're the reason we have a shot at the play-offs."

She knew that. She'd find comfort in it later.

With one last glare at Harper, he left to head up to

the owners' box. They still had a game to win for that wild card spot.

Harper fisted her hips and paced a few steps. "Iz, are you sure? We could force Dante's hand here. Believe me, he's got a few skeletons knocking around in the closet with those Armani suits."

Isobel smiled grimly at her sister. "I'm not going to play dirty, Harper. That's more your style. Dante is right. Hell, you warned me, and I still went ahead anyway. As for the coaching, I've been trying to force a square peg into a round hole. I don't fit."

Harper looked hurt, but then her expression softened. "You want to know my proudest moment?"

Oh, God. They were doing this now? "Acquiring Remy DuPre?"

Harper snorted. "No, it was the night my baby sister won silver at the Games."

"You watched?"

"Of course I watched! Dad couldn't go because he'd broken his ankle—"

"What the hell was he doing up on that roof anyway?"

She waved a hand. "There was no telling him what to do. So I went over to his place to watch the final with him. He'd just broken up with his latest girlfriend. Remember Cassie-Casey-Callie—"

"Caliope."

"That's right, Caliope! He was all by himself. And maybe I wanted to punish myself a little."

Isobel grasped her sister's hand. "I know it hurt."

No need to explain aloud what "it" was. She meant Clifford's obvious preference for Isobel over Harper, his dismissal of Harper's ambitions, his failure to support her after a Rebels player had punched her in this very locker room.

Violet was right. The guy was a complete asshole.

"I think we were both hurt in different ways. He expected so much of you, Isobel, while expecting nothing of me. Equally heavy burdens. But that night, when you sank that first goal against Canada—wow! Dad couldn't jump so I jumped for him. For you."

Isobel would have loved to see that. Instead, Harper had kept this to herself, for her own reasons. They'd wasted so much time.

"Then I went back to being a jealous shrew," Harper added, tongue firmly in cheek. She sighed, her eyes soft and shiny. "But, Isobel, if this is what you want, coaching, the Rebels—we'll make it happen. I'll make it happen."

Isobel believed her, but it wasn't what she wanted. Not like this. She had to stay through the play-offs, assuming they got there. Then . . . who knew?

No Games. No pros. No coaching.

No Vadim.

Oh, that hurt like a mother. "I'll be okay, Harper," she lied. "We'll be okay."

TWENTY-NINE

The mood in the owners' box was somber, each of the Chase sisters lost in her thoughts. Their future as the only woman-owned NHL franchise was on thin ice. (Bam!) Anything less than a win tonight would finish the team's season and their rule of the Rebels with it.

Isobel's phone buzzed with a message from Mia in New York.

What's wrong with him? It's like he's forgotten how to play hockey.

Halfway through the second period, the Rebels were down two-zero. Nothing was connecting, their moves sloppy, the pressure getting to them.

Mia had texted Isobel yesterday to say that Vadim visited them in New York and had reconciled with his mother. It did her heart good to know he'd made strides in their relationship, and Isobel was hopeful this would free up his game.

Not so far. One of her U-12s would be more effective than Vadim Petrov on that ice. He just couldn't seem to get it together. None of them could. It was like

Vadim was the bellwether, and as Petrov goes, so goes the team.

She slid a glance toward her sisters. Harper had a death grip on the armrest, while Violet was staring at Dante, her expression unreadable. He caught her looking and held up his hands in a gesture of *what?* Isobel wondered what was going on between those two.

Dante turned to Isobel. "Look, I'm going to voice something that no one else apparently has the guts to say aloud. You need to go down there and tell your boyfriend to get his stick out of his ass and start earning the shit ton of money we are paying him."

"He's not my—he's not the only player on the ice, Dante."

"No, but he's the only one playing like he's stuck in a fucking Siberian labor camp. He's a mood player. Always has been. And right now, he's in a bad mood."

This was true—and he wasn't the only one. Everyone was staring at her with doomsday expressions.

"What the hell am I supposed to do about it?"

Dante threw his hands up, displaying a lot more Italianness than his buttoned-up persona would have hinted at. "Oh, I don't know. *Be his coach.*"

"I quit, remember?"

"I unaccept your resignation."

"This can't be fixed with coaching."

Violet snorted. "Yeah, why should he listen to you anyway? You don't have two brain cells to rub together." This snarky statement focused the attention of the box's participants on the baby in the family.

"Well, she doesn't. Probably hit with too many pucks like all those idiots out there."

Harper and Dante shared a *Mom and Dad are curious* glance. "What's going on here?" Harper asked.

"Nothing," both Isobel and Violet muttered, like the eight-year-olds they'd reverted to, before returning to ignoring each other.

Harper smiled thinly at Dante. "Do you mind giving us a minute?"

"If it fixes the Shitfest on Ice, then not at all."

He stepped outside, leaving Harper to divide a look between her two younger sisters. "What's happened?"

Neither of them said a word.

"One of you had better speak, or I'm going to start emptying all the wine from the owners' box bar in the sink, starting with Violet's favorite Malbec."

Violet pointed at Isobel. "This crazy bitch tried out for the Games and is mad at Vadim because he threatened to shame Team USA in the media if they let her play."

Harper's mouth fell open. "Really? Did you actually make the team?"

"I would have. Except for Vadim sticking his big Russian nose in and talking to Coach Lindhoff."

"I'm sorry, Isobel," Harper said, touching her arm. "That must have really hurt."

"It—it did."

Violet shook her head, a sneer on her lips. "You people. This sport has brainwashed you into thinking your lives are nothing without it. How can you be okay with this, Harper? She could have died."

"This is her life, Vi."

Isobel's chest filled with gratitude. Harper was nothing but a boatload of surprises lately. "Thank you."

"And Vadim really should have tried to persuade her without talking to the coach behind her back."

"Yes, he should have," Isobel agreed, not that she was persuadable, but Harper was checking all the right boxes. *This is how family supports each other, Violet.*

"Not that it would have made a damn bit of difference, because she's always been stuck in the same cycle as me, wanting Dad's approval."

"Exactly—wait, what?" Isobel stared at Harper. "That's not what this is about. I'm playing hockey for me. Sure, Dad would have wanted me to take any chance I could, but that's not the issue here."

"What *is* the issue, Iz?" Violet asked with enough sarcasm to fell an elephant.

"The issue is Vadim thinking he can call the shots about my life and career. I know neither of you think *that's* kosher!"

Harper crossed her arms. "I think there are extenuating circumstances, Isobel. This man saw you crash on that ice. He saw that blade hit your skull, the blood pooling around your head." Harper seemed to shiver, her cheeks draining of all color, and her next words were barely above a whisper. "He saw you almost die."

Isobel shifted in her seat. Examined her nails. Sniffed. "On TV."

Harper shook her head. "Not on TV. He was in the

arena with everyone else. That's not easy to forget, especially for a man in love."

No, no, that wasn't true. It didn't happen like that. When she asked him if he'd seen the game, his answer was one of distance. He'd never said he was there in the flesh.

Something lurched in her chest. Unlocked in her brain. Still, her mind refused to go the distance. "He—he wasn't there. He would have told me. Later."

Harper continued as if Isobel hadn't spoken. "I'd never seen Dad so upset. The man wanted to murder everyone—the doctors, the nurses, the coaches. And Vadim. He was there in the emergency room right after the accident, and then the next day he came to see you. Dad ran into him in your room." She looked off in the distance, her mind returning to that horrific time. "I arrived to find Dad telling him to beat it. It was pretty clear there was bad blood between them."

Isobel had thought she'd imagined that. Imagined him.

Bella, I am here. Wake up.

Only one person called her Bella. Only one person. Vadim had come to see her in the hospital.

"Did you talk to him back then? To Vadim?"

Harper inhaled deeply, thinking back to this other lifetime. "Not the second time I saw him, but the first night—right after we found out you were going to be okay, but you were still in a medically induced coma—he approached me in the waiting room. It was pretty crazy with all the press and your teammates, but

Vadim was there, the Russian stare of doom cutting through it all. He came up to me and asked, 'She will live?' I mean, super dramatic. I nodded, and it was like this tiny sliver of misery dropped off him. But he still looked . . ." She hesitated.

Isobel's heart was beating triple time. "He still looked what?"

"Like he was suffering. Like he was deeply wounded, but I put it down to his being, y'know, *Russian*. Then I saw him one more time the next day in your room when Dad was threatening to sic security on him."

"He was at the game," Isobel said, not wanting to dare credit his presence to anything more than a passing interest, but knowing it was more. This was Vadim. The man was too passionate for passing interests. "Oh, God."

She stood and headed for the window that looked out over the rink, empty now during the last break. Her stomach was spinning, her head in a fog of confusion. Inevitably, her fingers reached for her scar like a talisman.

It had ruined her life. Built her up. Brought her here.

To him.

"He came to see me play and then—then—I heard him while I was under. He spoke to me." Lately she'd been dreaming about it, dismissing it as inconsequential when she would wake. She turned back to her sisters. "I thought it was my imagination, but, Harper, he was there."

Harper nodded, her eyes glossy. "I thought you

knew. When we traded him in, I assumed you two had history, but you were being a total pro. Ignoring it in typical Chase fashion."

Violet stepped in and gripped Isobel's arms. "I know you're scared of what you're feeling for him. That he'll turn out like Clifford or every other hockey douche bag, but you can't assume they're all the same."

No. Vadim Petrov was a man without equal. But that didn't excuse his most recent behavior, did it? And how would she get over her resentment at this and her jealousy over everything else?

"He screwed up my chance to win gold."

Harper squeezed her hand. "He did it because he loves you. And if I'd known about it, I would have done the exact same thing. Because I love you, too." Wet eyed, she divided an intent look between Isobel and Violet, stopping on the most recent addition to this crazy fucking family. "After your cancer diagnosis, you decided that you'd take control from here on out. Live life on your own terms. The year of the V, right?" On getting Violet's nod, she went on. "And it took me a while to figure out that letting Dad run my ambitions down along with one bad experience with an ex should not be enough to keep me in a rut. I had to break this cycle and become the captain of my own fate. We all do.

"You're probably not going to play competitively again, Isobel. Neither are you going to be a coach for the Rebels. In fact, after tonight, the Rebels as we know it might be no more. Times are turbulent, and it's tough to figure out where you fit in. But I'll tell you where you belong. Here, with us." She shot a glance at Violet, who was suddenly finding a thread on the carpet fascinating. "And that goes for you, too, Vasquez. Even if we lose the game tonight and the Rebels' strings are no longer ours to pull, this shouldn't be what drives us apart. Not when it's brought us together."

Violet sniffed. "You fucking bitch, Harper. I'm only sticking around this hellhole if you get me a photo of Remy's dick for my files. And not a sleepy peen shot, either."

They all laughed, grateful for anything to cut through the tension.

Reminded of her cavalier disregard for her sister's feelings, Isobel threw her arms around Violet. "I'm sorry I scared you. I wasn't thinking of how this would affect anyone else. I didn't realize that we'd reached this point." Where her sisters and one steel-eyed Russian meant more to her than going for gold.

Her younger sister hugged her back. "You pull a stunt again like that, and I will cut you."

Isobel could only nod at one of the nicest things anyone had ever said to her.

"So let me get this straight." Violet held up her hand and started a count. "In prehistoric times, Petrov took your virginity and 'forgot' to give you an orgasm."

Harper's mouth dropped open. "Uh, what?"

"Try to keep up, Harper." Violet continued, "He got chased off the property by Cliffie-boy wielding a hockey stick. Then a few years later, he shows up at your big game and sneaks into your hospital room to coma-stalk you even though he knows the maniac with the stick is probably looking to finish the ass-whuppin'. Two months ago, he's traded in, finally makes up for the lost orgasms big time, but then shoots himself in the dick by going behind your back and ruining your chance at golden glory." She punctuated the recap with a smartass grin. "Have I missed anything?"

Isobel gave a teary-eyed nod of acknowledgment of how crazy it all was.

"He's kind of dramatic."

"You couldn't make this shit up. Hell, Dante's not wrong. This family is a soap opera looking for a day-time network slot."

Harper gave Isobel a wobbly smile. "I think you have somewhere to be, sis."

Oh boy. There came a time in every girl's life when she needed to take a leap of faith. Isobel had always thought there would be ice under her feet when she landed. Not this time. This time, she was jumping into the air, but her fall would be broken—she hoped—by the arms of a man.

Vadim Petrov, czar of her heart.

Hell, the third period would be starting any minute. "I wish we had a closet of knee pads up here," she said as she headed toward the door.

"Why?" Violet asked.

"Because when a girl has to grovel, she likes to do it with protection."

THIRTY

Live from rock bottom . . .

In the final break of the game—and at the rate he was playing, likely the final break of the season—Vadim sat apart from the rest of the players, elbows on knees, head bent as if he might throw up at any moment. He couldn't focus. The puck was as small as a pea, and his stick was like a fork trying to chase it around on his dinner plate.

"Petrov."

He peered up, his vision sharpening to take in an angel in black. Bella.

"Outside. Now."

Obeying her command, he stood, tethered to her. No one offered commentary or even judgmental glances, not with a two-goal deficit and their dreams on life support.

Outside the locker room, she asked, "How's the knee?"

Disappointment washed over him. She was here in her capacity as coach.

He answered with a sullen, "Fine."

"You look tired. Did you take a nap today?"

He had tried, but he found it difficult to sleep when she wasn't there. He'd become used to her, he supposed.

"If you have no guidance other than to criticize my preparation, then this conversation is over."

"How's it going up here, Vadim?" She touched his forehead. "And here?" Her thumb drew a line along his lips. "And here?" Her palm on his chest yielded a jerk from his heart, the foolish lump sensing its owner. What was once intolerable had found a ready, willing acceptance.

"Isobel, what do you want?" The words came out rough.

Her hand remained, splayed flat against his thumping heart. "You came to see me in Buffalo. Not just to the game, but at the hospital."

"Of course I did."

"Why?"

"Why?" *Was she serious?* "Why would I not want to see history being made by the girl who set the ice on fire and my heart with it all those years ago? And it would have taken a team made up of every defenseman in the NHL to keep me away from your bedside."

"I didn't know you were there." Her eyes filled with tears. "I thought you saw it on TV with everyone else. Later. I—I didn't know."

He cupped her cheek and leaned in close. "When you were cut down, my heart was cut down with you.

At the hospital, I could barely speak English. Or Russian. The staff thought I was crazy, but they also knew who I was."

"Buffalo," she said on a sniff. "Big hockey town."

"Yes it is. They let me sit with you when I said I was your boyfriend. But your father returned and wouldn't hear of it. I knew that a public fight would get in the news, impede your recovery, so I stayed away, and then—" He shook his head. "It seemed better to watch over you from afar. You would have more chances to play, and I didn't want to distract you from your journey. This craving you have to excel. Deep down, I knew I had never meant as much to you as you meant to me."

Her career would always come first, even at the expense of his heart.

"Vadim, you're the best kind of distraction."

"Just a distraction, Bella?"

"No!" Eyes wild, she fisted his jersey. "What you did, talking to Lindhoff, I understand it was because you care about me. I hate it, but I understand."

"Not just care, Bella. *Ya ne mogu zhit' bez tebya.* That means 'I cannot live without you.' It took me a while to admit this to myself, but this amazing girl caught me all those years ago and I burn for her. Only her."

He raised his jersey and placed her hand over his favorite tattoo, the one of the skates in flames. "*Devushka s goryshimi konkami.* This ink was for you."

"This tattoo? It's—oh! The Girl with the Blazing Skates." She bit her lip, suddenly bashful. "That's me."

"I kept you here, all these years."

Her eyes fluttered closed, tears welling like diamond drops on her lashes. She opened them again. "Vadim, I've been feeling so lost. You know that. And I wasn't sure if I was using you as an anchor while I tried to right the ship or if this ship couldn't sail without you. I'm sorry about how I reacted. I needed someone to blame, to lash out at."

He brushed his lips across her forehead. "I can take anything you give me. We Russians are used to suffering."

"But you really shouldn't have to put up with my drama. It's so hard for me to admit I need you. Need anyone. I want to be the woman you deserve, but I also want to be the woman *I* deserve."

When would she realize her worth to him? Her worth to herself? Apparently he would have to spend the rest of his life showing her.

"Bella, they are one and the same. I will not be satisfied with a woman who has no dreams or ambitions. My woman is the North Star in my night sky, but also in her own. If she is not there to guide me, there is only darkness. For us both." He searched her face. "Talking to your coach, going behind your back, I know it was not the best way to handle it. This is not how we should resolve our problems. It was a decision made out of desperation, but also out of self-preservation. Without you, I am nothing."

"Oh, Vadim, you crazy Russian."

He smiled, sensing they were finally skating in sync at last. "Am I forgiven?"

"Sort of."

Perhaps not. "Sort of?"

"Well, you see, we have a problem." She pointed toward the arena. "Out there. We're two goals down, heading into the final period, and if we don't win, our season is over."

"I recognize this problem."

"Actually, there's a bit more to it than that. You see, if we don't make the play-offs, the team's going to be sold off. That's how my father set up his will."

She chose to share this information *now*? And people considered *him* dramatic!

"So there's a lot riding on this next twenty minutes." She peered up at him. "Probably shouldn't have told you that, should I?"

"It is an unusual coaching strategy, I admit."

The sound of voices rose. The players were about to leave the locker room.

"But here's the thing, Vad. I actually don't care about any of that. Sure, I'd like to get to the play-offs and hold on to ownership of the team, more for Harper, because this means everything to her. But if we don't, you're going to have other chances, either with the Rebels' new owners or with whomever you play with next, because you're too good not to lay your hands on that hardware. And on top of that, I can survive it because when the game is over and the interviews are done and the only sound on the rink is the Zamboni starting up, I'll have you. Wherever you are."

Remy emerged from the locker room, closely followed by Callaghan, Burnett, and the rest of the crew.

She tightened her grip on his jersey, pulling him close. "I *will* have you, won't I?"

"Past, present, future, Bella, I am yours. That will never change. I love you."

"Nice work, Petrov," Remy said with a wicked grin as he dropped Vadim's helmet, gloves, and stick at his feet. "But don't get cocky. Night's not over yet."

Isobel threw her arms around Vadim's neck and inhaled him.

"*Ty pakhnesh', kak zaplesnevelyy syr,*" she whispered in his ear.

The rest of the team trooped by with stupid grins cracking their stupid faces, all except an unsmiling St. James, who took up the rear and nodded at Isobel. "Coach."

She nodded back. "Cap." Then she turned to Vadim once more and repeated what she had just said. A very odd response to telling a woman you loved her.

"I have been working hard, Bella, so I know I am not as fragrant as I could be."

Her brow furrowed. "Excuse me?"

"You just told me that I smell like moldy cheese. Is this another of your unconventional coaching tactics?"

Her growl was so sexy. "Fucking Alexei, he's always hated me. I called him to get the correct pronunciation. You know he's dating your mom, right?"

Laughing, he kissed her hard and long, this woman who made him a man, and now the happiest person on the planet.

This woman who would make him a champion.

"My English is better than your Russian. Tell me what you meant to say."

"I love you," she said, her mouth in a beautiful curve.

That smile gave him life. "Again."

"I love you, Vadim Petrov."

"And if I lose tonight?"

A roar went up from the crowd. The last period was beginning. "I'll still love you. But I'll probably love you more if you win."

"Then I will win." And with his coach's rousing words echoing in his heart, he put on his helmet and headed out to do what needed to be done.

EPILOGUE

Isobel skated to the face-off circle and assumed the position. Stance wide, body bowed, blade at the ready. Her opposite stood a few inches taller than her, but that's where the superiority ended.

The puck dropped.

She touched it first, whipped it left to Gabby, and still found time to shoot a *gotcha* grin at the man she loved as she left him eating her ice shavings. One minute later, her team of U-12s—all girls—scored and won the game.

She called the entire class over to the circle and high-fived them all. "Nice work, guys! Remember what I said: speed will always win over might."

Vadim removed his helmet, his dark hair falling like glossy silk over his brow. The girls sighed, and Isobel's hormones joined in. He really was unbelievably dreamy.

And all hers.

The boys on the team, while not overcome in quite the same way by Vadim's perfection, gazed in wide-eyed wonder.

"Can you show us the goal from the Philly game?"

Vadim stroked the beginnings of a scruffy beard, another check in the hotness column. "*The* goal? You mean the one that got us to the play-offs?"

Isobel rolled in her lips. Vadim would be dining off that goal for the foreseeable future. Scored in overtime against Philly, it won the Rebels the last spot in the play-offs, starting in one week. They'd made it! Sure, during the first round, the wild card was up against the best team in the Western Conference, Dallas, but when had the Rebels ever gone the stress-free route?

The kids took the positions of the final play of the last Rebels game, and Vadim skated them through every pass, feint, and hit that got the win. Isobel watched her man, loving this playful side of him.

Happy Vadim plus happy Isobel equaled happy life. For them both.

She was considering her next career steps. Seeing the Rebels through to the play-offs, keeping the team in the family, and teaching the kids here were enough to keep her busy for now. Life had a habit of unraveling its knots. Supporting Vadim satisfied her, and when she was ready to figure out what came next—maybe her own foundation promoting leadership in sports to girls—she knew he'd have her back.

Finished with the reenactment of *only the greatest goal ever in a final regular-season game,* Vadim gathered the kids around.

"Who would like tickets to the first home game of the play-offs?"

Every hand shot up. "Me! Me! Me!"

"I will have a special box for you all to sit in, but only if you promise to do something for me."

A sea of bright-eyed faces looked up at him, ready to sell their souls for a seat in an executive box. Little hucksters.

"You must always listen to your coach. She is the reason why I am the success I am today, and she will make all the difference to your game. Okay?"

That's all? their expressions said. On a chorus of *okays*, they skated off.

"Did you let me win that face-off, Russian?"

He glided over and reached for the strap of her helmet. "This should be tighter, Bella. You know that." He removed his gloves, then her helmet, dropped it, and kissed her with enough heat to melt the ice beneath her feet.

Not so fast, Russian. She cut the kiss short. "Did you?"

"No. Your advantages over me are many, and I would not dream of giving you one more. You have always been faster." He grabbed her ass, pretty fast himself. "In every way."

That hand plus her ass: perfection.

Satisfied she wasn't being *totally* played, she threw herself wholeheartedly into being kissed by a pro, and probably would have risked freezer burn on her butt if she hadn't heard a cough behind her. Jax Callaghan had just arrived with his next group, older kids than hers, but still completely in awe of the Russian. While they crowded around Vadim with questions, Jax nudged her shoulder.

"Pretty surprising about Burnett."

Her heart lurched. "What about him?"

Jax pulled out his phone and tapped on the screen to show her a headline from the *Sun-Times* website: "Cade Burnett, Rebels D-Man, Comes Out."

Holy shit. "I had no idea."

"Yeah, just announced it at a press conference an hour ago. The media's going nuts." Jax shook his head, a wry grin on his lips. "The Rebels have never chosen easy, though, have they?"

No, they had not. Alamo was gay? And he had decided to unveil this nugget right before the play-offs? First in the NHL, too. Wow, the kid was brave, and bravery on the ice, in life, and especially in love would always be rewarded. The Rebels would rally around and support him like the family he was to them.

That exchange she'd witnessed between him and Dante at the fund-raiser opened a Pandora's box of speculation. These next few weeks were going to be most interesting.

"So how'd it go?" Jax asked, snagging her attention once more.

"How'd what go?"

"That shot you wanted to take?"

She watched Vadim, the man who loved her too much to bear the thought of a life without her in it.

Joking and laughing with the kids, he peeked up and delivered one of his patented Smiles of Destruction.

She fought her own grin—but not too hard—before giving Jax an answer.

"I took it, I scored big, and I won. The whole freakin' shebang."

ACKNOWLEDGMENTS

To the team at Pocket/Gallery—Molly, Marla, Melissa, Jean Anne, Kristin, Abby, Liz, Faren, and Lauren—thanks for being as excited about the Rebels as I am. Special thanks are due to my editor, Kate Dresser, for her awesome notes and insights. She didn't balk when I proposed the premise for *So Over You*: "Um, the hero of this book failed to rock the heroine's world the first time around. Okay with you?" Maybe she was faking it—ha!—when she said, "I can't wait to read that!" I'll never know, but it all worked out in the end—Isobel gets at least three orgasms to every one of Vadim's. The balance of the universe is restored.

Thanks to Lana Kart for her ongoing support, excitement about Vadim, and help with Russian phrasing. Any mistakes are mine.

Thanks to all the authors who helped me keep my sanity this last year: Gina L. Maxwell, Abby Green, Lauren Layne, Jessica Lemmon, Robin Covington, Sarah MacLean, Sophie Jordan, Kimberly Kincaid, Sonali Dev, Julie Ann Walker, and Avery Flynn, to name a few.

Every day, I learn something new from these amazing ladies, and I count myself blessed to be a part of this rocking romance community.

To my agent, Nicole Resciniti, thanks for always having my back.

And to Jimmie, my heart and my home, it's okay that you don't care even a little about hockey. ☺

Keep reading for a sneak peek at the sizzling next
installment in the Chicago Rebels series

Undone by You

A Chicago Rebels enovella

By Kate Meader

Available in March 2018 from Pocket Star Books!

ONE

Someone must have drugged his drink.

Dante Moretti shot a sharp glance at the Macallan in his hand, wondering if the amber liquid was truly blurring before his eyes or if he was just really fucking tired. A roofie seemed like the most logical conclusion, because the ass he had just been appreciating could not possibly belong to the last guy he'd expect to see here.

Here being a members-only gay club in the wealthy Gold Coast neighborhood on Chicago's North Side.

If Dante knew anything, it was that Cade "Alamo" Burnett, bulwark defender, All American, and pro hockey's class clown played for one team and one team only: Chicago's second-most successful hockey franchise, the Rebels. Dante was the Rebels' general manager—not to mention the first openly gay managing executive in the NHL—and it was his job to be apprised of these things.

Rebels defenseman or not, the object of Dante's attention carried himself with devil-may-care swagger, his stride sure, his head held high. If it truly was Burnett, then he clearly had no problem with the eyes of every guy in the place checking him out. Including Dante's.

It wouldn't have been the first time Dante had slipped up where Burnett was concerned. Surrounded every day by athletes in tip-top condition, he was fairly immune to the perfect abs, sculpted pecs, and bite-worthy asses. Separating his desires from his work wasn't just advisable, it was necessary. Ogling the players under his authority was a line he would never cross.

But Burnett? There was something about the amiable Texan that gave Dante gooseflesh every time he visited the locker room for a pregame pep talk or a postgame check-in. God knew why, because the man was a *polpetto*, a total meatball—a hazel-eyed, syrup-talking, built-like-a-tank meatball. Not Dante's type at all, although his teammates adored the guy for his ability to cheer a room and make a crapfest game feel like less than the end of the world. He had people skills. And shit, could he play.

"Earth to Hot Stuff."

Only slightly irritated, Dante turned back to the guy he had been considering fucking. Blond and urbane, he had an ethereal paleness, which Dante usually found contrasted nicely with his own dark Italian skin. Sex was as often about aesthetics as it was about pleasure.

"Sorry. Thought I saw someone I knew."

"Since you just moved to Chicago four weeks ago, that doesn't seem likely, now, does it?"

No, it didn't. This club only allowed entry by recommendation. Hanging out at rowdy gay bars held little interest for Dante. Something quieter and darker suited him, and a discreet, unnamed club in a Gold Coast brownstone fit the bill.

Cade Burnett's doppelganger had disappeared into the club's depths, but Dante's discomfort lingered. Taking another sip of his now suspect drink, he half listened to the guy beside him as he droned on about his job.

". . . *dealing with idiots who think diversification means add penny stocks . . .*"

It couldn't be Burnett. It made no sense.

". . . *portfolio . . . blah-blah . . . global equity funds . . . blah-blah . . .*"

Blond 'n' Boring looked up in surprise—up because Dante had stood suddenly, the itch in his body spreading to his feet. He needed to assure himself that one of his players wasn't about to blow up his career by being caught in a "compromising" position. Gay chief executives were one thing. The testosterone-soaked NHL wasn't quite ready for one of the first line to taste the rainbow.

"If you'll excuse me, back in a second," he said to . . . okay, he'd already forgotten his name.

The club was a maze of cozy rooms, secluded alcoves, and tight spots for all manner of hookups. Most couples—and sometimes threes and fours—

indulged their more private desires in the rooms on the next level. On this floor, it was subtle caresses, brief touches, soft kisses—all foreplay to test participants' boundaries and levels of interest.

Dante's pulse picked up as he moved further in. Not at the sight of men in sexual playtime, but at the thought of what he might find: Cade Burnett with whoever had thought it was a good idea to bring a famous pro athlete here. Cade Burnett with someone's tongue down his throat. Cade Burnett with his hand down someone's—*stop*.

Do not speculate. Just investigate.

He rounded a corner into a red room with velvet drapes, soft carpet, and lavish furnishings.

Dante's heart seized. It *was* him.

Burnett stood in a corner, one cowboy-booted foot raised to the wall, a lowball glass in his hand, an interloper trespassing in Dante's world. Three men surrounded him in a horseshoe of worship. Even others in the room watched, because Cade Burnett was so damn watchable. A little shy of six feet four, he towered over every man here. His hair was brown with coppery streaks, his jaw strong and square, his mouth permanently amused. Hazel eyes—not that anyone could see them in the dim lighting, but Dante knew their exact shade—flashed gold rings of fire around their irises.

His gift on the ice was brute strength and the best hockey IQ of any defender Dante had ever seen. But this was another type of magnetism.

Hockey smart was one thing. That Burnett was here

in the open proved he wasn't all that smart off the ice. The man had to have some fault.

Burnett laughed huskily at something one of his suitors said—a sound with a drunken tinge to it—and this was enough to change the dynamic of the group. The others shifted incrementally closer, jockeying for a position their conversation couldn't achieve alone. One of them, a guy in a Hugo Boss suit, laid a hand on Burnett's bicep and squeezed.

Something primal, possessive, and downright greedy reared in Dante's chest.

His overreaction shocked him, so much so that his instinct was to consider walking away. This was none of his business. He wasn't the team's baby-sitter.

Too late. If Dante had turned his back a half second later he would have missed Burnett capturing his gaze—and *capturing* was not hyperbole. Those eyes shone at him like a predatory cat's, all challenge, no fear.

Busted.

Continuing his original mission seemed best, but Burnett now watched him as he approached. Looking away was not an option.

"Dante," Burnett murmured, and, Cristo, the way he tasted his name made Dante instantly hard. His body flooded with awareness, along with a distinct desire to punch every man who stood between him and his defenseman.

"Could I have a word?"

Cade's mouth tipped up at the corner and he downed his drink in one go. He handed off the empty glass to one of the guys standing before him. Pushed another aside gently, all with a curious ambivalence.

"Lead the way."

Dante pivoted, having no clue what to do next. His cock had several ideas, all of them involving Cade beneath his body in one of the more private rooms upstairs. His brain, on the other hand, was still in charge, so he moved to a small sofa in the next room. He gestured toward the seat and waited for Cade to sit.

As if they were on a date.

"Do you want to tell me—"

Cade held up a hand, so assured. "I could do with another drink." He waved over one of the servers and ordered a Glenlivet. "Dante?"

Dante shook his head. Someone had to remain sober here.

With the server out of earshot, Cade gave Dante his complete attention. Complete wasn't quite right, though—more like consuming. Dante felt as if he'd been stripped bare, screwed senseless, and shown the door all at the same time.

"Come here often?" Cade asked.

"Not really. You?"

"A few times."

Dante's heart skittered with this new knowledge. No "accident" that he was here, then.

"We have procedures for this eventuality."

Cade narrowed his eyes. "Which eventuality is that?"

"An NHL player who'd like to come out. It hasn't happened yet, but every team is waiting for the first."

The slightest smile teased Cade's lips. "Kind of jumping the gun, aren't you?"

"You're here." Dante added a wave of his hand in case Burnett had somehow forgotten where *here* was.

"I'm here," Cade said simply, but there was nothing simple about the intent Dante heard in the words. Crackling energy licked between them, and Dante had the distinct impression that Cade was making some sort of statement, just not the one Dante had first assumed. He'd analyze that later.

Cade threw an arm over the back of the sofa. "So what kind of procedures are we talkin' about?"

"Procedures?"

"You said you have procedures for NHL players who are ready to come out."

Dante shook off his unease, glad to be back to more concrete specifics. "A PR plan. Press statement. Ways to handle the inevitable questions."

"Like how the *New York Times* prepares obituaries for famous people so they're ready to roll when they kick the bucket?"

Dante considered this, strangely charmed by the morbid comparison. "Well, there isn't a separate one ready to go for each player. We'd tailor our prepared statement with a few personal details."

Cade licked his lips, and Dante couldn't take his eyes off the slick, moist stripe that remained behind. With a tilt of his head, the younger man rubbed the dangerously appealing copper-tinted stubble on his chin.

"'He first knew he liked boys when, in the fifth grade, he told his momma he'd like to marry Johnny Sanderson.' That kind of thing?"

This was said with shocking equanimity, displaying a subtle humor Dante would never have attributed to a one-note clown like Cade Burnett. The guy was always so obvious.

"Cade, having your photo taken in a private club that caters to men hooking up with other men is probably not the best way to announce to the world that you're gay." Dante looked around, assessing the interest of other patrons. Conclusion: plenty. He might even place it at threat-level orange, not because a famous hockey player was in the house, but because Cade Burnett was simply beautiful.

And gay, Dante's cock happily chimed in. *He's fucking gay.*

"If anyone catches wind of this we can just say you were curious and asked me to bring you. It should be easy enough to spin that we're friends. Besides, no one would believe the truth."

Cade broke into laughter that drew a hundred eyes to drink them in. The sound was wonderful, the attention less so.

"Moretti, you are somethin' else, y'know that? You think I'm going to use you as my gay-buddy shield? Hell, I'm not too worried about anyone photographing us here."

"You really think you're safe?"

"I'm with you. That's as safe as can be."

Not even a little. "Why are you taking this risk?"

The server returned with the drink and handed it off with a wink at Cade. Smiling his thanks, Cade took a long sip.

"Sometimes I just crave company. Being a closeted gay guy can be exhausting."

"Being an uncloseted one can be just as tiring."

"I bet. But it must be nice not to have to hide. Even if you have assholes whispering behind your back."

So few people did him the service of whispering *behind* Dante's back. "Pros and cons to each position. But no, I wouldn't go back." He leaned forward because he needed to see Cade's eyes when he asked this. "Are you saying you're ready to go public?"

"No, but . . . I'm ready." He licked his lips again and Dante felt it like a streak of pleasure over his balls. His heart thrashed fiercely, so hard he was sure Cade had to see the pulse beating at the base of his throat.

Somehow he managed to ask, "Ready for what?"

Cade curled his hand around Dante's tie and hovered close enough that Dante could feel hot puffs of air against his lips.

"I think you know, boss."